Era of the Damned

Kay Marrie

i

Copyright

ISBN: 979-8-9910836-3-8

For those who have to be strong.

Books by Kay Marrie

Adventures: Into the Abyss

City of the Damned
Era of the Damned

A Court of Blood and Sacrifice

Trigger Warnings

Please be advised that this book contains material that may be disturbing or triggering to some readers. Read with your own caution. Content includes SA, torture, death, and gore.

Chapter One

The Beginning

There was a time when humanity was free. A time when the sun did not scorch the surface of the Earth, where the wind did not carry shards of glassy sand crystals through the air, and where the color of green and blue vivaciously decorated the trees and land around. People were free to travel. They didn't live under the torment and control of the demons. And most importantly, they were free to love.

Desti knew that she was now in the time before the Era of the Damned. How could she deny it being surrounded by a forest of crystal-clear rivers and luscious treetops? It had been three days since she and Tate jumped through the portal and stumbled upon her friends. And within those three days, she had done a lot of catching up.

"So, a demon spirit took over your body?" Anthony asked, an expression of utter disgust smeared across his face. The rest of the group was sitting in a circle, around a fire. They were telling their stories of when they were in Hell. Tess and Kaelen sat next to each other, Brandon and Seraph were on the opposite side of Desti and Tate, and Anthony was somewhere in the middle.

Desti shot a glance over at Tate. He was laughing, but she wondered if that was how he truly felt. She was there when that shadow took over him. When his body contorted and broke, and then turned into something that she would only imagine came from nightmares. It was still so new, the wound that went unseen, the scars that were etched into his soul, but he held up his façade like an armor, hiding any indication that anything was bothering him.

"Yes, it burrowed into me through my mouth."

Kaelen had leaned forward now, the orange and yellow flames outlining her pristine features as she said, "What did it feel like? You know, for that thing to be inside you?"

The air went frigid, it was as if time stopped the moment Kaelen asked that. There was a slight flicker of something behind Tate's eyes. Was he remembering the pain and suffering he went through? Desti reached out her hand and placed it on his knee.

"It was like being asleep but not fully gone. I could feel what my body was going through, I could hear what my body was hearing, but his voice, in my head, was louder. It was like watching myself act out disgusting things and not being able to do anything about it."

Desti had never heard the story of his experience during his possession. And now she felt guilty for not asking sooner. She too felt somewhat scarred from his possession. The memory of his hand against her throat, and the way his eyes were filled with so much evil, sent shivers down her back. Desti didn't realize that she had reached for her throat, as if her body was still trying to protect itself from him.

"That sounds terrifying," Kaelen said.

Desti looked over at Tate, admiring him. She didn't get a chance to do that much, but there she sat admiring every feature; his strong jawline, the way his eyes twinkled when he was engaged with someone, and his hair, which reminded her of something free in the wild, the way it blew in the wind with no restraint. She loved everything about him, but she loved that the most.

"Do you think the others are still after us? I mean, there is just more than one person that we pissed off," Tess said. The whole group fell silent and looked over to her. It was as if she had just dropped a bomb of realization.

"I don't know, Tess. I know that Amaros is probably after us because we took the Lux, but Elijah and the Master got what they wanted. They sacrificed us. They probably don't even know that we have escaped Hell." Desti thought about her parents. Her dad was the one who had given her up to the Master, and then she wondered where her mom was. Why didn't she come and save her? Why didn't she tell her about her *true* father? These questions were something that had been eating away at Desti, but she had come to terms with the fact that she probably would never know the answers.

"Does that mean that we all have the mark of the demons? Can't they control us now?" Kaelen leaned forward and pulled her hair to the side, spilling over her shoulder, revealing a red mark, shaped like a broken crown. It looked as if someone had taken a hot poker and branded the back of her neck. Kaelen's eyes glossed over. Desti shifted her body and said, "I haven't thought about that. My dad and the Master threw me into the pit while I was still twenty." She looked over at Tate, who she realized was staring at her with a soft expression. "Kaelen, how old are you?"

"I'm twenty-two," she said flatly. Desti could tell from the look in Kaelen's eyes that she was terrified. She would be too. Desti pulled her hair forward and turned her back toward Tate. "Look. Do I have the mark?" The moment Tate's finger brushed against Desti's skin; it was like an explosion. She closed her eyes, inhaling his touch. His fingers gently glided down her spine until she felt him pull away. "I don't see anything," he said.

She turned to face him. "When is my birthday? Come to think of it, it should be any day now."

"So, because you were sacrificed *before* your twenty-first birthday, you didn't receive the mark? But we who have already been twenty-one are now forever tethered to the demons." It was Seraph making an observation. He was older. Desti remembered him from their school. The school kept the kids divided up in groups, by age, until they felt that they were able to be controlled enough and let out into the desolate world.

The rest of the group started checking their skin for the mark. Desti was making a mental checklist; the marked and the unmarked. Kaelen, Seraph, and Tess were all marked. Brandon and Anthony, and Desti and Tate were unmarked.

"What does this mean? Does this mean that they can find us? Or bring us back there?" Kaelen started to cry. The energy had shifted the moment that the realization hit. It could possibly mean those things, but Desti didn't know for certain.

Memories of learning about being marked flooded her mind like a flowing river. Ms. Clyde's voice was clear as ever as if she were watching it happen in real life. *"You will be the property of the demon realm once you are marked. There will be nowhere you can go where they won't come to claim you,"* she had said. Desti shifted her weight where she sat and clenched her fingers into the palms of her hands. She thought about it. Could the demons still claim them, even if they are now in a different time? Desti slipped a glance to her left, just making sure that the Lux was still where she left it. She and Tate had set up their own section of their camp and kept the Lux always in sight.

Her gaze was locked on for longer than she expected. *Could I somehow free them of their marks?*

It was Tate who spoke up, trying to calm the tension in the air. "The demons very well could be searching for us, but I don't know how well they can track you here. We are in a different time now. Maybe you are safe."

"I know that Amaros won't stop until he finds us and the Lux," Anthony said. Desti shot eyes at him. Not a single flicker of fear showed in his eyes, instead, he was calm. She wondered if he had just mastered hiding his true emotions. He was too young to be so strong. But at least he was safe now.

"Well, that turned dark fast," Tess joked. She huffed out a laugh mixed with a sigh and stood from the stump she was sitting on. Seraph followed, then Kaelen, and then Anthony. When Desti looked to her side to see if Tate was getting up too, instead he stayed.

His eye twinkled under the glistening sun rays, illuminating the hints of yellow and blue that hid underneath the green. Desti traced his features all the way down to his half-smile. His curly jet-black hair was now freely blowing around with the tiny gusts of wind, making him look even more majestic. She could feel the beat of her heart increase the more she studied him. Then he was reaching for her, gently grasping her hands. She looked down, not noticing that he had said something to her.

"What did you say?"

Desti now refocused back to his eyes. He was trying to ask her something. "Will you come with me? I want to show you something." It was that smile that could cure any sadness that coursed through her veins, banishing any negative thoughts that clouded her mind, and warming her once-frozen heart. "Of course," she replied.

As the camp emptied, everyone going off to their own quarters, Tate led the way, following a little dirt path along the riverbed.

Chapter Two

Hope

"Where are you taking me?" Desti asked. She had tiptoed her way around the wildflowers that blossomed throughout the ground. She took every chance she had to preserve the nature of this forest. It was too precious not to. Tate had been walking far from the camp, glancing back with a peculiar smirk every so often. His gentle stride toward the unknown was something that Desti admired. The way his muscle flexed, the way his gilded hair looked like the night sky, lit by the twinkle of the stars. *Where is he taking me?*

"It's just a little farther," he said while reaching for her hand. Desti slipped her fingers into his and hurried her steps. There was something about the way his skin felt on hers, like an explosion of desire and comfort, cascading through her body like a shooting star. She inhaled, taking in the sweet aroma of fresh grass and pine. Gentle trills from the nearby birds whistled high above.

Soon, Tate slowed his pace and turned, facing Desti, with a grin so big, she knew that it must be straining his muscles. "Why are you smiling so big?" She laughed.

"I wanted to show you this." Tate stepped aside, carefully standing on the edge of the grassy path. Desti peered around the edge of a blueberry bush, and what she gazed upon then took the very breath from her chest.

She gasped, cupping her hands to her mouth. "Oh my God." She turned to look at him, watery-eyed. "You did this?" Tate simply nodded and took a step to follow her. What lay in front of her was something so beautiful that she would only assume to see something like this in a dream. On the soft patch of grass were hundreds of flowers, delicately laid out in a beautiful pattern, and in the center was a plate of fresh fruit he must have picked from the nearby blueberry bushes. She didn't know what to say. All her life, she had only known pain, suffering, and sorrow. Tate had been her only sliver of hope to break her away from all that, but he suffered too. Their world had no place and no time for something like this.

"Tate, I don't know what to say." She glanced back at him. "Thank you." And right then, it was as if all her feelings came bursting through the seams, exploding away any reminiscence of her old life. She repeated, "Thank you. Thank you. Thank you." After her lips slipped the last syllable, she began a slow and careful step toward Tate; toward her spark of hope in a dark world, her best friend who she could trust with her life. His eyes were fixated on her as she made her way slowly to him, and she knew what she was doing, eyeing him up and down. Taking in his scent that carried through the breeze, studying every flex of muscle under his glistening skin. She could feel the beat of her chest in her throat; faster the closer she came to him. He was electrifying. Captivating her like a black hole, sucking her energy into him until they became one.

She licked her lips, and she knew by the look in his eyes that he too was feeling the same. The way his body trembled, yearning to be touched by her. She knew just from the look of him. He wanted her. Bad. And she did too. It was too much to hold back anymore, and so she ran forward, breaking away from her slow and sexy stride, and crashed into his arms, into a fierce and fiery kiss.

She curled her fingers into his hair and pulled him into her, feeling his tongue slip between her lips. She gasped. "I love you," he groaned. And if she thought her desire for him couldn't grow any stronger, she was wrong, because the moment those words slipped out of his mouth, it was like a dam breaking free in her—everything. Her soul; her essence; her body.

She felt the roughness of his hands study the curve of her back, passionately making his way lower until he was pulling her up on him, wrapping her legs around his waist. She pulled away just for a second, gasping and moaning from the sheer pleasure of wanting him. Her body ached to be touched by him, and so, she let him lay her down on the soft green grass, clutching the blades underneath her.

"I love you," Desti whispered through a moan. The arch of her back just slightly lifted from the grass, inviting Tate to continue exploring. The gentle but strong glide of his hands started at her throat, carefully playing their way to her peaked breasts. He stopped there, kissing, and nibbling the warmth of her skin. Her shirt was half lifted from her body, exposing the goosebumps that lay across her. He was in a predatory mood now, zoning in on one thing, and that was her. His groan was low and pleasurable as if he could already feel what it would be like inside of her as he made his way down. Tate pressed a kiss on her stomach, following his hands down to her hips. He paused for a moment, panting, and kissing just below her navel. She pulled him into her with her thighs as a begging moan escaped her mouth. "I want you," she breathlessly spoke. Tate nodded as he willingly obliged.

The meat of her thighs was cupped under his grip, and she felt his head move lower, into the pulsating warmth between her legs. He had ripped her pants off in a swift motion; her bare skin now feeling the softness of the grass and the warmth of his breath as he inched closer. She couldn't bear to wait any longer. Desti needed him. She needed him so badly. "Please," she begged. Tate made one simple glance up just before diving into her, and when he did, it was almost an immediate explosion.

His tongue swayed in gentle motions, flicking Desti in just the right spots. Without realizing it, she had closed her thighs in on him, keeping him there a little longer. The pleasure was out of this world, cascading her through the galaxy and stars as the rush of pleasure traveled through her veins. Tate traced his fingers down her exposed thigh and slipped two fingers in, pulling her into him, and a gasp escaped her throat.

Desti had been so caught up in her pleasure that when she opened her eyes just for a moment, she didn't realize that Tate now stood before her, naked and aroused. The look in his eyes screamed, *'I want you'*. And she did too. She wanted every piece of him; his soul, his mind, but right now — she wanted to feel the hardness of him stoke inside of her. Desti curled her finger, inviting him to have her. She couldn't help but stare at his flexing muscles as he carefully crawled his way to her. She grasped for him, feeling the warmth of his skin, and then glided her hand down until the hardness of him was in the palm of her hand.

She had never done this before, and yet it came so naturally to her as if their two bodies were one. Meant to be together by some higher power or fate. Her legs shook with pleasure, and she could feel the wetness between her thighs only growing more the closer Tate came to her. One second, he was in front of her as she stroked him, desperately wanting more by the look in his eyes, and then, the next moment, she felt his body hover above hers as he slipped himself inside her, pulsating between her legs with steady strokes.

The pleasure was something out of this world as Desti struggled to keep quiet. But she didn't care anymore, and so she let go, begging for more from the rooftops. Birds flew from the trees from the echo of her moans, but she didn't care. All she wanted was him. The strokes grew harder and faster as she grasped her fingers in his hair, and then found their way to his back, clawing her way down in a pleasurable stroke. The fire inside her was building, warmth now rushing between her legs. It was as if the breath from her chest was sucked out as she gasped from the explosion that was happening between her. Together they were one, exploding with unimaginable ecstasy. Then after it had calmed, Tate lay there panting on her chest. Desti played with the strands of his hair that blew freely in the breeze.

"That…was…better than I expected," Desti breathlessly joked.

Tate glanced up with those glimmering eyes and huffed out a laugh. "I didn't know you were expecting anything."

"Oh stop," Desti said. She nudged Tate with her elbow and rolled over to her back, admiring the blue sky above. She had shoved away her true feelings for Tate for so long that sometimes she questioned if it was even worth it. Breaking the forbidden rules only got someone sent to the demons. It felt like she was stuck between two decisions. It could bring her eternal damnation, or she could be set free. But was that what she wanted? To always be on the run?

Desti grabbed her pants and slipped them back on, and Tate followed. She was quiet for a moment, just staring at the clouds above passing by. The breeze had blown in a little harder now, whipping around loose strands of her hair. She felt Tate scoot closer to her. His warmth. He leaned into her until his shoulder was touching hers.

"Tell me."

"What?" she said.

Tate glanced over at her and repeated. "Tell me what is going through your mind." Desti looked over at him and sighed. "Everything is so different now. Part of me feels like maybe we are in over our heads." Desti traced her fingers along the cracks of the pebbles that lay next to her and continued. "Because of me, people died. People suffered. I don't want to cause any more pain." Desti's voice was caught in her throat. She thought of Lyra; her torn limbs just lying in her own pool of blood. She should have just stayed home, Desti thought. And there were so many more people.

Tate reached for Desti's chin and lifted it until she was staring into his eyes. "Because of you, people are alive. *Anthony* is alive. Tess, Seraph, Kaelen, and Brandon are alive." Desti shivered and closed her eyes, a single tear now streaming down her cheek. "In our world, no matter where you are, or who you are, there will always be people suffering. You have saved people, Desti." Tate grabbed her hands now and cupped them firmly in his grip. "We actually found the Lux. We got our friends out of Hell. Don't forget how brave you are."

Desti inhaled. "Do you really think we can stop it from happening? The war, I mean." This thought weighed heavily on her. Stopping the Master—stopping Amaros and Elijah was one thing, but the entire world—it's too much.

"I think that there is nothing that we can't do when we are together." Tate picked up one of the blooming flowers from the ground and gently placed it in Desti's hair. He gave her a soft smile and stood, holding out his hand to her. She slipped her hand into his as he pulled her to her feet.

"We should get back to the group. They are probably wondering where we are."

Desti just nodded and let Tate lead the way as she admired him from behind.

Chapter Three

Ahead

"It's over here," Seraph shouted from ahead.

It had been a few days now since Desti and Tate jumped into the portal, landing themselves in the time *before* the Era of the Damned. This new world was everything that Desti imagined it could be—treetops souring to the tips of the sky, melodies of chirps and buzzing from various birds and insects, and even the air had a fresh scent of jasmine and pine—nothing like the smog-filled sky back in the city of Mors.

These past few days had been something she could only describe as magical, but she knew deep down that this wouldn't last. Because she knew what was to come. It was just a question of when.

"Are you okay?" Tate must have noticed Desti faltering in her thoughts. She blinked and gave him a half smile while walking toward wherever Seraph was calling from.

"I'm fine."

Tate cocked his head to the side. "You are most definitely not fine. What is on your mind?" He had turned his body until he was now facing her and held out his hand to slow her pace. "Hang on, we will catch up to them," he said. "Now, tell me. What is wrong?"

Desti was silent for a moment. She didn't want to worry anyone with her intrusive thoughts. The past few days had been magical, getting to know her friends better and seeing Anthony doing so well, but she mostly just loved the time alone with Tate. In her city, it was forbidden to love, to show affection, and ever since she had gotten a taste of what it felt like to be close to the person that she loved, she wanted to savor every kiss, every touch, without corrupting it with her fears and worries. But when she glanced up into Tate's eyes, all she saw was the deep worry in them.

She huffed and pulled him to the side to sit on a tree stump. "This place is amazing and beautiful, and—" she stopped.

"And what?" asked Tate.

"And this world is everything that I prayed for, but we both know that it won't last." It was as if something had a hold of her vocals as she tried to speak. The anxiety of thinking about everything came rushing to the surface.

"What do you mean, 'it won't last'?"

Desti rolled her eyes before answering. "We both read the same history books. We both know that the Rapture is going to happen. This world is perfect because *it* hasn't happened yet. What if we jumped ourselves right into the beginning of a war, Tate?"

Desti noticed a change in Tate's eyes, once beaming with love and hopefulness, were now shrouded with the same despair that she was suffocating from. "You know I am right. I can see it by the look in your eyes."

Tate didn't say anything at first. He only let out a large breath and stood from where he was sitting. "We can't think like this Desti. We should be grateful for where we are. All of us could have easily been dead, but we made it out—*alive*." He continued to pace in front of her, stirring up hues of dirt particles, and continued, "Maybe that won't happen this time. We could figure out a way to stop it from happening."

Desti sighed. The time in the Beginning of the Era of the Damned was a horror story that she was forced to learn growing up. The world eradicated most of the population with catastrophic weather, and once that had subsided, the real terror began its reign—demons flooded every city, and every country, ripping people apart, and capturing the ones they felt would suit their needs for a new world. To Desti, it sounded like the most terrifying thing to experience.

Desti clutched the Lux that was nestled on her hip, noticing Tate's gaze flick down to it. "What? You think that because I have the Lux that I somehow can stop the end of the world?" She scoffed and stood up, now walking to catch up with the rest of the group.

"Wait." Tate lunged forward and grasped Desti's free hand and pulled her close to him. His eyes were fixated on her as he drew his fingers upward, tracing the outline of her face. Desti leaned into his touch, closing her eyes just for a moment. She felt the tips of his fingers brush the edge of her lips until he had made his way to her hair. "Whatever it is, I will be there, right by your side, fighting for you." Her pulse was now electric, beating up into her neck. Desti inhaled, shivering from his touch.

"What if this is something that we can't fight? I don't want to lose you." Desti placed her hand over his until their fingers laced together. "You are my everything… I didn't know it back then, but I know it now. I can't live without you, Tate."

Her hair blew freely in the breeze, strands of brown and gold dancing across her face, but that didn't stop Tate from leaning in and capturing a kiss. The moment his lips pressed against hers, the world stopped. She melted into his touch until she found herself tangled into him; his hand effortlessly gliding its way down the small of her back until he was pulling her body into him.

Desti pulled away slightly and gasped. "We really need to catch—"

Tate stole a kiss, and then another, until her words were muffled under the slight moans that drifted from her mouth. "Shhh…" he kissed her, then pressed his lips to her cheek. "I'm here. I'll never leave you." Tate then kissed his way to the side of her face until he nibbled at her ear, and then softly whispered, "I love you, Desti."

"Okay, you two love birds. I think we have given you enough alone time for the day," Tess called, emerging from the bushes. Desti stepped back and laughed. Warmth flushed to her cheeks as she glanced back at Tate, who didn't seem to have the same embarrassed expression. He gave her a slight smirk and nodded his head. "Come on, let's catch up with them."

Tate then tugged her along until they both disappeared through the bushes.

The first thing that Desti noticed when emerging through the bushes was the glistening city that was nestled beneath the mountainside. It seemed to stretch for miles, and now that the sun was beginning to set, it was as if the gilded houses were painted with hues of gold and orange. Seraph and Kaelen stood ahead, staring out at the vast life beneath their feet. Desti thought that they too must be admiring how breathtakingly beautiful this view was. Anthony was sitting on a large boulder, swinging one leg over the other, just twirling a leaf in his hand. He lifted his gaze and smiled once he made eye contact with Desti and Tate.

"Hey you," he said.

Desti strode forward and inhaled. "So, this is what a real city looks like." Anthony took another glance at the houses along the streets and then looked back at her. "I prayed just so that I would one day be able to take a breath of fresh air again; feel the wind on my face; the sun warm my skin..." He trailed off, glancing away as if he were reliving the torture he had to endure, but then continued, "And then you came along, and you answered all my prayers. But I never thought that I would ever get to see something so...perfect."

Tears almost began to well in her eyes as she listened to Anthony speak. He had become like a little brother to her. Someone that she truly did love and want to protect. Desti placed her hand over her heart and ran forward, pulling Anthony into a hug. "I'm so happy that I was able to give you all those things."

Tess was standing off in the distance when she spoke, breaking up the side conversations that were going on. "Uh— I hate to interrupt, but what should we do now? We have no idea how to speak to these people, let alone live among them."

Brandon nodded his head in agreement; he had a mouth full of blueberries. He kept one foot in front of the other as if she were still trying to walk away and get to the city.

Tess's wild, bright orange hair bounced with the gusts of wind, making her look like a fierce animal. Her eyes flashed with a sense of worry, which made Desti question their next steps as well. She turned to Tate. "She's right. We can't just go down there and say 'Hi, we are from the future. Your world is about to end.'"

Tate laughed but quickly sucked in his breath as Desti scolded him with fierce eyes. "Sorry, uh, maybe we could start with walking the streets. Then maybe we can talk to someone, and *maybe* they will be able to point us in the right direction."

Chapter Four

A New City

The path down to the city was traitorous, and Desti and the rest of the group had endured numerous cuts and pokes as they slid their way down to the bottom of the mountain. Her leg stung from the thorns that had somehow managed to wrap their way around her ankles.

"I'm never doing that again," Kaelen said as she brushed off withered, dry leaves that clung to her clothes and hair. Seraph stood at her back, plucking each leaf—one by one—until her golden mane was clear of the debris.

Seraph walked toward Tate with an urgent look in his eyes. "Should we…you know, bring weapons down there with us?" Tate cocked his head to the side, glanced at Brandon in a silent motion, arching his eyebrows. Brandon mirrored the same expression. Desti could tell by the glimmer in his eyes that he was considering Seraph's suggestion, but before Tate could answer, Desti jumped in. "Actually, Seraph, I think it is best that we go unarmed. If we come waltzing in there with sharp sticks in our hands, no one will want to help us."

Tate chuckled, and Seraph gave Desti a half-nod. Kaelen skipped over to Seraph, giggling, pulling his hand into hers as she began to walk down the path leading toward the city. Desti tilted her head. *Are they…together?* She wondered.

"What are we going to say if someone talks to us?" Tate asked. Desti could tell he was nervous by the change in his voice, but he would never admit it. She was nervous too. This was new territory for her. For all of them. "We just…keep it simple," she said, smiling at him.

"Keep it simple. Okay. I can do that."

Anthony and Tess were trailing slightly behind, talking, while Kaelen, Seraph, and Brandon had already begun their adventurous walk. Desti guessed that Anthony had forgiven Tess for what she did to him. After spending so much time with her—not poisoned by the demon blood—she actually turned out to be quite friendly.

Desti held out her hand as a gesture for Tate to take it. His gaze slipped to her empty palm. He hesitated for a moment, flicking his gaze to her eyes. "We don't have to hide anymore. It isn't forbidden here," she said.

The moment his fingers slipped into hers, it was like an electric current shooting through her body, freezing time in that moment as she let her body explore the power of his touch on her skin. Who knew that one touch from someone could make you feel so alive again? She squeezed his hand and pulled him forward.

Above the lingering trees, white, fluffy clouds soared above them. Sunlight and shade danced together in harmony, blanketing the pathway with bouts of warmth. Desti tilted her chin, soaking up the warm rays that beamed down upon her. "It feels so good," she said. Tate had a look in his eyes that Desti couldn't pinpoint what he could possibly be thinking about.

"What? Why are you staring at me like that?"

He cracked a smile and laughed. "Nothing…I just never thought that we would be here. Doing this." He gestured to the trees and forest around him and let his gaze fall back to Desti, a glimmer of hope and peacefulness lingered in his eyes, flashing gold and green, and then slowly his gaze shifted to something more primal, hungry, as his eyes traced Desti's arm and then up to her mouth. He stopped there, and by the way Tate bit his bottom lip, Desti knew that he was thinking of one thing—she couldn't help but think of it too.

Desti snorted and swatted his arm. "Tate, not here. *That*…will have to wait," she joked, eyeing him up and down. Damn, did he look good like that—his gilded hair shimmering like a moon-kissed starlit sky, and eyes burning with a fiery desire. One look at Tate had ignited a rush of warmth into her core. All she wanted in this moment was to be alone with him;

to feel his biceps pull her in; to smell the pine and breeze in his hair; to hear gentle moans escape from his mouth but—

Desti blinked, trying to shake away these thoughts. *Not right now. We are too busy and in a hurry.* The rest of the group had already started on the path down to the city, so, Desti inhaled and took off running after them.

"Hey wait! We're coming"

She could hear Tate panting behind her, but he did catch up rather quickly. Oh, we shall work on our stamina; once we find a safe place to lay our heads, she thought.

"What is it?" Kaelen was asking Brandon, poking something that looked dead with a stick. Tess had peered over her shoulder in a contorted and creepy manner, and Seraph looked just as perplexed.

There was a gentle breeze that blew in from the rolling white clouds, but this time, a waft of something decaying smacked her in the face. She recoiled and covered her nose, grunting. "Ugh, it smells dead whatever it is." And whatever *it* was, did look like a ball of dead something. Black coursed hair covered half of—whatever— that thing's body was, but there were patches of crusted, flaky skin too.

"Well, if it's dead, maybe we should just leave it alone. If someone sees us poking a dead thing, then no one is going to want to help us," said Tate. Just as Kaelen dropped her stick and stepped away, there was a noise coming from behind the alleyway that the group had somehow found themselves in.

Desti held her breath in a moment of tiny panic. She had to keep reminding herself that this world wasn't just plagued with demons at every corner, but still, she stepped back in retreat as the noise grew closer. Tate had placed his hand softly on the small of her back, as in a way to say, *I will protect you.* Her eyes found Anthony; she couldn't help it but to worry for him. He had almost become like her little brother, her child even, and she would do anything to protect him.

Suddenly, in the shadows of the alley, a figure emerged, and…it was grunting. Desti sucked in her breath. Maybe there were demons in this time too, she thought, but just as fear was about to unravel her, the figure—a man—stumbled into the light.

"Who the Hell is that?" Tess asked. Her bright orange hair was wild with questions, and her eyes too. Brandon took a defensive stance, as did the rest of her friends. Desti had to remind herself that Tess was a fighter, a warrior, a machine trained to kill, if need be, and she had that look in her eyes now.

"What are you kids doing with my dog?" the man grumbled. He was covered in filth and stains; even Desti had better clothes than him. Her gaze traced him up and down until his eyes met with hers. *Oh shit, he is looking right at me.*

"*That* is a dog?" Kaelen asked, pointing the stick toward the black ball of *whatever* that was lying on the ground. The man looked seriously pissed off as he took a step forward. "Of course it's a fucking dog. Are you blind?"

Suddenly, the black ball unfolded its body and began to wag its tail. It lifted its head and made a sound that Desti had never heard before. She felt Tate lean closer to her until his breath kissed her neck, and he whispered in her ear, "I have never seen one before. Only heard of them." She nodded slowly. The city of Mors didn't have animals, except for the very small selection of pigs and chickens that kept the people from starving to death.

A dog.

Desti was actually looking at a dog…and it was *alive.*

Anthony broke his silence and walked closer to the man and said, "Sir, sorry about your dog. We aren't from here and we don't see many dogs where we are from." The man grunted and cocked his head to the side. He whistled, and his dog jumped up and took off, running into the shadows. The man eyed Anthony up and down, then slowly gazed upon the rest of the group. "You kids look like Hell. You're not from around here, are you?"

Tate slipped a glance at Desti, and in his eyes, he was saying, *don't say anything,* but before Desti or Tate could say something, Seraph spoke. "No, we are not. We are from—"

"Seraph!" Tess yelled.

Seraph stopped dead in his tracks and swallowed. He looked at Tess, then Brandon, and then at Desti, and then back at the man standing before him. "Hmmm," the man grumbled. "You kids in any kind of trouble?"

Do we say yes? Desi wrestled with the thought of telling him the truth, but she knew that she would sound crazy. In her hand, Desti still had the Lux clutched tightly within her grip, but she held it off to her side to keep it hidden. It seemed that every day, the Lux felt more powerful as if it were connecting with her in a sense. She couldn't explain it, but a connection was forming.

"We were hiking up the mountain," Tate pointed to the mountain behind them, and continued, "We got lost, and stumbled upon this city. Do you know where we can find somewhere to rest our heads for the night?"

Tate still had his hand placed gently on Desti's back. He hadn't even slightly removed it from her. His touch was electrifying, and sensual, exploding a type of hunger and desire in her core that she had never experienced before.

"You got money? Cause to me, looks like you ain't got it."

Anthony, Brandon, Tess, Kaelen, and Seraph all shot a look at Desti. "Uh…"

"I'll take that as a no." The man took a swig of a bottle that he had clutched in his grip and burped. "You ain't gonna get far without money. S'pecially in this town. He has got everyone under his spell." The man pointed his bottle at a poster that hung on the brick wall, splashes of the brown liquid hitting the ground. She hadn't noticed it until now, but the moment her eyes fell upon the picture, her heart dropped to her stomach.

"Who is that?" Desti had stepped closer. She looked at the rest of her group, and she could tell that they were also experiencing an internal panic. She would recognize that face anywhere. His voice practically haunted her at every waking second, and those eyes, she could see the evil that seeped from them, even in this picture.

"That bastard is Rospinity Gage," the man spat. "That fucker owes me." Desti heard Tate suck in his breath; his hands began to tremble on the back of her shirt. It was as if her throat was being crushed by the overwhelming feeling of despair, because whoever Rospinity Gage was, Desti knew him as someone else—she would never forget those eyes.

"The Master," she breathed.

Chapter Five

Rospinity Gage

"How is this even possible?" **Tess threw her hands up. She had** been pacing back and forth for the past hour now in a sheer panic. Kaelen was at the point of almost hyperventilating, Brandon was off in the corner sulking in silence, and Seraph and Anthony stood in the corner like zombies.

"Tess, calm down." Desti stepped forward, arms stretched out. Tess gave her a frantic look and continued to walk in circles. "Calm down? How the Hell can I calm down? You saw who was on that poster! The Master…he…" Tess's voice croaked; she sat down and began to cry.

Desti sat next to her and placed her hand on Tess's shoulder. Tess's eyes were glossed with tears as she glanced up at Desti through her frizzed tangles of hair. "When Elijah burned down the camp with his army of demons, the Master was with him. He took me, and the others, and before he cast me to Hell, he…he…tortured me. But not just me. He made me watch as my friends were ripped limb from limb as he sat there and *ate* them." Was that what happened to Clara? To Tilly? And all the others? Even though Desti didn't know them well, she still considered them her friends. Tess was now in a full-on cry, but Desti didn't blame her. She knew how horrible it was to watch someone get eaten alive.

The day she had found Tate, she saw a man's leg get ripped off as the Master sunk his teeth into his flesh. It made her want to hurl just thinking about it. That was a memory that she had shoved way down, and for good reason.

"So, the Master's name is really Rospinity Gage?" Kaelen snorted. "What a weird name." Seraph had chuckled at that, but Anthony and Tess's faces were stone cold.

"How is this possible? How could he be here, and back in our time?" Anthony asked. Tess furrowed her brows and huffed. "It's his fucking dark magic. If he is working with Amaros, then who knows what kind of crazy shit he can do." Tess scoffed. "Maybe there are two of him."

Anthony cocked his head to the side. He didn't seem to disagree, rather, agree with what she was saying. Maybe Tess was right. Were there *two* of the Master? Or has he somehow figured out a way to travel back in time? Come to think of it, why did Amaros send Desti and her friends back to the beginning of the Era of the Damned? This was a thought that lingered in her mind more often than she'd liked to admit. She should be happy that she didn't have to go back to that insufferable world, but something didn't feel right. Something about being sent here, to this time, felt calculated, and knowing Amaros and the Master, they always had a motive.

"This can't be a coincidence. This must mean something. If The Master is really here, then we must lay low and keep our eyes out for him; we will come up with a plan on how to deal with him later."

Seraph had leaned back in the chair he was sprawled out in and took a sip of a bottle of brown liquid, almost choking as he swigged it back. "Well, good thing that smelly man let us crash at his…uh…" Seraph glanced around, and continued, "…place."

It wasn't much of a place, Desti thought, but it was better than sleeping in the streets. The smelly man had offered Desti and her friends to stay at his "bunker", which he had hidden within a closed down part of a building. It was abandoned; however, it was now a hive for all the dirty crazies that lived in the city. He even had electricity, which to Desti, was almost unbelievable to see with her own eyes. Back in the city of Mors, only the schools had small amounts of electricity, and even then, it was scarce.

"That smelly man's name is Peter, and he is letting us stay here. Don't go ruining that by insulting him," Tess scoffed. "Don't forget that his smelly little dog is named Jet," Brandon added, and then shrugged his shoulders as Tess shot him a glare.

Peter had told them his name while he led them to his hidden home, and he told them about the man he hated so much—Rospinity Gage—the Master. All of this was too much to fathom. How in the Hell was the Master here? Now? *And*, to top it all off, Peter said that he was the mayor of the town, whatever that was; but Peter had explained that Rospinity basically was in charge of the city.

Great, Desti thought. Just what he needed. More power.

From the cracks that sporadically decorated the withered brick walls, a dim, orange glow seeped through, spilling into their room like strings of gold. Desti took a moment to admire how beautiful the sunset was, even from inside, and then stood. "We should all get some rest."

Seraph was already half passed out in his chair, and Kaelen was curled up next to him, her head delicately placed on his shoulder. Brandon nodded and walked his way over to what looked like an old room; however, the walls were half torn down. "I'll sleep here tonight," he said. Tess and Anthony had found a corner to sleep—small pads of cushions were laid out as if this place were expecting people to be staying here. "Anthony, will you be okay sleeping out here?" Desti asked. He just simply smiled and nodded.

Peter had told Desti that he had something important to do, but that she and Tate could use one of the empty rooms. Once Desti established that her friends were safe and comfortable, she grabbed Tate's hand, pulling him to their room.

"This is our room?" Tate said. His face expressed a mixture of displeasure and shock. Desti didn't blame him—their room, if you would even call it that—had three and a half concrete walls—not four—and a broken, wooden door that clung to the frame as if its life depended on it.

"Well," Desti said. "It's better than nothing, and at least we have *some* privacy." Desti went to shut the wooden door, leaving only a sliver of a crack open. When she turned, she noticed Tate had lay down on one of the mattresses on the floor.

"You look comfortable." She laughed.

Tate smiled, his eyes flashing her with intensity. He looked gorgeous, she thought, in the most masculine way. Through his shirt, the rifts of his muscles danced with every movement, and damn did it look good. He looked like a freaking god lying under the beams of moonlight. "Come lay next to me," he replied, patting on the bed.

With one foot in front of the other, Desti took a couple slow and steady steps, and once she met the bed, she kneeled onto the cushion until she found herself leaning over Tate, her hair spilling over her shoulder. He brushed it back and kept his hands delicately placed along her back. His touch…oh it was electrifying. Even the faintest of touches from him sent Desti swirling.

Back in the city of Mors, it was forbidden to love. To do so would mean being sacrificed to the demons, with a lifetime or more of torment. Desti didn't know how terrible that reality truly was until she saw it for herself. She had known for a long time her feelings for Tate were more than just friends, but she had no choice but to push it way down. But she couldn't pinpoint when that obsession had drowned out her feelings altogether.

This was new territory, and she had to tread cautiously. It was dark now, moonlight eventually faded to a sea of black as the starry sky enveloped the world. It was beautiful, she thought. The peace. The clear skies. Desti closed her eyes and drew in a breath, feeling the touch of him. Tate traced idol circles along Desti's back, and she melted into his touch.

Thum. Thum. Thum

This is the sound of the man that I love. His heart. She could listen to it all day long; the way it unraveled her until she felt raw and vulnerable in the most desirable way.

"What are you thinking?" Tate broke the silence.

His voice was like velvet. Like the spring water flowing through her fingers; smooth and crisp. He stopped tracing his fingers along her back and brought them up now to her hair. "I'm thinking about Mors…about our lives there."

Tate made a grunting sound, and Desti lifted her head to glance at him. "I think about that often too. Our world was so…"

"Terrible?" she finished.

"Yes, and then some. But without you, I don't think I could have survived it. I don't think I would even want to."

Desti knew that his words were true. It had always been her and him, since they were young, and it would be her and him until the end.

She was now lying halfway on the mattress with her leg wrapped around his torso, resting her head delicately on her hand, and the other, she tiptoed up his arm until she met his face.

His face was the most perfect and beautiful thing she had ever seen—his sharp jawline, pointed nose, and those eyes…God, those eyes were to die for. She cupped her hand around his cheek and let herself fall into his gaze. It felt like an eternity staring back at him, and she wondered in that moment what he thought of when looking at her. Was it pain and suffering, and all the torment she went through? Did she remind him of the horrors of their world? Or did he see something more?

His lips parted, and she got a glimpse of his tongue underneath, and that was when a warmth rushed to her core. A primal hunger that she had spent years trying to lock away, but she felt safe now, and so, it was time to let the predator out of its cage. His eyes flashed with something predatory itself in that moment; there was no denying the electric pull in the air. His smell—pine and oak—was like a drug to her. Desti inhaled the scent of him and ran the palm of her hand down his chest.

"You are all that I ever wanted, Tate, my best friend…" she nipped at his neck. "My Savior…" Gently, her tongue grazed over his skin until her mouth lingered just above his ear. "My love…" The minute the word love escaped her lips, Tate had tightened, flipping her over onto her back. She felt his grasp on her pull her body into him. His breath kissed her shoulder as he leaned into her touch, kissing the peaks of her collar bone, until he found himself venturing farther downward. Just the sounds of his gentle moans got Desti wet. In less than a heartbeat, Tate had Desti pinned beneath his body, grinding into her with an aggression that Desti desperately craved.

"I would do anything for you," he purred. "I would kill for you, and if I had to die to save you, I would take the knife and do it myself."

"Oh, Tate," she gasped.

His fingers had found their way to the spot that craved him the most; gentle circles teased her as his teeth grazed the hollow of her neck. A rush flooded over her just from the sheer sound of his hushed groans, so, she could only imagine how her body would react once it got a taste of him. Her fingers locked into his hair, pulling him in. She couldn't hold it back anymore. She needed him, and she needed him now.

Their lips crashed together like a star falling into the Earth. She breathed him in, tasting the sweetness of his lips. Oh, he tasted so good. So, fucking good. Desti could barely contain herself with his cock grinding up against her like this. Her tongue explored his in a dance of desire, their breaths mingling until they became one.

"I want you," she managed to beg. "Now."

Tate pulled away just for a moment and smiled. *Oh God!* She couldn't wait anymore. Desti reached for the hardness that was so desperately trying to find its way to her center. If she had to guide it there, then so be it. Tate's fingers had slipped beneath her shorts and between her legs.

"God, Desti," he breathed. Tate went in for a kiss, and his fingers went deeper. Desti gasped, her back arching and writhing, until she couldn't take it anymore.

"I need you," she breathed.

His body was warm, soft, and hard all at the same damn time; he was perfect. "You're mine, forever, no matter what," he groaned, kissing his way down until he stopped just above her hips. He was like an animal, ripping her pants off, and before she had a second to move, he dove into the wetness of her.

Her world stopped in that moment as she clawed her way at the sheets beneath her, trying to scream from the pleasure he was inflicting on her. Tate was like an animal, and she embraced his primal instinct. Her thighs wrapped around him, holding him into her as he flicked his tongue exactly where she wanted him to.

Heat and pressure was building between her; she could feel it in her core. Her moans grew louder and louder, and just before Tate had Desti over the edge he slowly pulled away, kissing the inside of her thighs.

"Oh, God! You're fucking evil," she hissed. Tate laughed and flashed a wicked smile of enticement. "Can't have you coming yet. I want to make you scream my name and beg for more." Even the way he talked made Desti's legs quiver. He could fuck her with the smoothness of his voice, and she would be satisfied, but now, she needed him, and she wanted him—inside.

"You better fuck me then." The corner of her mouth twitched and that was when she saw the change in his eyes. He was going to fuck her until her throat was hoarse, and that was exactly what she wished for.

His cock was long and hard, peaking up at the sight of her sprawled out body on the bed. Desti bit down on her lip and opened her legs, slowly grazing her hands up her thighs. "Do you like what you see?" Tate only nodded slowly, not once breaking his gaze on her. His magnificently chiseled body leaned over her like a god.

And…when the Hell did he take his shirt off?

She couldn't take it anymore. He was her kryptonite, and she was his. The moment he slipped himself into her, the very breath of her chest hitched at the pleasure he invoked in her. "Oh my God, Tate." At first his strokes were slow and steady; his breath caressing her skin like silk. With every passing second, she only grew wetter; every stroke slipping in effortlessly. Desti dug her nails into his back and pulled him into her, and the strokes then grew faster and harder.

Her moans matched his strength, but he caught them with his mouth, kissing her swollen lips until only muffled cries of pleasure escaped between shallow breaths. It was building again, the heat in her core and in her legs. Desti arched her back in an effort to beg for more; more pressure, more of *him*.

"Fuck! Tate, I love you," she cried, and that got her exactly what her body desperately craved. He fucked her until she was screaming his name, and soon she was going to get the release she was begging for.

"Please," she breathed. "Keep going…fuck." Ugh he felt so good. Soon, she was tingling as it grew and grew, and Tate seemed to be getting close too by the way he was moaning in her ear. And just like that, an orgasm so intense rolled through her body, leaving her shaking from the pleasure, Tate climaxing at the same time, and once it had passed, Tate kept his body entangled with hers, placing gentle kisses amongst her arm.

He had a twinkle in his eyes when he looked at her. "What are you thinking?" she asked. Tate was silent for a moment, as if he were pondering about what to say. "I'm thinking about you…" his voice trailed off and he glanced away, breaking his gaze. "You look sad. Why do you look sad?"

Desti had pulled Tate's face toward her, and his eyes were glossed over. Desti sat up. "Tate, what is it? What's wrong?" He drew in a large breath, reluctant to speak.

"I can't get it out of my head. The things that you went through. The things that *I* did to you, *down there*." It was as if he couldn't bear to speak of their time down in Hell; the way the Shadow had swallowed him and used him like a slave. Desti grabbed his hand and said, "Hey, that wasn't you. Okay? *You* got us out of there. *You* got us here, where we are safe. We are safe now, Tate."

He was her savior; the man who broke her free from her life of torment, even before she had gone to Hell. He hadn't known it, but without him, she wouldn't have survived. But sometimes, she forgot that he needed her too, and it was in this moment that she truly saw how much he needed her to guide him out of the darkness of his mind.

"Listen to me," her voice was firm. "You did nothing wrong down there. You got us out and kept us alive. I will never stop fighting for you, and for our friends. Together, we are stronger." Desti's voice choked. Tate had blinked away the tear that gathered in his eye, and pulled her into his chest, breathing in the scent of her.

"I love you. From the moment we met, I knew you were going to be special to me," he said. Desti didn't say anything, instead, she soaked it in; his scent, his voice, his touch, until a darkness of her own took over her mind, pulling her into a much-needed sleep.

Chapter Six

Something New

"What exactly am I eating?" Anthony asked Desti. He sat at a large table, with a plate of food that Peter had given him. Desti poked her food with the same perplexed expression plastered on her face. Brandon held up his fork and sniffed his portion before nibbling at it.

"Peter said it was called 'poor man's breakfast'," she said. Whatever that was. Anthony was only a young teen, and even before then, he was a prisoner to Elijah's sick and twisted game. It was only natural to assume that he hadn't had much experience with food the past few years or so, and back in his city, who knows what kind of things they served there?

He glanced up at her and grunted. "It looks like something threw this up on my plate." Desti laughed because he wasn't wrong, but that didn't stop Seraph, Tate, and Tess from scarfing their food down. Kaelen, her, and Anthony approached with caution.

"Just eat it. We need the energy. See," she said while regretfully taking a full spoonful of her breakfast into her mouth. "Mmmh, delicious." Anthony didn't seem too convinced, but he took a bite of his anyway, making an awfully disgusted face.

"Where did Peter go?" Kaelen asked, poking her food with her fork.

"I think he said that he wanted to introduce us to some of his friends," Tate replied. He was guzzling down some water and giving Desti an intensely seductive glare through the glass. She held in a laugh and glanced away from his *looking*. *Not now*. But she couldn't get him out of her mind either.

"Great, so we are going to meet more crazies?" Seraph joked. Tess laughed at that, but Kaelen looked displeased at his remark. "Seraph, just because they are homeless and a little dirty, doesn't mean that they are crazy." She lifted her hand, gesturing to everyone sitting at the table, and continued, "*We are homeless and a little dirty.*" Brandon scoffed and Kaelen shot him a deathly glare. "What?"

"Speak for yourself. I happened to clean myself off in the river the other day," Brandon replied, a slight smile pulled on his mouth. Kaelen's tightened face calmed, and she even huffed out a chuckle, rolling her eyes.

She had a point. Desti was just glad that they had someone be kind enough to share their place, even if their place was a crumbling, withered building that smelled like God knows what. Seraph leaned forward and asked, "So, are we going to just not talk about the fact that the Master is here? Do you think he would recognize us if he saw us?"

The air went frigid the moment Seraph mentioned the Master. Desti sucked in her breath and reached for Tate's hand beneath the table; his warmth was the only thing that could bring her body back to a normal state. "Either it's him and he would recognize us the moment he sees us, and who knows what he will do to us, or there are two versions of him. Maybe this version hasn't experienced all of the horrible things that he has done yet."

"So, what? Do you want to kill him before he gets the chance?" Tess asked so bluntly. Desti spit out her drink, spraying water onto the table. "Tess, we can't just go around talking about *killing* someone out in the open like this. This is a different time." But Desti knew the pleasure she would get from slitting his throat, watching his blood choke and gag him while he tried to beg for her mercy; she practically dreamt about it every night. She wanted to do terrible things to the ones who tormented her, but that was a thought that she hadn't even shared with Tate yet.

"Peter seems to hate him. I wonder what he has done to him," Anthony added. Tate glanced over at him and smiled; the kind of smile a proud father would do. Anthony was so kind, so pure. It pained Desti to her core that he had suffered all those years, alone, and if there was one thing she would do in her life worth fighting for, it was to give Anthony a chance to be happy.

"Maybe we have a chance to change the future. Maybe we can stop the rapture from happening altogether," Seraph had added, and Brandon grunted, "Mhmm," in agreement. But Tate, in the most calming voice, spoke, "The rapture will happen, whether we like it or not. Unfortunately, we don't have control over that, but we might be able to take care of the Master before he gains too much power." Tate pointed out his thumb and did a slicing motion across his neck at the mention of the Master.

Suddenly, Kalen hunched forward with a searing pained look on her face. Desti was the first to notice and reached for her. "Kaelen, what is it? What's wrong?" The rest of the group stopped what they were doing and were now focused on Kaelen. She was hurled almost in a ball, shaking from something causing her pain. But before she could speak, Seraph and Tess, too, had begun to shake and hunch forward.

"Fuck, it burns!" Seraph yelled through gritted teeth. *It burns?*

"What burns?" Desti asked.

"My neck. Check my neck." Tess had turned her body, facing her back toward Tate, and pulled her hair forward. Even from where Desti was sitting, across the table, she could see it clearly—the mark—and it was red hot, almost glowing with its intensity. Desti gasped, cupping her mouth. Tate slipped a worried glance at Desti. His eyes said it all, and she knew what he was trying to say—*we need to help them.*

The three of them were shaking so badly that they could barely speak, and Desti panicked, not knowing what to do, but Anthony stood from the table and ran off. "Anthony, where are you going?" Desti yelled. "I'll be right back. I am grabbing something!"

All Desti could do was watch her friends suffer, and it was a terrible feeling she knew all too well. Anthony came running up with a small pearlescent orb in his hands. "I saw where you hid it. Maybe you can help them with this."

"Anthony…I don't know how to use it yet." Anthony shoved the Lux in her hands and said, "You healed Tate's cuts with it. You told me so. So, why can't you do the same here?" Desti looked to Tate for reassurance, and he gave her a nod, his eyes glimmering. She'd better hurry quickly before Peter came back with his friends. The last thing they needed was to have to explain…*this.*

"Okay. Seraph, give me your hand." Seraph obliged and placed his shaking hand on the table, and Desti placed hers onto his. She closed her eyes, clutching the Lux with her other arm, holding it into her chest. She closed her eyes and slowed her breathing, drowning out the noise of the world, escaping to a part of her mind that was rarely explored.

Please take their pain. Please make it go away. They don't deserve to suffer anymore. Desti repeated this in her mind, hoping that something would happen, but she could still feel how tense

Seraph was under her hand. She tried again, breathing and focusing even more deeply.

There was silence at first, but something she was not expecting happened—it talked back.

We cannot. It must be you.

Desti almost dropped the Lux and gasped, and when she glanced around, Tate, Brandon, and Anthony were staring at her with curious eyes. "What? What is it?" Tate asked. Her voice caught in her throat. "It spoke to me…"

Tate blinked and Anthony leaned forward even more. "What did it say?" Desti's fingers were trembling. The Lux had now begun to feel warm to the touch as if she had activated it somehow. With hazy eyes, she looked at Tate and said, "It said they can't. That it must be me." Desti peered over at her friends; they were curled into themselves and clearly in pain.

"Tate, I can't do it. I don't know how to." He grabbed her hand and looked at her fiercely. "You can do it. You healed me back in the forest. I know you can do it." Desti gulped down her doubts and tried again. This time she asked for all three of them to place their hands on the table. "I want to try something. Anthony," she said. "Put your hand on the Lux with me.

She had the Lux in the center, her hand and Anthony's touching it gently, and in her other hand she held her friends'. *This has to work. Please. It has to.* Desti tried again, clearing her mind, bringing herself to that place of peace, and spoke again.

Heal my friends. Rid them of their pain and suffering. Set them free of their bindings. She demanded it this time, the voice in her headstrong and clear. This time, nothing spoke back, but something *was* happening. A warm rush of electric pulses flowed through her fingertips, and she could see it, the light, melting into their skin. Brandon made an audible gasp and just briefly Desti dared to break her focus to see the expression on his face.

Seraph was the first to relax and exhale a sigh of relief, followed by Tess and then Kaelen. They all sat back in their chairs for a moment, and Desti was frozen in disbelief. "Tess opened her eyes and said, "What the fuck what that?"

"What? The searing pain in the back of our necks, or the crazy electricity that Desti shot out of her fingers?" Seraph joked. "Both," she replied.

All eyes were on Desti now, probably wanting answers on what the Hell she was able to do, but she didn't have the slightest clue about the things she might be capable of.

"Uh…I don't know what I did, you guys. I just told it to free you of the pain. And I had no idea that this thing could actually talk to me."

"You heard it? In your head?" Kaelen had asked. Desti nodded but kept her gaze on Kaelen. She looked troubled, terrified even, and Desti knew there was something that she wasn't saying. "Kaelen, what is it? What's wrong?"

"I heard a voice too…" Kaelen trailed off, but the moment she finished speaking, Tess and Seraph froze as if they saw a ghost. "You heard it too?" He asked.

"Heard what?" asked Tate.

Tess gave Kaelen and Seraph the side eye, speaking up before they managed to. "It was like static, and whispers. It sounded as if its voice was something that was searching for us; it was far away, I could tell, but I could feel how badly it wanted to find us." Tess clenched her fingers into her arms and shivered.

Kaelen nodded and Seraph's mouth was parted. "It felt like it was getting close, but whatever you did, Desti, you must have pushed it away."

Desti's breathing hitched as she drew in a ragged breath. Realization was hitting her now, that the marks were something dangerous, and they knew nothing about what it truly meant to have them. *Holy shit*, she thought. This was a situation.

Chapter Seven

Introduction

Peter was kind enough to lend Desti a small bag and a change of clothes that he said he had found dumpster diving. Considering the new situation with the marks that Seraph, Kaelen, and Tess had, she thought it would be best to keep the Lux with her at all times.

Thank God for this bag.

After Desti had rid her friends of the mark's effects, they sat there for a moment in silence, and that was when Peter walked up with some of his friends, Jet happily following alongside him.

"Desti, I would like for you to meet Jake—he gestured to a young man, maybe mid-twenties, with shaggy dirty-blonde hair—and this is Lauren, my second in command."

Desti nodded her head and then looked them up and down. Jake seemed like any other sweet homeless man walking the streets; timid and shy, maybe even a little slow, but Lauren was the complete opposite. She was fierce, Desti could tell, just by the way she stood and held her chin high. Desti thought she was beautiful, her eyes a piercing golden-brown color.

"Desti it's nice to meet you. Peter told me a little bit about you and your friends." Lauren held out her hand and Desti shook it. "I didn't know you guys had a hierarchy here. I thought this was more like a community of—"

She stopped herself. "Of homeless people?" Lauren added. She laughed, a smile tugging at her lip. Desti huffed out a sound of embarrassment and immediately retreated. " I didn't mean it like that."

"It's okay. But yes, to answer your question, we do have people in command here. It keeps the order."

"I'm sorry, and what exactly are you guys doing again?" Seraph had so rudely interjected. Desti rolled her eyes and Tate stiffened, but neither Peter nor Lauren seemed offended by Seraph's question. And that was when realization dawned on her. Peter still hadn't explained exactly his situation, or the history of him and Rospinity, and Desti was eager to find out.

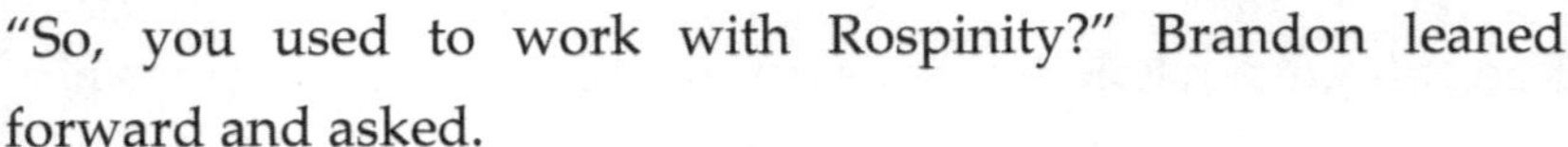

"So, you used to work with Rospinity?" Brandon leaned forward and asked.

Peter nodded his head simultaneously with Lauren. "Yes, I was his partner in his campaign. Desti had almost forgotten that Peter mentioned that Rospinity was the mayor of the town. Desti arched her eyebrow and asked, "So, he is in charge of the city?"

Lauren nodded but the look in her eyes told Desti there was more than what she was saying, and Desti was curious as to what it was. Desti held her gaze on Lauren, and she knew that Lauren could sense her curiosity and mistrust. Lauren glanced at Brandon, then Tate, and stopped at Desti. "Our city hasn't been doing well, ever since the First Fall, and Rospinity took that as an opportunity to gain control and power."

First Fall? What did she mean by that? To Peter and Lauren, they were just a group of young adults who got lost hiking, so naturally they should know what the First Fall meant, but Anthony—thank God for Anthony—he interrupted and asked, "What is the First Fall?"

Lauren glanced at Desti and Tate, probably waiting for them to explain what it was, but when they sat silently, Lauren nodded and proceeded. "The First Fall was the collapse of our government after the west coast was destroyed by the Earthquakes." When no one spoke up, Peter placed his elbows on the table and said, "Surely you remember that. The whole world has been crumbling and going to shit since then."

The sun rays were now spilling into the room, gilding Kaelen's golden hair; it was practically blinding. She flipped her hair off her shoulder and said, "We aren't from here." Desti wanted to smack her on the back of the head, and the confused expression on Lauren's and Peter's faces confirmed Desti's feelings.

"Right, but like I said, the whole world knew about this. Everywhere on the planet has been crumbling."

"Who did you kids say you were again? Where did you come from?" Peter asked.

Oh shit, Desti thought.

"You kids ain't one of his spies now, are you?"

Desti had to think quickly or else their only place to stay could soon become just a forgotten memory. She needed time. Time to figure out what kind of powers the Lux truly held, what Rospinity—the Master—knew about them, if at all, and maybe, just maybe, she might have a way to change the course of history, stopping the rise of the demons altogether.

But first, she needed to see Rospinity. Desti blinked and quickly interjected, "Of course, we know about the First Fall. It was horrible to hear about…that." Desti glanced up but the look in Lauren and Peter's eyes was unconvincing. She couldn't tell if they were buying her story. Her breathing hitched, and Tate must have sensed her internal struggle, so, he jumped in and changed the subject.

"I don't think we have officially given you our thanks for the hospitality, and I must admit, we are quite intrigued to hear about your plans with this city and your history with Rospinity. Maybe we can help."

Desti blew out a breath of relief and leaned back into her chair until her shoulder blades were touching the hard plastic. She looked at Tate and smiled. He always knew how to wear that mask when he needed to. He could convince anyone anything if he tried. Lauren and Peter seemed to have taken the bait and now engaged in their own hushed conversation with Tate about their plans for the city. If he could convince them to let her and her friends in on their plans, then that meant that she would be able to get close to the Master; and maybe even kill him before the world began to fall apart.

Brandon and Tess had sat in silence off in the corner, sort of listening, sort of not, but Desti was grateful for that; it was less opportunity to mess up *her* plans. She couldn't help but think of how crazy it was that she had stumbled upon an underground rebel group trying to take out the Master; even if they were technically homeless, their home was far better than most places Desti had seen growing up.

But Peter's plans for taking down the Master were different than what Desti had planned for. If only he knew that stopping the Master—Rospinity—could potentially save the future; he only thought that he was trying to make a small difference in his city.

For now, Desti decided to keep the Lux a secret from them and to keep her knowledge of Rospinity to a low. Her first step would be figuring out if this version of the Master would recognize her; if so, then she would be royally screwed, but if not, then there would be her first step in her plan: Take Down the Master.

After Peter and Lauren had talked Tate to a complete state of boredom, they finally whisked away, off somewhere doing something *important*, they said. By the end of the hour-long conversation, Tate's eyes were bloodshot, and his shoulders were slumped.

"That was a lot, huh?" Desti said while slipping into a clean shirt that Lauren had found her.

"What? The fact that they talked to me for over an hour straight, or the fact that they just pretty much told me their entire mission and what their group stands for?" He huffed out a laugh, sliding his fingers through his hair. Desti had glanced up after putting her shirt on and did not expect to see Tate shirtless.

"Woah…"

"What? You've seen me without a shirt hundreds of times."

"Yeah, but now it's different."

Tate cocked his head to the side, a smirk tugging at his mouth. "Different how?"

Desti rolled her eyes, reluctant to give him the satisfaction of admitting that his hot body did all sorts of things to her. She bit her lip and then said, "Now that we have…" her eyes fell to his *area* and then locked back into his gaze. He was smiling but silently waited for her to finish.

"Now that we have done…that, it's all I can think about when I see you, like this…"

Tate came closer now, and he had finally slipped his clean shirt over his head. The warmth of his body pulsated off him, caressing Desti as he leaned into her ear. Just a few more inches and his lips would have kissed the part of her ear that would completely undo her. Just thinking about it sent a rush to her core. "It's all I've been thinking about too," he purred.

Before Desti could respond, Anthony peered around the corner, saving her from getting too hot and bothered. "Desti?"

"Yes, Anthony, I'm over here."

Anthony was holding a plate of food that she assumed he got from Peter or one of his people. "Peter gave this to me. He said that one of his scouts found a good stash of food and supplies while out in town."

"Thank you." Desti took the plate from Anthony but noticed that his face lingered with curious eyes. He glanced back up at her and asked, "What exactly did Peter tell you and Tate? They keep telling me that it isn't safe to go outside."

This was something that she hadn't had a chance to talk with Tate about yet, but she was also curious. When Desti had wandered from the mountain to the city, it had looked beautiful; grass and life burst through every crevice of every structure, but maybe that wasn't how it was supposed to be here. She had only ventured to the very outskirts of the city, so maybe the rest of the city was unsafe somehow. She didn't remember seeing that many people walking around. Come to think of it, Peter was the only person she had seen on the outside, besides those hikers a few days back. She smiled back at Anthony and led him to a small table where Tess and Brandon, and Seraph and Kaelen were sitting. "Let's eat first, then Tate can catch us up."

Desti sat down her plate and pulled out an empty chair, taking a seat and before she dug into her food, she glanced back at Tate and nodded her head. "You coming?"

Chapter Eight

The Plan

"So, we were pretty much dumped at the end of the world, and now people have resulted with creating their own governments within their cities due to their fear?" Seraph had asked with a mouth full of food.

Kaelen, wide-eyed, nodded her head as she listened to him speak. Tate had gone over the details of what Peter and Lauren had told him. The city was mostly destroyed by terrible Earthquakes, seemingly abandoned by most of the locals; however, the ones that stayed eventually split into two groups: Rospinity and his clan wanted to rule the city; he wanted power, while Peter and his friends wanted peace and a simpler way of living. He had been in hiding for the past two years now, scavenging what he could and recruiting people to his group after seeing the evil in Rospinity grow like a wild vine. He believed that Rospinity was up to no good and that eventually, he would be the reason for the destruction of this city.

If only he knew how close to the truth he really was.

"Pretty much, yeah," Tate replied.

Tess leaned forward, a hint of fear lurking behind her irises, and asked, "Do you think he would know who we were if he saw us?" This was a fear that ate away at Desti. It was unrelenting and tortuous, but valid because he very well could be the same version of the Master back in her time.

When Desti was in Hell, she witnessed creatures and magic that she had never thought would have existed, and yet, they did. With the Master having access to that kind of power, who knew what he was actually capable of?

"Isn't he a High King of Hell? There are three, right?" Brandon had broken his silence, speaking with a mouth full of food. And then he continued, "There is Amaros, the Master, and there must be a third…"

New fear unlocked.

A third.

Desti hadn't thought about a third powerful demon king, but now, holy shit, that was another thought that would eat away at her confidence.

"We don't know that for sure, Brandon. If there is, then let's hope we never have to meet him. And as for the Master, I suggest we try to see if we can spy on him; see what he is up to."

"How are we going to do that? Do we even know where he is?" Tess asked.

"I'm sure Peter can tell us. He has spies all over this city. One good part of living underground is that you get very good at sneaking around," said Tate.

"Well, he said that he was going on a run today but would be back later for dinner. Maybe we can talk to him then," Kaelen suggested. Desti nodded, and glancing around the table, everyone else seemed to be in agreement with their plan. So, until then, she decided she would try to relax and enjoy herself.

"Come here, little guy!" Desti cooed, crouching on a small grassy patch in the alleyway where she had first met Peter.

"You're going to scare him away with that voice," Tate laughed.

Desti shot Tate a deathly glare and said, "Well you get him to come to you then." Tate didn't have to do much except kneel and make a clicking sound. Jet had bolted from the shadows he was hiding in and lunged himself into Tate's arms, tail wagging vigorously around. "See, he likes me."

Desti rolled her eyes. Jet licked Tate on every inch of his face and bounced around as if he were finally happy to have someone to play with. His mottled black coat was caked in gunk and was smelly, but Desti didn't care. She had never seen a dog in her lifetime. They were only a myth growing up, and so, dirty coat and all…Jet was adorable.

"Good boy. Go get the stick." Tate had tossed a small stick that he found lying between two walls. Jet seemed to love this game as he leaped and jumped in circles, although he wasn't very good at it.

"I don't think he knows what to do." Desti laughed. Tate smirked, petting the top of Jet's head. "Maybe no one has played with him like this before." There was a glow about Tate that Desti rarely saw in him. A smile spread across her face, and she tilted her head in silent admiration of the simplicity in his features. His hair was wild and free, tousled with jet-black strands that danced around his green eyes. Desti had never met someone so breathtakingly good-looking. Seemingly sucked into a daze, Desti didn't first realize when Tate had said something; his voice was a mere whisper that flutter through her mind, until—

"Desti?"

She blinked.

"Sorry. What did you say?"

"I said I could feel your eyes undressing me. Are you that eager to get me naked again?" Tate flashed Desti a wicked smirk. Her breath hitched at the thought of his naked body on display again. She ran her tongue across the tip of her teeth, imagining all the things she wanted him to do to her.

Tate snapped his fingers and laughed.

Shit. I did it again. A warm rush flooded her cheeks, knowing that she had just gotten caught—again—picturing Tate naked. Totally in denial, she said, "I don't know what you are talking about. I was thinking of something completely ordinary." Before standing up, and giving Jet another gentle pat on the head, she smiled back at Tate and then went back inside.

There was something on her mind that had twisted its way into her core, causing an unnecessary amount of panic. Tess, Seraph, and Kaelen were exactly where she thought they would be, lounging around in the corner of the dining room, laughing and talking.

"There you are. I was hoping to find you guys."

Kaelen glanced up at Desti with bright eyes and a smile, her golden mane tucked neatly into a bun. "Hey, come sit with us. What did you need?" Kaelen patted a seat next to her and Tess. Desti sat and drew in a breath.

She was silent for a moment. All eyes were on her. Tess was the first one to break the silence, her eyes almost as intense as her wild, orange hair. "Desti, are you okay? What did you need to talk to us about?"

Desti locked gazes with Tess, slowly tracing her way from Tess to Kaelen and then to Seraph. "We all never got to really discuss what happened with you all over dinner." At the mention of 'what happened', everyone stiffened as if they all knew what she meant. Kalen instinctively touched the back of her neck.

"You mean our marks?" Kaelen asked. Her once vibrant, blue eyes, now dulled to a lifeless gray-blue. This was something that Desti could tell was weighing heavy on her. Desti nodded. "Yes, I don't want us to ignore the fact that all of you are marked. I don't know what it means yet, but the fact that it practically burned you last night is not good. I'm scared that there is more to them than what we know so far."

"Well, you were able to ease the pain for us. Can't you just keep doing that if they start to burn again?" asked Seraph.

"I could…and I will. But that isn't the problem. I was thinking…what if your marks are somehow like a tracker; a way for Amaros and the Master to find us. I don't think it was a coincidence that he sent us to this time and this location. It must all be connected somehow."

"So, what do you suggest we do then? If they are going to be coming after us, then we need to find a way to get rid of these marks." Kaelen's voice was now shaky, etched with fear. Desti felt it too. The fear of the unknown. That time spent as Amaros's slave was something that will haunt Desti for the rest of her life. Shivers crept over her nerves at the thought of him; of his torture arena; of his creatures that he would use to do his bidding.

The shadow.

The beast.

The serpent.

All those grotesque and horrifying faces would never leave Desti's mind. But the one memory that haunted her the most was the one of the fading of Tate's eyes, going from *him* to something so black…so evil; Desti cringed at the thought of it. *The Shadow*. Every night, she practically had nightmares of that moment; the moment Tate had been forced to consume the evil darkness of that *thing*; and it almost killed her too. She knew this was what was keeping Tate up in the middle of the night with cold sweats. He didn't have to say; the heaving breaths and shakes gave it away.

Desti had kept the Lux hidden for the most part and hadn't really practiced what kind of things she could potentially do with it. Yielding celestial power was a new and uncharted territory for her and quite frankly, it terrified her.

She blinked, coming back to her surroundings. "Kaelen, I will find a way to get rid of your marks. Don't worry." All Desti could do right now was offer her friends a friendly smile and a hopeful solution to their problem and maybe it was time to face her fears and try something new.

"Here, let me help you," Tate purred in Desti's ear while she held the Lux between her hands. The warmth of his hands wrapping around her waist sent a heat throughout her body. She pressed her back into his chest and tilted her head so that she could feel his breath caress the hollow of her neck. With her eyes shut, she was heightened by the sweet sounds that drifted from his mouth; low and feral.

"How is holding me going to help me?" she bargained.

Tate chuckled and leaned closer to her, whispering in her ear, "Don't make excuses. You can do it. I just want to feel you while you yield that power." As his voice lingered on that last word, Tate tightened his grip on her, and she could feel the hardness of him press into the small of her back. Her body quivered and she sharply inhaled. With the faintest of touches from him, it was like sending her body exploding with tingles.

Tate silenced his comments and placed his chin resting on her shoulder as she lifted the Lux into the air. Having him here and holding her did give her a sense of security and comfort; maybe he was right that him touching her could somehow help with yielding the powers.

"So, what do I do? Do I just talk to it?" she asked.

"Is that what you did before?"

She lifted her brow and tilted her head. "Sort of. It was more of a prayer."

Tate pressed his lips against her ear, ecstasy exploding down her arm, and he said, "Then pray." It was difficult to focus with such distractions snatching her mind from what was in front of her, but she blinked away her intrusive thoughts and focused on the glowing orb in her hands.

Pray. I can do that.

At first, her mind was shut off, like a prison door slamming shut, but that wouldn't stop her. "Focus," she whispered. "Focus." The weight of her eyelids pulled down until a curtain of blackness enveloped her vision; the only light she could see now was from her imagination. She thought of wanting to end the suffering of her friends; of wanting to free them of their bindings to Hell.

The words came effortlessly, fluttering into her mind like a river of whispers and thoughts.

Angelic beings, please release the tethering that holds my friends hostage.

She opened one eye, peaking at the Lux to see if anything happened, but it was stagnant. Nothing changed. Frustrated, she huffed out a breath of curses.

"It's fine, Desti. You can do it. I've seen you make it work before. Try again." Tate's breath kissed the back of her neck, and she closed her eyes, inhaling the scent of him. He was always the one who could bring her back to a sense of peace and comfort.

Try again.

Angels of light and the divine, I reach for your mercy, begging you to undo the demonic bind on my friends. Reach down and heal them of the torment that is to come.

First, there was warmth, and then a dim glow just under her fingertips emerged as if it were placing its own hand on hers. She sucked in a breath. "Tate," she breathed. Afraid to move, Desti only peaked slightly from the corner of her eyes to see Tate also lit up with the same exhilaration.

"I see it," he said. "You are doing it." But as quickly as the light came, it faded until the Lux was again just a cold, dull orb.

"Did it work?" she asked while glancing at Tate, his eyes flashing with intensity. Before Tate could respond, Desti shoved the Lux into his hands and took off toward her friends.

Anthony was playing with Jet, throwing some kind of stick—Jet still had yet to master the game fetch. "Desti, what's wrong?" he called, but Desti only waved her hand, yelling back, "I think I did it!" She was air and wind, leaving only a breezy trail behind, in her path.

When Desti turned the corner, there sat Kaelen and Seraph, and Brandon and Tess, around the table, setting up plates for dinner. Bright-eyed, Kaelen smiled, noticing Desti's eagerness. Between heaving breaths, Desti asked, "Do you feel anything? Anything different?"

Tess's eyebrow arched. "What do you mean?"

Desti walked forward, breathless from the running. "Your marks. Did it work? Are they gone?" Seraph almost stood from his chair in excitement. "Did you figure out how to—"

"Here just check me," Kaelen interrupted, pulling her gilded hair over her shoulder. Seraph traced his fingers over her skin gently until he was peering at the back of her neck, and what Desti thought would be a look of joy on his face soon fell to disappointment.

She knew that look.

She knew what it meant. "It didn't work, did it?" Desti somberly asked. Seraph shook his head, and Kaelen turned her shoulder so that Desti could see, and there it was, the bright red mark, shaped like a broken crown, etched into her skin.

Desti frowned, feeling utterly defeated. "Desti, it's okay. We will figure something out," Kaelen said. Desti sat down at an empty seat and was silent for a moment. "I don't understand. I felt its energy. I *saw* its energy touch my fingers."

"Well, there must be something you did differently this time. Peter says that we are safe in this building. Most of the city has been abandoned and the Master and his people live in the other part of town. No one is coming for us."

Tess jumped in, her bright orange hair now a gentle sunset color from the shadows of the enveloping night. "We have time. Take it day by day. Learn what we can, and hopefully, you can master the Lux, and we can take out Rospinity when that happens."

Desti scoffed. "So, you are calling him by his name now?"

"What? You don't like using his name?" Tess asked.

Desti tilted her head, nose scrunching in a disapproving face. "I don't know. It feels wrong to me to even acknowledge him like that. Something about being sent back to this time and this place seems calculated. And the fact that the Master is here, just proves that there is something that Amaros knows that we don't."

Suddenly, Desti was startled by a pair of hands grasping onto her shoulders. She gasped but soon relaxed into the touch when she realized who stood behind her. "Geez, Tate, you scared me."

He chuckled. "Sorry. You ran out of there so fast. I had to come to see what was so important."

"Not before stopping to play a little fetch with me and Jet, though," Anthony spoke from the background. Desti smiled, her reservations slowly melting away at the sound of their voices. "That dog doesn't seem to know how to play fetch yet,"' Desti joked.

Jet barked and Desti assumed it was him objecting.

Her auburn hair fell flatly across her shoulder, spilling into her face. Come to think of it, Desti couldn't remember the last time she was able to truly wash herself. There was a gentle caress of Tate's hands gliding over her shoulders, pulling her hair back so that he could lean in and whisper something in her ear. "I know what you are thinking. Let's take it one day at a time. I'll be with you the entire way. First, let's eat, second, I am going to get you naked and give you a proper bathing."

Desti's body tingled at the velvety smoothness of his voice. And Tate was right, that was exactly what she was thinking…dinner then a nice bath, and maybe…

Her imagination traced its way down a memory of Tate's naked body, but she broke that focus quickly and opened her eyes when she heard a familiar voice come from the distance.

"Supper is served," Lauren said, holding a platter of food. Peter quickly ushered everyone to sit down, with a smile plastered on his face. "I've got eyes on Rospinity. Would you like to see what we have been doing out here, tomorrow?"

Chapter Nine

Close

" I forgot what a bath felt like," Desti breathed. She inhaled the warmth of the mist that hovered above the water.

Tate had carefully slipped her dirty clothes from her body until she was bare and exposed. Her initial instinct was to cover herself. She would never let her body get to this point of filth back in Mors, but their journey had been extensive, and this was something that unfortunately had slipped through the cracks. As she lifted her arms to cover her breasts, Tate grasped her wrist, ferocity glimmering in his unbroken gaze. "Don't even think about it. You are perfect just the way you are. Dirt and all."

Instinct told her to turn her head, but Tate caught her chin with his other hand and guided it back toward him. No words were spoken, but looking into his eyes, she knew he was only seeing her at this moment, and by the way, he slipped a peek down her, she also could tell that he wanted to see her, just like this—naked.

The water was perfectly warm; people at this time actually had running water, which was baffling to Desti. In Mors, you would have to gather water from the watering well, and then heat some over a fire, if you were lucky enough to even have a fireplace.

The moment her body slipped through the barrier of the glassy surface, it was as if all her pain, all her worries, melted into the steam. She tilted her head back in pure bliss.

Soon, Tate followed, and Desti felt his body fit snugly into hers as they submerged themselves. "So, what do you think about Peter's mission tomorrow?" Tate asked while grabbing a sponge and wiping the dirt off Desti's arm.

His touch…God his touch felt like fire and ice, sending her through time and space and to a whole new reality. When she opened her eyes, he was staring with a peculiar smirk on his face.

His brow arched.

"I want to see him. Rospinity. I want to know what he is up to. From what Peter told us at dinner, it sounds like he is preparing for something."

"Well, we know what that something is."

Right. The apocalypse. How could she forget that she was sent to the time, right *before* the end of the world happened? "So, you think he has been trying to gather as many people as possible for when the demons come to the Earth? Maybe to be his slaves?"

"Or their food," Tate purred, placing gentle kisses along her forearm. How did he do that? How could he always make the energy shift to his liking? A smile tugged at Desti's mouth. "oh, yeah. Which one do you think it is?"

"Army or food?" Desti said while crawling into his lap. Tate's hands rested on her hips as he traced idol circles along her spine.

"You know, it is really hard to focus when I've got such a goddess sitting on my lap like this." Desti snorted and leaned closer, her fingers now cupping the sides of his face. "Maybe I want you to lose focus. Maybe I want us to just be here…now…" She placed a gentle kiss on his cheek, but that ignited a hunger in Tate's eyes.

"I can do here and now," he purred. Within a heartbeat, Tate had flipped Desti onto her back, gliding her to the edge of the tub, hovering his body over hers. "You're trembling," he noticed. For a moment, a glimmer of worry lingered in his eyes, but Desti soon snatched that worry away with a fierce kiss. She crashed her lips into his, breathing in his moan as she pulled him closer to her.

There wasn't enough of him. She had to have Tate. All of him—like a drug her body so desperately craved. Water splashed like a wild storm spilling onto its neighboring land, but that didn't stop their bodies from exploring each other. Tate's tongue danced with hers and she pulled his hair as she nibbled on his swollen bottom lip.

A low growl reverberated from his chest and that was the moment the predator came out from him. Desti felt herself being lifted from the tub and gently placed on the sheeted floor.

With one hand he had managed to pin her arms above her head, and she let him, breathing in the desire and heat in the air. Just the hint of Tate's breath touching her skin sent Desti's body swirling. It was almost unbearable to wait any longer to see what the rest of his body was going to do to her.

Between ragged breaths, she moaned, "Tate…oh God….I need you…" He let go for a moment and her arms came over his shoulder as she dug her nails into his back, pulling him in, feeling his body tense and flex in excitement. With his free hand, he began exploring her naked and wet curves.

"You're so fucking beautiful," he growled.

"God…you're perfect." Tate took just a moment to admire the beauty that lay before him. And just before he dove back into his hunger, he flashed a smirk.

The world stopped the moment his perfect mouth kissed the wetness between her legs. Desti gasped, writhing and arching her back in the process, but Tate snatched the meat of her thighs, holding her hips in place. He was like a hungry lion who had finally won the prize of its prey.

Pleasure exploded to every nerve of her body, her heart slamming into her chest with matching breaths. And before she thought it couldn't get any better, Tate took his two fingers and slid them in, only to intensify her pleasure to a whole other level.

"Oh my God….Tate…fuck!"

Desti's moans grew louder and louder; she bit down on a towel to muffle the echoing cries for Tate's tongue. She was getting closer now, warmth rushing between her legs, but Tate loved to tease her, so he pulled away, flashing a wicked smile.

"Not yet, princess," he purred while wagging his finger.

Tate hovered over Desti, the shaft of his cock hung heavy, pressing against the hollow of her belly button. His black hair hung freely on his face. She brushed it back so she could see into his eyes—green and gold, full of so much love and strength hidden beneath the waves of his irises.

"God, Tate. I love you." Desti pulled him into her, embracing every ounce of him into a fiery kiss, and in that moment, she felt the hardness of him slide into her and shove its way in, deep. A gasp caught in her throat, muffling the cries that Tate swallowed with his lips. Everything about him, she craved. His scent—pine and oak, his guttural moans and growls, and God…his eyes were like looking into a window to heaven. And as she admired and studied all these things that she loved about him, his thrust grew stronger and quicker, snatching Desti's focus and forcing her into a state of one thing—bliss.

He kissed her neck and then her shoulder, still slamming his hardened cock into her like his life depended on it. Desti was sweaty now, but she didn't care. At this moment, the only thing on her mind was the hotness that was fucking her brains out. She could hear his moans building; hers too, and she knew that together, they were going to climax.

And suddenly like a cresting wave, Tate's body shook and trembled and Desti scratched down the flexing muscles of his shoulder blades until the roll of her orgasm faded away into echoing tingles. Breathless, Desti lay there entangled in Tate's legs, her hand placed gently on his chest.

"I can't believe we never did this….you know….*before*," Desti laughed.

Tate looked up at her and chuckled. "Well, I definitely thought about it, but…"

"The forbidden rules. I know," Desti finished.

"No, that's not it. I would have broken the forbidden rules over and over again if you wanted me to. I'd do anything for you, Desti. I just never thought you felt that way and I would never pressure you."

Her heart sank to her stomach. How long had Tate been in love with her and held onto that secret, letting it weigh him down? She had wished she'd seen the signs and known sooner, but maybe it was for the best that they waited until escaping Amaros before being intimate.

"If it could just be us, and this, every day, then I would be happy," Desti whispered.

"I'm happy no matter what when I have you with me, my love," he softly spoke.

Night had soon enveloped the sunset sky, and her friends had all gone off to bed by this point. And so, Desti savored this moment, in Tate's arms, and just lay there skin to skin, drifting away into a slumber.

Chapter Ten

Chaos Ensues

"So, what exactly are you doing today?" Seraph asked Peter and Lauren. Peter turned and smiled, clutching a large iron bar and Lauren had some kind of shank that she clearly made out of building debris.

"Y'all kids would do best if y'all just listen and stay quiet. Let me and Lauren handle this. There was something in Peter's eyes that Desti noticed; an intensity to them that she recognized; she had seen that look before back in Mors—it was the look of someone feral, someone who had been forced to do horrible things to survive. It changes you at some point until your mind becomes so twisted that you don't even recognize who you are anymore.

Desti sucked in a shallow breath but didn't speak. She clutched a small knife that Lauren had given her and just nodded. Tate's hand was pressed firmly on her shoulder and then he leaned into her, pressing his lips just at the edge of her ear. "Whatever happens, stay close to me. You understand?" Desti nodded slowly, slipping a glance at Anthony and the others. Tate's voice was a mere whisper, like a ghost caressing her skin. "Don't let Anthony out of your sight."

Desti stiffened at the thought of losing Anthony. She couldn't, wouldn't. It won't happen, she thought.

"So, what usually happens on these runs of yours? Like what is the purpose of them?" Kaelen had asked.

Lauren glanced back with an intense stare. "These people used to be good…caring, but something has changed. At one point in time, they were normal, but something was different. He has changed them somehow…like a bunch of mindless zombies walking around out here." Lauren scratched her head and Peter only nodded while he listened.

This all sounded way too familiar. Flashes of memories at the Resistance camp flooded Desti's mind. Could it be? She thought. Was the Master using demon blood to create his own slaves? Desti kept this thought to herself, but she was intrigued. The only way to know for sure would be to see them for herself.

"So, are we just spying on them then?" Kaelen asked. Tess nodded her head in agreement but didn't speak. Peter looked at every one of them before replying, "No, we are going to take someone."

"What? Why?" Anthony broke his silence.

"Cause, people have been disappearing around here, and then they pop up on the other side of town, looking like Hell. Something is going on. Something is coming; I can feel it."

Seraph didn't seem too worried. He cleared his throat and flicked his hair out of his face. "Oh, something is coming alright." Tess jabbed Seraph in the side with her elbow and shot him a deathly stare.

"Right. Shall we go then?" Lauren said more as a command than a question.

Eventually, they all left the safety of their fortress and ventured outside to the withering town, and this was the first time that Desti felt…scared.

The town was nothing like the mountainside that Desti had ventured from. What was once seemingly a lively, beautiful city now looked like somewhere plucked from the aftermath of an atomic war. The farther she ventured deeper into the city, the more the surrounding land was destroyed.

"Woah, what happened here?" Anthony asked while glancing around, mouth gaping open. Lauren snickered and while twirling her shank between her fingers she replied, "Mostly the Earthquake…that's what made all these buildings crumble, but that…" Lauren pointed to blackened, ashy remains of *people*, scattered around like some sick decoration. "That was Rospinity and his people."

Desti gulped down a lump in her throat and glanced at Tate with burning eyes. His face was expressionless, but she knew that he felt it too. "Why would Rospinity do this?" Kaelen asked. "At first, he seemed like the savior of the town…acting like he cared, *saving* people from the collapsed structures. Once he got enough people on his side, he took over half the city, claiming he was the new mayor of the town, and people just let it happen. Slowly, I saw a shift in him…he was evil to his core. Once I realized that, I packed my shit and waited for the right time to get out. Found Lauren in one of his holding chambers on my way out and took her with me."

Lauren smiled at that. She must have felt truly loyal to Peter if he had saved her. Desti racked her brain trying to think of what the whole purpose of Rospinity doing all of this, but a feeling deep in her gut told her that she already knew the answer.

"Why would anyone be okay with doing this?" Tess cried. Her bright orange hair was now gilded with streaks of sunlight peering through the clouds above. She was picking at her fingers in a nervous tick, eyes darting from one horrible thing to another.

"That my Dear is the ultimate question, and why we must capture one of his people," Peter replied.

Desti frowned. She knew it had to be the same way Elijah took control of the people of the Resistance. It was like a virus, starting off slowly, seeping its way into their thoughts, and eventually when there was no more humanity left, they became his slave. If Desti was right, then Rospinity was creating an army of loyal soldiers, preparing for what she feared to come—*now*, Desti was scared shitless.

Peter crouched down and slowed his pace. They had crossed half the city in just an hour. He got low and so did Lauren. "Why did we stop?" whispered Anthony.

Desti gave him a smile and returned her attention to Peter. His finger lifted to his mouth, and he only pointed with his metal pipe at what was ahead. It took a moment, but then she saw it—a group of people, men and women, gathering around what looked to be some kind of torture area.

Splatters of dried blood covered the nearby concrete slabs like a sick and twisted pathway made just for them. Desti's breath caught in her chest and her heart began to beat heavily. Tate must have noticed the shift in her, his hand gently pulling her hair to the side before placing a kiss on her cheek. He lingered for a moment just before speaking softly in her ear, "Are you thinking what I am thinking?" She knew what he meant. He could see it too, the empty hollowness that lingered in their eyes. It was the same damned look that the people at the Resistance had. Desti only nodded and that was when she heard Tate inhale sharply.

"You people are all fucking crazy!" a man yelled, chained and shackled to a concrete slab at the center of an intersection. A woman with wild curly, brown hair flashed the man a wicked smile, playing with a whip in her hands.

Desti tensed at the sight of that whip. It was too familiar, too raw in her memories to not react to such a thing. It was a whip that had torn Tate's flesh from his chest, and hers too. The scarlet trickles of blood still haunted Desti in her dreams at times. "They are going to whip him," Tate whispered and Desti just nodded. She reached out her hand and locked it through Tate's elbow and forearm.

Desti's glance shifted to the rest of her friends who were quietly ducked behind building debris: Kaelen and Seraph, Brandon and Tess, and Anthony, all sharing the same horrified expression in their eyes.

"The Master says that you need to drink," the woman said harshly. In her hands, she cupped a small flask, silver and about the size of a book. The man only shook his head violently with a wild look in his eyes. "You promised that this was going to be a sanctuary. An Oasis! The rest of the world has fallen. I thought you were my savior!" he cried.

"Trust me," the woman said. "If you don't drink from this flask, then you'll regret it." Her eyes were consumed with darkness, the irises of her pupils engulfed in a storm of blackness.

"Did you hear her say 'the Master'?" Desti whispered to Tate. Tess and Brandon flashed Desti the same worried look that Tate had on his face. They heard it too. And so, her fears had unfortunately come true. The Master was here at this time, and he was creating an army. The only lingering question now was, did he remember her? Did this version have the same memories of his battle with Desti and the others?

Peter turned around and in a hushed voice said, "We need to get *that* woman, right there." Of course, he was pointing to the crazy woman with the whip. Why did it have to be her? Tate nodded and Lauren readied her stance. Peter looked as if he were about to pounce, and Desti almost had the instinct to pull him back. Something in the back of her mind was telling her to wait. It was almost like a voice, whispering distant echoes throughout her head. If she closed her eyes and focused, she thought she could hear it more clearly.

"This is your last chance. Drink or I will slit your throat." The woman raised her whip and slashed it down on the man; agonizing screams reverberated throughout the city. Desti flinched the moment she heard the crack of the whip rip his flesh. Tears began to well in her eyes. She had to do something.

Before anyone could hold her back, Desti lunged forward and screamed, "Stop!" The woman froze, probably in shock that she was seeing Desti emerge from the rubble and flashed her an evil smirk. The man was bloody and slumped over, shaking and whimpering from the pain.

"Looks like we have company," the woman said. One of the men in the back scoffed and stepped forward. "Who the Hell are you?" In his hand, he held a broken glass bottle, sharp, serrated edges flashed under the sun's rays.

More people emerged from the shadows, like cockroaches, surrounding Desti and closing her in. She glanced over to where Tate and the others were hiding, hoping that they wouldn't come out or be seen.

The woman held up her flask and smiled. "Looks like we have a new member of our group. Who thinks we should make her drink?" There was an echo of grunts and grumbles from the men and woman that stood around her, their eyes even more intensely hallow than when she had first seen them.

"I'm not drinking anything from you, and neither is this man."

The woman laughed. "Looks like we have another feisty one. Listen, lady," she said, stepping forward, "You will do as I say and drink from this fucking flask or the Master won't be happy."

Desti flinched at that name as if hearing it caused her body physical pain. Immediately, Desti regretted that she let it show. The woman cocked her head to the side with a curious look in her eyes. "You know the Master, don't you?"

Shit.

Desti didn't answer, instead, she stepped back until she was blocking the man from being exposed to the whip. "Kill her!" one woman yelled.

Another man screamed, "Make her drink!"

"Whip her!"

"Let me slit her throat!"

It was like a sea of endless threats that sent Desti's body into a total panic. Her heart was slamming against her ribcage, and her body began to tremble. This was bad. Very bad. The woman raised her whip, preparing to slash it down onto Desti—a feeling she was all too familiar with, but just as she was about to do it, Peter had chucked his metal pipe, like an arrow ripping through the air, smacking the woman straight in her head.

Blood instantly gushed from her cracked skull as she dropped to the ground, choking in a pool of her own scarlet liquid. Chaos ensued, and people from every direction hurtled forward with their weapons, as did Desti and her friends.

Just before the man with the broken glass came at Desti, Tate slammed into his chest, knocking him to the ground. "Get the man, Desti!" Tate yelled. The dagger in her hand was too small to break chains that thick, and so she chucked it. Frantic, Desti searched for something to break the chains that held that man hostage, and then she noticed Peter's pipe lying off in the distance.

In the frenzy, dodging and weaving through bodies, Desti snatched up that pipe and jammed it into the chains, twisting and yanking until she heard it snap. A sigh of relief briefly escaped, and then she grabbed him by the arm. "I'm getting you out of here. Let's go!"

Desti pulled the man away from the fighting and that was when she dared to gaze upon the battle. Tess was on the ground, tumbling with a woman with short black hair, blood was splattered all around, and she couldn't tell whose blood coated the gravel. Brandon and Seraph were fighting off two men with makeshift swords with their bare hands, and Desti couldn't help but gasp at the fear that she would lose more friends.

And then—

Where is Anthony?

Like a swirling black hole of despair, Desti's mind was in sheer panic because Anthony was nowhere in sight. Her head darted around in a frenzy until she heard a slight *psst* coming from the distance. Kaelen poked her head out from behind a shattered car and waved her over. Before taking off, Desti glanced back one last time, making sure that she wasn't seeing her friend's spilled blood on the ground. It was difficult to tell who was fighting who, but no one seemed to be dead…yet.

Desti hurried over to the car and behind it, ducking, was Anthony. Kaelen had her arms wrapped around his head to block him from seeing the chaos. "Take him, I need to go back in there and help them," Desti said, shoving the battered man into Kaelen. He hissed at the pain but obliged and sat right there next to her.

She was like lightning, weaving through the shattered debris of the city, jumping and hurtling toward her friends like her life depended on it. Just as she made it to the perimeter, screaming, so loud, so terribly shell shocking, ripped through the air—and everyone stopped.

That screaming…it sounded familiar. Only a moment passed until she realized what was happening. Seraph and Tess were on the ground, whimpering in pain. All of them as if something were causing them to hurl over, and that was when it hit her.

The marks.

They must have been activated somehow. But how?

Tate, Brandon, Peter, and Lauren all slowly stepped back and walked to where Desti was standing, completely shocked at what was happening.

"What is happening?" Lauren asked.

"It has to be the marks." Desti replied.

Lauren and Peter both shot Desti a furious glare. "What marks?" Desti inhaled, but before she could explain, one of the men stood and locked gazes right upon Desti. His eyes were black, soulless, empty…devoid of any humanity.

She sucked in a breath and held it in her chest. Everyone turned their gazes to her, curious as to why he was looking at her like that. The man tilted his chin in the air and inhaled deeply, almost moaning as he leveled his head back down.

"The Escaped One," he hissed. "Oh, we've missed you." The man licked his lips intensely as if he were tasting the fear that was imbued with the copper, tangy scent of blood in the air.

Oh fuck.

Tate stiffened and she knew that he was thinking the same thing. The Master knew that she was here. Tess and

Seraph were still hunched into a ball on the ground, shaking from their lingering pain. Brandon was white as a ghost and blankly staring, and Lauren and Peter had a look of pure fury and confusion entangled in their eyes.

"What does he mean *'escaped one'*, Desti?" Lauren's voice for once caught in her throat. Before Desti could explain, she heard a heinous chuckle echoing from afar. It was a voice so sinister that it sent her body into a sheer panic. Her instincts told her to run, but where to? For all she knew, the whole town could be infested with the Master's slaves.

And then he appeared from the depths of the shadows, lurking from the corner, and the moment she gazed upon him, seeing that hunger in his eyes, she knew that he knew exactly who she was.

"Desti, at last..." the Master spoke.

Chapter Eleven

The Master

The moment the Master stepped into the light, Desti knew it was him. The same Master that she had been so close to…before he had hurtled her into the portal to Hell. But as Desti traced her eyes along his body, she noticed something different.

Where are his hooved feet? And claws?

This version may have looked *human,* but there was no doubt that his consciousness was the same. It was without a doubt the same cambion that tore a man's flesh with his teeth, eating him raw to the bone; the same creature who stole her friends and sacrificed them to Hell. Desti couldn't see her face, but she knew it must have had the look of utter disgust for him.

One question still lingered on her mind, which was how was he here when she had just seen him days ago, before jumping into the portal? Maybe he traveled back in time years prior, knowing that Desti would end up right here, right now. Or maybe there were two bodies but one mind. So many possibilities racked her brain as she stood there paralyzed with fear.

"You know him?" Peter asked, confusion smeared all over his face. Lauren made a snickering noise and kept glancing between Desti and the Master. A single tear formed in the corner of her eye, but she blinked it away, ignoring Lauren and Peter's prying eyes.

Desti went to step forward, but Tate flinched as if he were going to hold her back, but she shoved out her hand for him to stop. "Don't worry," she said.

"It's me. When I saw your picture on the building, I almost couldn't believe it was you."

The Master smiled, his teeth were now sharp and serrated, and Desti knew this must have been the first time that Peter had seen any kind of feature of a cambion because he flinched at the sight of it, gasping. "What the Hell are you Rospinity?"

The Master didn't break his focus from Desti, taking a slow and steady stride forward. With a wave of his hand, his minions fell back and formed a small half-circle behind him. Desti glanced to her right, noticing Tess and Seraph still hunched in pain.

"What is happening to them?" Desti demanded. The Master only scoffed. "That my Dear, is the power of the mark.

They can feel when I am close, and the more they fight it, the more pain it shall cause them. Surrender, and the pain will ease." The Master was now directing his voice to Tess and Seraph. They aggressively shook their heads, cowering at the sight of him.

"No one is becoming your slave anymore. You got what you wanted, didn't you? My father…Elijah…they let you sacrifice us. Wasn't that enough for you?"

A heinous laugh boomed from his chest. "You must be really stupid, little girl if you think that I will ever be satisfied with that. What is the fun in sacrificing you if I can't have you?"

Desti inhaled sharply. And as if she were watching it happen in slow motion, the Master began to morph into something far more sinister; claws broke through the skin of his knuckles, blood trickling through the cracks of his fingers; hooves emerged and that was when she noticed Lauren and Peter stagger back in a panic, falling onto the ground.

"This," he yelled, "Is the real me." His eyes narrowed and then he growled like a freaking rabid animal just before lunging at Desti. His titanic body came hurtling for her so fast she almost didn't have time to react. Tate must have expected something like this to happen because he was already at her side, shoving her out of his way.

Her hands hit the gravel. A sharp pain shot through her arm as she caught the brunt of her weight. "Come on, we need to get out of here," Tate said, pulling her up. Peter and Lauren had already readied their stances to fight, and Desti didn't want to stay to find out what happens next. "Where is Anthony?" she asked. Tate glanced back at the half-burned car where he had left him, blowing out a sigh of relief. "He's back there still. Come on!"

Tate yanked her out of the chaos and ran toward Anthony and Kaelen. "Wait! We can't leave them!"

Desti yanked her arm free and turned her direction toward Seraph and Tess, yelling, "Get up! Come on!" Desti held out her hand and they took it as she pulled them forward. There was screaming and a sharp growl that snatched Desti's focus just for a moment, and that was when she saw the Master had picked Lauren up with one of his claws jammed right into her ribcage. His head tilted back, teeth sharpened, and he bit down on her side. The scream that echoed around her was the worst imaginable scream she could have possibly imagined hearing. "Oh my God, Tate. He is eating her," she cried.

Tate didn't lose focus, not even once. He ushered them out of the crosswalk and began to run as fast as he could, now gripping Anthony with one hand and Kaelen with the other. Desti had her grip on Tess and Seraph. "What about Peter!" Anthony yelled.

There was no way Desti had any chance of fighting the Master. It ate away at her that she just left Peter back there to die but if she had stayed, she too would have been dead. Eventually, the screaming faded, and they slowed their pace when they had run through about half the city. In between heaving breaths, Tate asked, "Where the Hell is the guy we saved?"

"He ran off when Kaelen started screaming." Kaelen was hunched over, hands on her knees, gasping for a good breath of air, but despite that, she looked to be feeling better. "Yeah, what he said."

"Do you know where to go?" Tess asked through gritted teeth. Tate took a moment and glanced around, nodding his head to his right. "It's this way. Come on."

Desti didn't argue. Even if it wasn't the right way, any way was better than staying in the same spot. Under the glistening sunlight, they ran, ducking and weaving through fallen buildings and piles of dead, ashen bodies, for what seemed like hours.

Then Desti noticed something familiar off in the distance. A poster. And on that poster was Rospinity—the Master. Desti frowned at the sight of him, but she knew that their building was just around the corner now. Anthony turned the corner first, then Kaelen and Seraph, followed by Brandon and Tess, and then Desti and Tate.

Some of Peter's people were gathered around the main sitting area, talking and sifting through piles of what looked like junk. Desti practically collapsed onto the concrete ground as she rushed inside. Time stilled, and everyone stopped what they were doing. A man with dreads arched his eyebrow and looked her up and down. "Where is Peter?" he asked.

Her voice choked as she tried to tell the guy that Peter was dead, but by the way he was looking at her, he must have seen it on her face. He inhaled. "What happened? I thought you were just going on a quick run."

Did Peter not tell his people about his plan to kidnap one of the Master's members? Desti tilted her head slightly, still trying to catch her breath. "We were attacked," she said.

A woman laid down a shirt she was holding and interjected. "Attacked! By whom? Rospinity?" Desti only nodded her head, and then she slipped a glance at her friends, all seemingly paralyzed with guilt and intimidation.

"Peter wanted to take someone…a woman back with us, but she was about to kill this man, and so, I—"

"So, you got him killed?" the woman sneered.

"What? No…I…uh…"

"Rospinity would have attacked whether Desti tried to save the man or not. Don't blame this on her." Tate had now stepped closer, standing next to Desti. She could still smell the sweet scent of pine lingering from him. The scent of him always brought her back to a sense of calm.

"I'm sorry. I wish I could have done more." Desti wanted to finish but instead, her words drifted into the air as she watched the people in front of her—Rospinity's people—break down and cry. Desti flinched and immediately retreated to the small room that she and Tate were staying in.

"I think we will stay and help them," Brandon said, ushering Anthony and Seraph over to the table to help sort through the materials their scavenger must have found.

Chapter Twelve

Surprise

The events that unfolded last night haunted Desti just as much as memories of her time in Hell did. After she had bolted off to her room, Desti had skipped dinner and instead cried herself to sleep while Tate stroked her hair.

Too many people have died because of her. She tried to save Peter, but she couldn't. It was morning now, assuming, since gentle, warm golden beams peaked their way through the cracks in the boarded-up window. "Desti, you can't lay in bed all day," Tate whispered.

His voice was like silk, caressing her mind until it felt better. She sat up with bloodshot eyes and looked at Tate with a flat look. "He is dead because of me, Tate."

"Desti, that is not true. You couldn't have avoided any of that from happening. You got Tess and Brandon out safe, and Anthony and the others." Tate had placed his hand over Desti's and cupped it gently. His touch was soul-soothing. Electrifying.

She closed her eyes, and Tate pressed a loving kiss right on her temple. "Come on. Let's go eat, see the others, and maybe we can talk strategy."

"Strategy?"

"Yes. We still need to figure out what we are going to do, especially now since the Master knows that we are here. He will be looking for us."

Desti grumbled, but got up anyway, slipping on some clothes from the pile of stuff that Peter's people had been sifting through. Tate was grabbing a shirt, his bare skin flashing its fading scars that ran along his ribcage. Desti sucked in a shallow breath at the sight of it. She had almost forgotten the abuse that Tate had endured growing up.

"You coming?" he asked while holding out his hand to her. Desti nodded and followed Tate out into the main room.

Distant chatter echoed around the bend of the walls and as Desti turned the corner she saw everyone sitting at a large table, seemingly in a deep and serious conversation. Tess glanced up and offered a friendly smile, but Desti could see the sadness that lingered beneath. Seraph and Kaelen were sitting at the edge of the table talking with a woman, and Brandon was playing fetch with Anthony and Jet.

Desti smiled at that. Jet ran up and down the hall, barking and wagging his tail. "Desti, he finally can play fetch," Anthony called out while throwing a stick. Jet bolted off and grabbed the stick with his mouth and brought it back to Anthony.

Before she could say anything, someone interrupted.

"Desti," a woman called.

She quickly turned her gaze to her left. A woman with short brown hair was sitting at the table, eating. Desti walked over. "Yes?"

"Please sit."

Desti took a seat across from the woman. "Your friends told me a very interesting story last night." Desti raised an eyebrow.

The woman leaned forward, placing her elbows on the table. "Tell me, is it true?" Desti traced her gaze between Seraph and Kaelen and the woman and then gulped.

"What did they tell you?"

"Oh, you know. That y'all are from the future and that Rospinity is some kind of demon king."

She'd guessed that sooner or later she would have had to tell them the truth but now that she was facing this woman, she couldn't help but feel uncertain if it was for the best that Peter's people knew about it.

Desti nodded. "Yes, it is true. We come from one hundred years in the future. Your world…our world ends, and

Hell will spill onto our lands, infesting it with its demons. The end of days are coming."

The woman didn't even flinch, but her eyes lingered with a hint of fear. "How did you end up here then?"

Brandon came from behind and answered her. "The Master sent us to Hell, and from there, after pretty much escaping with our lives, we were sent here, thanks to her." Brandon patted Desti on the back. This was the first time that any of her friends had recognized the sacrifice she had made for them. A smile pulled at her mouth but soon faded when she glanced back at the stone-cold face of the woman. She cocked her head in confusion. "Who is the Master?"

Right. She only knew him as Rospinity. Desti cleared her throat and said, "Rospinity." *Now* the woman seemed intrigued. "So, Rospinity is from your world, and he is—"

"A cambion," Seraph interrupted. "You know...part demon, part human. He apparently *also* is a High King of Hell. Probably why he was able to be here and there. You know...his dark magic and all."

"If this is true, then we must prepare for what is to come."

Desti thought of the Lux. Was this the tool that could change the course of history? Could she give these people a fighting chance now? She had hidden the Lux back in her room and hadn't touched it since the last time she tried to heal her friends' marks. "Half of your world's population will disappear, and that is when the ground will split, and the creatures of the dark will swarm every city on the planet. You will either be eaten and tortured or enslaved by the higher demons. I don't know how we can stop this from happening."

"It seems as though the Master has a big part in this. We should try to kill him and free his horde of slaves. Maybe that will do something," Brandon spoke.

"But how do we kill him?" Kaelen asked.

Tate cleared his throat in a confident sanguine approach and said, "We kill him with her." And Tate was pointing right at Desti.

She gasped and swiftly turned her head. "Me? No, no, no…I can't, Tate."

"Why do you think she is the one who could do this?" the woman asked. Desti was squirming with uncertainty, but Tate was poised and confident. He rested his hand on Desi's shoulder and replied. "Because, I have seen her fight the Master before, and what she did was incredible." Now his attention was on Desti as he got down to eye level, lowering his voice to almost a whisper. "Desti, if you could learn how to do what you did in Rotten's Crude, then you could potentially save us."

Before she could answer, a curious voice from behind interjected. "What did she do?"

Tate arched an eyebrow giving Desti a peculiar smirk. She shook her head no but knew he wouldn't take it for an answer. "We can show you," he said.

"Tate, I don't know what I am doing."

"Just breathe and focus. According to the legend, this thing has the power to eradicate the demons from the world."

Desti scoffed, clutching the translucent orb between her palms. "This *thing* is called the Lux, and I barely have been able to make it work." Tate's body was so close now that she could feel the warmth of him. He leaned in, almost pressing his lips to her ear. "This power is within *you*, Desti. It's not the Lux that is special. It is you." A stream of shivers crept down her spine. Tate did make a point. When Desti had somehow broken her friends out of the Master's chambers, she didn't have the Lux then. So maybe the Lux was just a tool she could use to harness her energy better.

The woman, who Desti now knew as Lorie, had shown her an empty level of the building, which she said was perfect for this kind of thing. All eyes were on her. Literally. Lorie had grabbed every single member of Peter's group to come watch Desti yield angelic magic.

No pressure.

Tate wanted to start Desti off with an easy task, so, he placed a small can on a concrete slab about ten feet away and told her to hit it with the Lux's light. Desti was surrounded by a crowd of curious and hopeful eyes, and she knew that she was probably the only one who wasn't that hopeful.

"You got this!" a girl called out.

"Desti, you can do it," Kaelen said, smiling at her. Desti had really grown to love her new friends, and she didn't want to let anyone down. If she were going to break their bonds to Hell, then she would have to start to learn how to yield these angelic powers sooner or later, and so, she inhaled, readied her stance, and closed her eyes.

This time, she tried something different. Instead of praying in her mind, she thought about commanding the Lux to do what she wanted. Only a handful of times had Desti gotten it to work; probably more out of sheer luck than skill, but she remembered the way it felt on her skin when it did—warm and tingly.

Anthony and Jet were off in the far corner in case something went wrong, but Tate stood right by her side. "I've got you," he said.

In her mind, she thought about light and power and all the pain she had endured, hoping that this would fuel it. Her body felt like it was going to explode with rage as the memories and thoughts came bursting through her mind, thinking of her commands for the light to emerge. She thought that maybe this would actually work, but when the Lux stayed cold and dull, she huffed out in frustration.

"It didn't work."

"It's okay. Try again."

Small, delicate claps echoed around the large room, and that made Desti smile. These people barely knew her, and they were rooting for her. They believed in her. And then she thought about her friends and how much they meant to her; Anthony…Tate…Kaelen…and—

Suddenly, a tingly pulse vibrated through her fingertips, and white and yellow light grew bright around her grip. She sucked in a gasp. In her chest, a warm festering sensation developed, and it was as if the energy from the Lux was coursing through her body now. She felt it now. More powerful than she had ever before.

"Oh my God, Tate. It's working."

"Shhh. Just focus."

Desti obliged. With this newfound energy, she opened her eyes and shifted her attention to the metal soda can on the slab ahead of her, thinking of only one thing, and that was *hit the can*.

The room fell deathly silent, not even a whisper escaped the throats of the people who surrounded her. Suddenly, a soft humming sound trickled its way into Desti's mind. Then it grew louder and then louder until she almost couldn't take it anymore, and just as she was about to scream a burst of bright holy light blasted from her fingertips. She dropped the Lux, but the energy still flowed through her, like a running river of heavenly power.

The beam of light shot forward and exploded the can into dust. Desti pulled her hands down and the light retreated back into her fingertips. She held her hands, palms open, facing up, completely in disbelief at what she had just done.

"Holy shit, Desti! You did it!" Tate yelled. He had literally jumped in the air and pulled her into a crushing hug. Everyone else was clapping and cheering. Some people were completely frozen with their mouths hanging open.

"How did you do it?" Tess ran forward with her arms open for a hug. Desti embraced her and pulled back. "I don't know. I was thinking about you guys."

"Really? About us? That's what did it?" Tess laughed.

"About how much I loved you all." All of their eyes softened when they heard her say the word love. Love was a forbidden word back in their world, and to hear someone say it to you was unexpected.

Anthony rushed Desti with a hug and grumbled into her chest, "I love you too." Once all the commotion simmered down, Desti stood there in a circle of new and old friends. "So, that's it then. That is the key. Love."

To make it work, all she had to do was love.

Chapter Thirteen

Together

Over the next few days, Desti had gone to that level of the building at least once a day to practice using the Lux, and what she discovered was that, all along, the power was within her, even without the Lux in her hands. It only amplified her energy, which made her think that it was some sort of battery of angelic powers.

Lorie had set up a memorial service for Peter and Lauren and then cooked dinner for the entire group. No tears were shed by his people, but instead, they gathered to show their appreciation for him and what he had done for this city.

The world was coming close to the end; every city in every country was facing the same despair and corruption.

Peter had established something safe for the people of his town, maybe even something capable of fighting back.

Desti had done a lot of healing these past few days, reflecting on the good that she hoped would come rather than sulking about what had been done. Anthony seemed happy too. For once, he had somewhere he could feel safe and welcomed. To see him teaching Jet how to plat fetch, or to see him assisting Lorie and her people with their duties, it warmed her.

On the rooftop of the structure, there was a secret oasis hidden between four walls. Open bright blue skies soared above, rolling white clouds whisked by, blowing the gentlest breeze and freshly scented air around.

Desti closed her eyes and inhaled, gently grazing her fingers along the rubbery blades of grass that she was lying on. Chills ran through her body the moment she felt the touch of Tate's fingers twirl her loose strands of hair around.

"Tell me," he said. "What does it feel like?"

Desti arched her head so that she could see Tate's eyes, his arm cupping her body into his chest. Beneath the hues of green and gold, there was a glimmer flickering in his gaze.

"What?" she asked.

"When the angelic powers are in you. What does it feel like?"

Desti smiled and turned her gaze down now as she watched a butterfly flutter around, dancing between blooming petals from the garden. "It feels like a river of energy. It's nowhere and everywhere all at once, and sometimes it feels like it is trying to speak to me."

Tate sat upright and Desti did too, and he grabbed her hand. "It speaks to you?"

"Well, not fully, but I think so. It's like a whisper in my mind, but it sounds far away as if it is lost or something."

"What do you think it is trying to tell you?" Tate asked, curiosity now growing in his gaze. The wind had picked up slightly, now blowing his black hair like back silk caught in a storm. His mouth tightened.

"I don't know but the more that I practice, I can feel the voice getting closer. I think it could possibly be someone *from* the angelic realm."

"You mean like Heaven?"

Desti nodded but didn't speak this time. Suggesting that the Heavenly realm of the angels was trying to speak to you through your mind sounded crazy to admit, but everything in her life at this point sounded crazy, and yet it happened.

Tate cupped the side of Desti's face, running his thumb across her bottom lip. "I knew you were always special."

She inhaled, closing her eyes, feeling his touch, and just as she opened them, she felt Tate pulling her in. Desti followed the flow of his hand until her lips met his, pressing a gentle kiss to his mouth. His tongue explored hers, passionately. In between breaths, she gasped, pulling away just for a moment before deepening the kiss into something more feral.

"Fuck, Tate. You always know the right thing to say to get me like this." She laughed. Tate huffed out a slight chuckle, a small smile tugging at his mouth, but he didn't speak. His eyes were set on her and his mouth wanted more.

He kissed her and then trailed those kisses up her jaw until his mouth hovered above her ear, whispering, "I say these things because I mean them. You are the light that brightens my darkest days, the calm that drowns out my storm. You are my savior and my queen. I would do anything to protect you, Desti."

She couldn't hold back anymore. Desti crashed into Tate with her body heating to the core. She wanted every part of him, now. Tate pulled her shirt off in the heat of the moment, exposing her peaked, hardened nipples. He smiled and continued to remove the rest of her clothing. Desti ran her hand over Tate's shoulder, sliding off his shirt as she let him undo her pants. His skin was velvety soft, and she couldn't get enough of it, tracing idol circles along the rifts of his chest, gently stroking until her fingers found the tousles of his hair.

She leaned in and kissed the peak of his shoulder, then traced gentle kisses, pausing at the hollow of his neck. He tilted his head back and let out a guttural groan. Both her hands were placed on his bare chest now, slowly guiding him back until he was lying on the soft grass. The wetness between her legs flowed out with desire for him like a trickle of rain escaping the pressure of the clouds.

But this time, she wanted to be in control. Desti followed her gliding hands down until her mouth grazed the shaft of his erect cock. It was throbbing for her touch, aching to feel what the inside of her felt like, but she didn't grant that just yet.

With the faintest smile, she glanced up at Tate just before he closed his eyes and leaned his head back from the pleasure of just her breath caressing it. Desti opened her mouth and took him in; just the tip at first, licking and sucking, until she heard his moans grow louder.

"Fuck, Desti…keep going," he begged, and she obliged. Desti swallowed the length of him down until she felt the tip in the back of her throat, swooping her tongue around as her head bobbed up and down. She felt the hardness of him intensify, and she knew that he was close, but she wasn't done yet.

Desti pulled back and spread her legs until she was hovering over that beautiful creation, and then plunged herself onto him, feeling his cock fully inside her. His energy was everything. His power and kindness and love radiated from his soul and into her and as she sat there with him, she felt as if she was one with the man that she loved. Tate firmly grasped the meat of her hips and thrust his waist upward, plunging himself even deeper to her core.

She gasped and moaned and almost couldn't take the immediate pleasure that she was feeling. "Oh my God. It feels so good."

She could barely speak between the moaning that forced its way out of her mouth. Desti's hips thrust forward and backward, feeling the length of him hit the one spot that made her toes curl. She couldn't stop. She wouldn't. The pleasure was like a building wave in the open ocean, flowing and free, but soon it would crest and come crashing down with its roaring intensity. Tate had taken a handful of her ass in one hand and the other was gripping the small over her back, guiding her motions to go faster.

Breathless, she tried to give Tate a kiss during her time riding him, but the pleasure was too good to do anything besides keep going. Tate tilted his head back again but this time he let more than his moans escape his mouth. "Fuck me like the goddess that you are." His voice was guttural, but he continued. "I want to hear you scream and beg for more of me."

Her moans grew louder and faster along with Tate's, and she tried to beg for more of him. She wanted every inch to be inside her, pulsating into that wetness that gushed just for him. She knew that they both were getting close to the end. A warm rush of tingles flooded their way to her core and the center of her legs. She felt every part of her tense just before the climax came crashing into her.

Desti almost screamed from the intensity of her orgasm, riding the wave of it, using Tate's erect cock to keep it going just a little longer, until the wave of pleasure simmered down, and then she collapsed onto his heaving chest.

Tate held Desti in his arms, breathing heavy, deep breaths. "Shit, Desti." He laughed. "I think you are getting better at this." Desti sat up and chuckled. "Yeah well, I could say the same about you too."

"We should probably get back to our friends, don't you think?" he asked. Desti nodded. She knew that she couldn't stay up here forever, and sooner or later, someone was bound to come looking for them, and the last thing she wanted was someone like Anthony walking in on this. Desti threw on her clothes, as did Tate. "So, what do you think everyone is up to today?"

"Last I heard, Seraph, Kaelen, and Brandon were going to train with some of Peter's people. Anthony and Tess were playing fetch with Jet."

"Well, shall we go join them then?" Desti asked softly, holding out her hand for Tate to follow her. Tate offered a friendly smile and said, "We shall."

Chapter Fourteen

Worries

There was a sharp, ear-pitching buzz, steel clashing against steel, as Tess brought down her sword, slamming it into one of Peter's men. Echoing cheers reverberated around the room in praise of Tess's immaculate sword-fighting skills. Her hair was a frizzled mess, heaps of dirt and sweat smudged across her face and neck, and the look in her eye was that same look she had seen when she first saw Tess fight, only that time, she was fighting demons.

Desti smiled at Tate and ran forward toward the commotion. "You look like a real badass over here," Desti joked. Tess twirled the sword in her hand and nodded.

"You think? I feel like I just look very sweaty." Desti snorted and then tilted her head, looking at Tess's sword with curious eyes. "Where did you get a sword?"

Tess pointed behind her to a woman with a long blonde braid, talking with a group of people. "She has like a whole chest full of them. She mentioned something about raiding a weapons store. Who knew they actually had weapons stores here?"

The glistening sweat on Tess's brows refracted the sunlight that streamed through the broken beams hanging from the ceiling. Desti covered her eye with her hand and briefly glanced up. In Mors, it wasn't common to gaze at the sky and admire the blue and white that rolled on by, but she found herself doing just that quite often, but this time, the beautiful sky didn't give her a sense of peace, but instead acted as a reminder of the horrors that she knew were inevitable.

There was a war coming. The end of the world. And she may be the only thing that could save this planet and the people living here. When Desti returned her gaze down, Tess had been pulled to the side by a group of admirers.

"Looks like she fits in pretty well here. Don't you think?" Tate's voice came from behind. Desti jumped a little and turned around, staring right at that gorgeous face of his. "I think all of us are." Desti placed her hands on his chest and let her eyes shift to the corner of the room where Anthony and Brandon were playing fetch with Jet. For once, Anthony was a kid, and that made Desti's heart feel so full.

"I can see it in your eyes that you are holding something back." Desti narrowed her eyebrows at Tate. How did he do that? How could he see through her smiles and laughter, seeing the raw and hidden thoughts that lingered?

"You are too observant," she said, giving him a playful shove, but Tate caught her hand and held it to his chest, never breaking his gaze. "What is it? What aren't you telling me?"

At first, her instinct was to hold it in. Don't tell him, she thought, but what good would that do? After breathing out a few curses under her breath she caved. "We aren't safe here, Tate," she said. "I mean, right now it may seem safe, but a *war* is coming, the *end of the world* is coming, and we have no idea what the Master has planned for me, but I know he won't stop looking for me. I have no plan on how I am going to keep us all safe, let alone save the world."

Tate pulled Desti aside and sat down on a small ledge away from the people. "Come sit with me." Desti rolled her eyes but listened, taking a seat right next to him.

"Tess can kick some ass, don't you think?" Tate asked. Desti looked at him confused that he changed the subject. She nodded and watched Tess from across the room. "yeah, she can. All those years as Elijah's slave, forced to fight those demons, just so he could use their blood to create more slaves…it's crazy to think about, but at least she learned a valuable skill all those years." Desti scoffed.

"Brandon too. I've seen some of his secret meet-ups that he would have. Half of it was talking concepts and strategy, but the other half, well…they would fight." Desti hadn't heard Tate talk about his friendship with Brandon much. "How many meet-ups *did* you go to?"

"I went to enough to know that he could protect you if you needed it." The faintest of smiles pulled at his mouth. Now Desti knew where this conversation was going. She reluctantly looked his way, but his eyes were set on her, a fire burning in them that she hadn't seen before.

"My point is, Desti, that you are surrounded by strong capable people, and out of everyone here, you are the one that outshines the most. You are the blazing sun…the light that shrouds the dark…the fire that will burn the Master and Amaros and Elijah to the fucking ground." Tate leaned forward, resting his forehead on Desti's, closing his eyes. "You are the one thing that gives me the strength to keep fighting in this world, because without you, I would have given up long ago."

Desti sucked in a shallow breath.

"Don't give up on yourself, Desti. With you, we have hope."

The very breath in her chest got caught in her throat as she went to speak. A single tear began to form but she tried to blink it away. Tate caught the stream on the tip of his finger a wiped it away. "Don't cry," he said.

"How do you do that?" she asked in a half cry half laugh.

"Do what?"

"make me feel so…special."

He grabbed her cheek, eyes intensely staring into her soul. "Because you are."

"Desti!" Anthony called from across the room. He was smiling and running toward her while Jet followed along. Seeing him so pure and so free was all that she could have asked for, but sometimes good things need to come to an end.

"Yes?" she asked.

"Are you going to practice? We all are…you know, so we can prepare." He scratched his head and Jet barked.

"Anthony…come sit with me."

Desti shot Tate a glare that said *leave us alone*, and so he got up and walked over to Seraph and Kaelen who were having a sword match off in the distance. Anthony sat next to her, and Jet jumped up in his lap and he looked over to her with curious brown eyes.

"What is it?"

"I've been putting this off because I don't ever want to make you do something you don't feel comfortable with, but after what has happened, I think that you should practice with the Lux too."

"Really? I didn't think you would want me to—"

"I didn't," she interrupted. "I mean, I didn't want to make you feel like you had to be the one who must save everyone. It's not a fun burden to carry."

"But because of the Master and the rapture coming, you know that I would be able to protect myself better if I could learn like you," he finished. Desti laughed and shook her head.

"Yeah, pretty much. How did you—"

"I doesn't take a rocket scientist to guess that one. Besides, I've been thinking about the Lux a lot. I would like to try it."

Desti leaned in closer, speaking in a hushed tone. "These people don't know about your blood yet. Are you sure that is a secret you are willing to give up?" She hadn't thought about it until now, but maybe keeping Anthony's Nephilim heritage a secret could benefit them in some way, but Anthony was already shaking his head.

"No, I am not worried. I want to do this."

Desti stood and held out her hand. Clashing and banging echoed around from the group members all having their turns with their swords and weapons. Tate was now off in the distance joining in on some takedown moves with Seraph and Kaelen; Tess was with Lorie and her friends and Brandon was now sitting in the corner, sharpening a small knife. There was no better time than now to go practice with the Lux.

"Come on. Let's go before they notice we are gone."

"Okay, so you just hold it like this. See?"

Desti held the Lux between her palms, showing Anthony the best way to grip it. A bead of sweat trickled its way down her neck as she stood there. She swiped it away and blew out a huff. "Whew. It sure is getting hotter, isn't it?"

Anthony nodded but was too focused on the Lux to do anything else. He had grabbed it from Desti's grip and gazed upon the translucent orb that lay in his hands. The irises of his eyes reflected the shimmering that emitted from its glossy surface.

"What does it feel like?" he asked.

Desti tilted her head slightly and furrowed her brows.

"You know, when the energy flows through you. Does it hurt?"

She stiffened at that. The energy was heavenly and brilliant but also equally terrifying and something that made her feel like she was no longer in this realm. But that would be too much to dump on him, so Desti instead offered a friendly smile and replied, "No, it doesn't hurt."

Ahead, was a small metal can, about the same size as the one that Desti had first practiced on. Anthony stood about ten feet from it, his hair wildly dancing with the gentle breeze that blew in from behind the withered, broken wall.

"Just clear your mind and think of something happy. Something that you love." Desti hoped that Anthony could at least think of one happy memory, but growing up how they did, happy memories were a rare thing to come by. She held in her breath as he prepared himself.   "Thinking   of   happy thoughts is a way less painful way to do this than the way that Elijah brought my powers to the surface," Anthony said so nonchalantly as if his years of torture hadn't caused him pain to relive or speak about, but to Desti, it was as painful as if she had experienced it herself. Desti hated Elijah for what he did to him, for betraying his people. Betraying her. And for what? All because he wanted power. Desti scoffed quietly before returning her attention to Anthony.

Desti watched his eyes close, his breathing stall, and at that moment, it was as if the world went still with him. Not a single breeze or single sound made its way to disturb him at this moment. At first, the silence was almost deafening, so quiet that it almost drove her mind mad, but then the faintest of whispers fluttered into her mind.

Anthony twitched. Did he hear it too? Desti didn't dare reach out and ask. Instead, she kept her distance so that she wouldn't disturb him. The whispers grew louder, sounding like they were whirling around her and inside her at the same time. Anthony tensed and cocked his head to the side making a small grunting sound.

Suddenly, his eyes shot open but the look in his eyes wasn't his. They were glowing. Fiercely white, the blacks of his pupils were completely drowned out by the intensity of what every power was flowing through him.

"Anthony?" Desti called.

He didn't answer. His body lifted from the ground, frozen. Desti sucked in a gasp, completely regretting letting him try this. "Anthony! You can stop now." Desti ran forward but when she gripped onto Anthony's arm her heart skipped a beat and then she was somewhere else completely.

At first, there was just white light. Light that seemed to emanate from nowhere and everywhere all at once. *Where am I?* Distant melodies sifted through the air, enticing Desti to follow, but as she went to take a step, something seemed off. Glancing around, she didn't see anything. Not even her own body. And—

Was she floating?

What the Hell?

Immediately, Desti hit solid ground and was thrust down in a small garden. The sky was a breathtaking expanse of brilliant hues, a perpetual dawn painting the heavens with shades of gold. Desti curled her finger into the blades of grass beneath her—the most brilliant shades of jade.

Then, the scenery expanded until she was gazing upon a vast valley, decorated with thousands of different kinds of flowers. Desti inhaled and for a moment had forgotten what she had been doing before, but then a booming voice broke her mind from the serenity that infused itself into her.

"Desti," the voice said.

She gasped. "Who said that?"

"Do not fear, child of light and darkness, for I am Seraphiel, the divine one." The voice that resonated in her mind was both ethereal and commanding, sounding like a thousand whispering prayers all at once. It coated her mind like the first rays of dawn breaking through the night.

Desti couldn't help but squeak and cower at such an incredibly profound voice, but as she glanced around, there was no one in sight. The only thing that graced Desti with its beauty were opalescent butterflies fluttering through the meadow that stretched beyond.

"Where are you?" she asked.

"I am everything. I am all around and nowhere."

"Can I see you? Do you have a physical form?" Desti was now picking at her finger nervously, her heart slamming into her chest, and almost instantaneously, a figure appeared before her—a man. A very beautiful man.

He strode forward reaching out one of his hands. There was an eccentric glow around the outline of his body and his eyes were the same fiercely glowing white as how she saw in Anthony's eyes. "Child," he said.

Desti flinched, but then took his hand. Touching him was like touching a thousand Luxes. Feeling that energy pulse through her body like a running stream of light was nothing short of a miracle.

"What am I doing here?" Desti asked.

"Your time has come. The prophecy must be fulfilled."

The intensity in his eyes was too much for her to handle, and so Desti kept her gaze forward as she listened and followed. "What prophecy?"

"The child of light and dark, born into the realm of the wicked shall carry the blood of the heavenly and bring forth a wave of light back onto the Earth."

Desti pointed to her chest, eyes wide with disbelief. "Me?" She began to shake her head. "There is no way that *I* am the one in your prophecy. I can't be."

Seraphiel let out a gentle chuckle and paused for a moment, standing beside the most magnificent field of flowers and stream. He kneeled and plucked a flower from the grass. "Your world has been destroyed for many years, Child. The cursed one, bringer of darkness, shall no longer reign the humans of your planet. It is written that the child of light and dark shall be born, raised in the realm of the Cursed One's reign, but shall find their innate powers and cast the evil back into Hell where they belong."

"How? How am I supposed to cast the evil back to Hell?" Seraphiel only smiled. "When the time comes, Child, you will know."

Desti began to shake and tremble. It couldn't be her. There was no way she was the Child of Light and Dark, but if it wasn't her, then how come she was the one who found the Lux? She was the one who had escaped Amaros and the Master. Could it really be *her*?

"I see you fear the prophecy, Child. You don't need to worry. I brought you here to give you a gift."

Desti tilted her head with a curious face. "Oh?"

Seraphiel let go of Desti's hand for a moment and reached into a large pocket on his white robe, pulling out a small silver cross necklace. It dangled between his fingers as he brought it closer. Desti instinctively reached out for it. She recognized that necklace.

"Is this…Ms. Joan's?" her voice lingered on her name. Seraphiel smiled. "Yes. She wanted you to have it." Desti pulled back, brows furrowed. "Wait. How did she get this to you?"

Seraphiel didn't answer but instead placed the necklace around Desti's neck. Desti touched the silver pendant that hung just above her collarbone and breathed. "She is dead, isn't she?" she cried. Another person in Desti's life…dead.

"There is no death. Only transition. She has transitioned to the kingdom of light. With this gift, you shall hold the power of my touch within you. Seraphiel stepped away, his body now a beautiful, magnificent silhouette, illuminated by an ethereal heavenly glow.

"I can't accept this, Seraphiel. It's too much." Desti went to take the necklace off, but Seraphiel held out his hand and spoke. "One gift for another." And just like that, in his hand sat the Lux; the small opalescent orb that everyone had seemed to be fighting over. It was almost relieving to have it off her hands now.

She knew that he was taking back what belonged to him, and he had given her something in return. Desti wanted to cry. She wanted to shed tears for the lost, and for the suffering, for the ones who hadn't even experienced their suffering yet, but Seraphiel wiped away the tears that gathered and offered her one last smile before disappearing into the light.

Everything went black.

A gasp forced its way into her lungs and then all of a sudden Desti was lying on the ground next to Anthony. She sat up gasping and panicking, glancing around her until her eyes met Tate's. He kneeled close to her and helped her sit upright.

"Desti, it's okay. You're safe. What happened?"

"Uhm…I don't know," Desti said reluctantly. Anthony was still lying on the ground, a stillness holding his body. "Is Anthony—"

"He's alive," Tate said. Desti immediately relaxed, knowing that Anthony was okay. She refocused now.

"I went somewhere else." Desti looked over at Tate and he cocked his head to the side. "What do you mean? Where did you go?" In the irises of his deep green eyes, she could see the worry that clouded them. Desti cleared her throat and said, "I think I went to Heaven."

He didn't speak, but his eyes said it all. Worry, fear, sadness, and confusion, all swirled around in the twitching of the muscles in his face. "Are you sure?" he asked.

"I met an angel…named Seraphiel. He said that it was my time, and he gave me this." Desti held the necklace that hung around her neck, tiny beams of light refracting from it, creating a warm golden waterfall. Tate touched the necklace and grunted. "This looks familiar. Is this—"

"Ms. Joan's," Desti finished. His eyes went big, and he leaned in closer. "Is she dead?" Desti almost found herself crying at the thought of Ms. Joan but knowing that her soul had passed to the kingdom of light kept those tears at bay. "Her soul is free now and she is at peace."

Before Tate could answer he was stopped by a bloodcurdling scream that was coming from Anthony. His voice ripped through the air as he jolted forward, sweat now profusely beading off his face. Desti immediately reached for him but the moment she touched him, he flinched. His eyes now were back to their normal color but there was a hollowness to them. What did she do to him? She thought.

"Anthony." Desti cupped the side of his head. "What happened? What's wrong?" He was shaking under her touch but then slowly turned his head until his eyes met hers. In a whimpering cry, he said, "I saw what is coming. What the world will endure. It's worse than anything you could imagine and there is no way to escape it."

Anthony sobbed into Desti's chest, and she held him, stroking his hair until his sobs calmed. Tate had an expression of complete panic on his face as he hovered anxiously above them. Desti didn't know what to say. She too almost wanted to cry, but Tate reached down and held her as well, and in that moment, just the three of them sat there and cried.

Chapter Fifteen

Horrors to Come

They barely had more than fifteen minutes to calm Anthony down before Brandon came rushing through the door screaming that Peter was back.

"What?" Desti whipped her head around. Brandon was franticly waving his arms for them to follow him, eyes wild and untamed. Tate immediately pushed back, stiffening his face, and got up. He crossed the room in less than a second and was already bolting out through the door.

"Are you okay to go downstairs now?" Desti asked Anthony, clutching the sides of his cheeks. He nodded and stood. "I'm okay now. Come on," Anthony said while pulling Desti to her feet. Anthony took off running too, leaving Desti behind.

"Wait up!" she called breathlessly.

A chaotic commotion echoed through the stairwells as she ran as fast as she could to the first floor. It grew louder the closer she got and then she too was rushing into the room in a haze.

"Where is he?" she called, glancing all around the room. It was a mad house down here. People were screaming and arguing, others were crying, and everyone was gathered in a circle, creating a barrier that Desti had to break through. She pushed her way in and that was when she saw Peter hunched on the ground, shaking. Filth, blood, and dirt clung to him like a second skin. His body was decorated with lacerations the size of Desti's hand, and some went as deep as his bone. A knot formed in her chest, and she almost couldn't speak between her heaving breaths.

"Oh my God. Peter, I can't believe—"

"Don't," he rasped, holding his hand out. Fury and rage burned within his eyes as he turned and looked at her. "You left me," he growled. Desti immediately gulped down a knot in her throat as all eyes were on her now, their gazes shifting to something far more red.

Tears began to well in her eyes as everyone glared. "I'm sorry…I didn't know what to do—"

"You could have used your light to save me!" he hissed.

Desti gulped, palms now sweating. "I still don't know how to control it. I'm sorry…"

"You left him to die!" a lady yelled.

"Coward!" another man shouted. And eventually, it was like a ripple of screams and curses, cascading their way around the room until Desti felt like she was drowning in their anger. She was shaking now, breathing became difficult, and her heart started to skip beats.

Tate ushered through the people and before he came closer to her, he tried to help Peter to his feet, but the moment he touched Peter's arm, Tate winced in pain. Desti rushed forward, arms stretched out, but Tate held out his hand and said, "I'm fine. Let's go." Desti glanced around for her friends. *Where are they?* She thought. But then a bright orange, wild mane caught her eyes, giving her an immediate sense of relief.

Tess.

Tess must have seen her panicked look and by the way the room was, she probably could have easily guessed that Desti didn't feel safe. Tess and Brandon came running through the sea of people, reaching out to her. "We should probably get out of here, Desti," Brandon said. Desti nodded but something kept her still.

"Where are Kaelen and Seraph, and Anthony?"

Anthony shouted from behind, his voice barely audible in the screaming crowd of people. "Desti, I'm here. Kaelen and Seraph are with me." Tate gave her one final nod and pulled her away from the screaming people, and the last thing she saw before leaving the room was Peter's vicious eyes.

Something happened to him, and she wanted to find out what.

The moment they all made it outside to the alleyway, Kaelen started first. "What happened? They all look like they want to kill us. Don't they know that it wasn't our fault?"

It wasn't anyone's fault, but people do and think crazy things in times of panic and suffering. Desti would know more than any of them. In the city of Mors, Hell, in the entire world where Desti lived, every life of every human suffered immeasurably. She saw firsthand, experienced the pain through her own eyes, knowing what that could make any person do. You would go crazy at times from the pain and the sorrow that infected your life.

Desti didn't blame these people for the way that they were reacting, but it didn't mean she wanted to stay anywhere close to them right now. There was a heavy heat that hung in the air. Not like how it was when Desti and Tate first arrived in this world. It felt familiar in a terrifying way.

"We need to find somewhere safe to go," Seraph croaked. He had a small knife dangling in his grip, and Desti shot him a curious glare. "Where did you get that knife?" Desti asked.

"I managed to sneak one from their weapons chest. I got all of us one." Seraph turned around and started pulling daggers from the inside of his waist belt. Desti almost laughed with a mixture of fear and relief swirling around in her.

Tate smiled and took the knife that Seraph handed him. "Thanks. This will at least offer us *some* protection out here."

"The only real threat is the Master. Anything else, we can easily handle with these." Desti held up her dagger, it flashing fiercely under the sun's beaming rays. The brilliance of the white light that protruded through the clouds was picking up its heat day by day and Desti had noticed.

"This heat," Desti started. "It feels just like—"

"Like the demons' world…" Kaelen's voice drifted off. Her eyes were empty as if her mind had gone back to a place of pain and torment. She refocused with a new fear burning within her eyes. "You don't think it's happening, right now. Do you?"

By *"it"*, she meant the rapture. The end of days. The most brutal time in human history. It was terrifying to think about.

Tate shook his head. "No way. There were signs that led up to it. I remember the lessons we had. The world was pretty much at its end even before the demons showed up."

Tess glanced around at the rubble that surrounded them, the burnt buildings, and the bodies that littered the crevices of the once beautiful city. "Umm…this looks like it pretty much has ended if I do say so myself."

Everyone stopped what they were doing to take a look for themselves. Tess wasn't wrong. This city had been through Hell and the only people that remained now were Rospinity's people and Peter's. Everyone else probably either evacuated or perished in the chaos of survival.

"Where are we supposed to go?" Kaelen whined.

Desti had absolutely no freaking clue and by the look on Tate's face, neither did he. Brandon started to walk down the alleyway, back toward the street, twirling his dagger in his hand. "I guess we start walking and keep an eye out for something that seems fit for us to stay in."

The rest of her friends followed but Tess lingered for a second. "Wait, we need the Lux." Desti instinctively played with the cross necklace that hung on the hollow of her neck. She hadn't told them yet about what she experienced or where she went. "Don't worry. It's back to where it belongs. I don't need it anymore." Tess cocked her head to the side, confusion plastered all over her face, but Desti just simply smiled and said, "I'll explain later. Okay?"

It was time to get out of there before Peter and his people came looking for them because the way that they last left them, everyone looked like they were going to rip the flesh right off her bones. Desti and the rest of her friends took off around the corner, now wandering the ruins of the city.

It had been hours of painstaking treading down the streets; blown-to-piece buildings, dead animals, and human bodies randomly scattered around, but the worst thing that Desti started to notice was an awful pungent smell that seemed to radiate through the sky—tangy and sour.

This wasn't normal. Something was changing the city right before her eyes, and this terrified Desti to her core. This smell…this heat…it was all too familiar, and Desti didn't want to speak it out loud, but she felt as though this really was the beginning of the end. The apocalypse was going to happen and by the way the shift of the world was happening around her, she could feel it was going to happen sooner rather than later.

"So, tell me again," Desti said to no one specific. "What happened again? With the rapture, I mean. What was the first sign of the end?" Desti walked with a languid pace, her movement deliberately slow as she navigated through the relentless heat. The fabric of her clothing clung to her damp skin, but there was too much sweat to even wipe it away. And so, Desti distracted her mind with conversation.

Kaelen was walking to Desti's left, her golden hair bouncing between steps. She glanced over with a painful expression, looking awfully exhausted, but nonetheless, she answered. "At first, there were the little signs that led up to it according to our lessons: the Earthquakes, the storms, famine, disease…it pretty much was ending before the really bad stuff happened. Then half of the people just vanished into light and the other half, our ancestors, were the ones left to suffer."

Everyone was silent, staring at Kaelen as she told the history of the beginning of the Era of the Damned. Her voice began to shake and quiver because now she was getting to the gruesome part of the story. "Then the lesser demons infested every city of the world, devouring the innocent and the damned, and once they all had their fun, that was when the higher demons came upon the Earth to enslave the remaining humans."

Tess cleared her throat. "I heard that most of the beginning, all women were used as sex slaves, to ensure the repopulation the way the demons wanted it." Anthony stiffened at the sound of that. Desti reached for him, placing a gentle hand on his shoulder. "Tess, maybe that isn't the best to speak of right now."

"Right. I'm sorry. It won't happen, Okay?"

"It *will* happen, Tess. Because it already did. We can't stop it from coming," Brandon interjected. Tess scoffed and flung her hair off her shoulder. "You really think that we are going to relive the same fate as our ancestors? We have weapons now. We can stop this from happening!"

"Tess, I hate to break it to you, but your little dagger isn't going to do shit to a bunch of demons coming at you."

"I wasn't talking about my dagger. I was talking about them." Tess flicked her gaze to Desti first then it slowly shifted to Anthony. Desti straightened up and felt Tate bring his body closer to her now, the heat of his core hugging the small of her back. She inhaled, breathing in the energy that his body emulated. Even the faintest of touches from him sent her swirling.

"Anthony and I need more practice with our powers. We are just discovering what we can do," Desti replied. Seraph quickened his step, narrowing his brows. "And what happened to the Lux, Desti? You haven't had it since back there."

Desti shared a glare with Anthony, both of them speaking through their gaze, and a simple nod from him gave her what she needed to feel comfortable with telling them what happened. Desti drew in a breath and said, "The angel Seraphiel took it back."

Everyone stopped in their tracks, but Desti kept going a few more steps before realizing that all eyes were on her now. "You didn't tell me this," Tate spoke. Desti didn't have time to. There was too much chaos happening and then Anthony screaming…she hadn't been able to give Tate or anyone the details of what happened, and so that was what she did in that moment. She told her experience from start to finish about the angel Seraphiel and about her new gift and newly improved powers.

Most of her friends that stood before her had hope lingering in their eyes, and for once, Desti felt that maybe, just maybe, she really could help save them. If not the world, then at least save her friends.

Chapter Sixteen

Hideout

"Just kick it in," Tess hissed.

Seraph was pondering over how to break into a house that the group had stumbled upon. All the windows and doors were boarded shut; glass scattered all around like a warning for intruders. Seraph kicked one of the wooden beams that clung to the basement window. It didn't budge. This wood was thick. His leg reverberated backward as he fell on his ass and Tess couldn't help but slip out a chuckle.

"Here, let me try, Brandon stepped forward. Brandon craned his foot back and slammed it into the beam, hard. A tiny snap echoed and Desti sucked in her breath. Brandon cracked a smirk and said to Seraph, "See. That's how you do it."

"Whatever." Seraph waved his hand at Brandon as he pulled himself to his feet. Kaelen was quietly giggling at their bickering from the corner. It was nighttime now, and Desti was honestly surprised that they hadn't run into the Master or one of his people yet. There was no way that the Master was just going to let her go. He had to be looking for her, but he must have known where Peter's hideout was, right? Why didn't he just break through the doors and get Desti himself? The silence that crept its way through the night was more terrifying than if Desti was to face the evil that sought to hurt her.

That was when you should fear the most, when the wind stops howling, when the bugs stop buzzing, and when the world around you goes still. That was when danger lurked around the corner and in the depths of the shadows, waiting to pounce on you at your most vulnerable and unexpected.

Desti glanced up at the midnight sky, ignoring the beauty of the splatter of stars that hovered above. She was too worried that something was coming for her. She could feel it in her bones, but Desti kept that thought to herself and waited quietly in the distance.

"Come on. I want to get inside before someone sees us," Tess said as she stepped over the broken shards of wood and lifted herself through the window. Kaelen ran forward, her blonde hair gilded by the trickling moonlight, spilling over her shoulder as she was the second one to crawl through. Brandon and Seraph both walked forward simultaneously and glanced at each other for a second before Seraph stepped aside to let Brandon go first.

Desti watched Seraph slip into the shadows next followed by Anthony, and now it was just Desti and Tate left outside. There was an oppressive blanket of a sulfur smell in the air, which frightened Desti because back in the city of Mors, that only meant one thing and one thing only—demons.

She glanced around anxiously, heart beating wildly in her chest, and she thought that Tate would maybe save her from her worries with one of his gentle touches, but what he did next sent a shockwave of horror to her gut.

Tate snatched Desti's jaw with a firm grip, but he didn't say anything. He just stared at her with a wicked smile plastered on his face and then after a second, he released her and said, "Come on," disappearing into the basement.

What the fuck was that?

What *was* that? Why did Tate grab her like that? Was it some kind of sexual thing?

No. No way. He wouldn't get off with being so aggressive. Maybe he was mad, but Desti tilted her head as confusion swirled around her brain, thinking of what she could have done to upset him. All she knew was that that was weird, and she didn't like it.

As Desti lowered herself into the basement, the first thing that smacked her in the face was the awfully pungent smell of moldy stale air. She covered her nose with her hand as she peered around the room. A small single lightbulb dangled from the ceiling, casting a dim orange dome of light in the center.

"I guess this is better than nothing," Anthony spoke. Desti offered a smile to him, but she knew that the sadness on her face couldn't be hidden anymore. Anthony smiled back but his eyes told Desti a different story. "At least we aren't outside anymore," Desti said while taking a seat on an old cushion that was lying on the ground.

Kaelen and Seraph were trailing the perimeter of the room, probably curious if there were any hidden doors or compartments, Brandon was messing with the lightbulb, Tess sat down in the corner of the backside of the room and rested her head between her knees, and Anthony sat right next to Desti.

Desti glanced up, tracing her gaze up Tate's body. He stood like a statue, staring at the depths of blackness in the corner of the room as if he were watching something. Desti's lips parted slightly, and she drew in a shallow, ragged breath as fear took hold of her.

"Desti?"

Anthony snapped Desti from her thoughts for a moment and she turned her gaze to her side, looking into those big innocent eyes of his. Immediately, Desti relaxed a bit and smiled.

"Yes?" she said.

Anthony's eyes changed to something more empty, dark. Desti reached for him, placing her hand on his knee.

"What is it? What's wrong?" For a brief moment, Desti did a quick glance at the room to make sure no one was truly paying attention to them; and they weren't.

"We never got to talk about what we saw back there…" his voice trailed off. When he said, *"Back there"*, she knew what he was talking about. Anthony was talking about the Lux and whatever place that he had gone to. Desti's experience was pleasant and weird, but mostly pleasant, but she saddened when she remembered the horrifying scream that ripped from Anthony's chest as he sobbed in her arms. He had cried to her of the things he saw briefly before she really had a chance to ask him more about what it was that he experienced.

Now should be a good time.

Desti's brows drew together in a compassionate worry for him. "I've been wanting to talk with you about it. What exactly happened to you? Where did you go?" Desti's hand was resting on his shoulder now and she could feel the vibrations rattling up her arm as his body trembled. He was never like this. Something must have really frightened him.

"I saw…" he stopped as if it were too painful to continue, and Desti leaned in slightly to encourage him to keep going. He blinked away a single tear and glanced her way really quickly before continuing. "I saw it happen…like I was there. I saw the demons crawl from the depths of the Earth and tear away at every person who was still alive on this planet. And then I saw you, and Tate, and Tess, and everyone else. There was so much blood that I couldn't tell whose it was. I was so scared," his voice croaked. And now Anthony was crying, silently, a stream of tears glided down his cheek.

"Sweety, I know it probably felt real, but it wasn't. Okay? You are here now, and we are all safe." Desti was now patting Anthony's back with the palm of her hand, going in idol circles. She shifted her gaze slightly to make sure no one was paying attention to their conversation. Seraph and Kaelen seemed to have dozed off, as did Brandon who was now slumped over. Tess looked bored and tired as she picked at her fingers. And Tate was—

Wait a second. Where was Tate?

Desti's eyes darted from corner to corner of the dark room, but she couldn't see Tate anywhere. Desti turned toward Anthony and said softly, "Try to get some rest, okay? I'll be right back." There was a sadness that clung to his eyes, but Desti just gave him a gentle kiss on the top of his head and stood from where she was sitting. Anthony lay down now and closed his eyes, and as Desti took one more glance around the room, she noticed that now everyone was asleep—except for Tate, who seemed to be…missing.

There was a staircase at the far end of the room, so Desti stepped over the sleeping bodies of her friends and ventured up the staircase, pushing open the door that was at the top slowly.

"Tate?" she whispered.

It was dark up here. Like really dark, but someone had lit a trail of small candles and left them along the floor. Desti followed the trail of flickering candlelight until it led her to a room off in the distance, down the hall. With every footstep she took, she could hear the slight creak of the old wooden floor crying out. Desti took shallow breaths and the closer she came to the room, the quieter she was trying to be.

Desti placed the palm of her hand on the door and cracked it slightly, peering her way in before walking in fully. Was Tate in here? She thought. There was a shadow—a silhouette—standing by the boarded-up window. Desti blew out a sigh of relief and walked in.

"Tate, what are you doing in here?" she whispered.

At first, he didn't answer. He didn't even move. Instead, he stood there silently still peering through a tiny crack between the wood. It was dark, so it was difficult to see fully, but Desti was sure that there was something off about him. Maybe Tate was finally having a mental breakdown and needed some alone time with her.

"I can hear you breathing," he said quietly but firmly.

"I didn't want to startle you," she replied, walking fully into the room and shutting the door behind her. At the center of the room, there was a large bed, blanketed with a dark blue quilt. Desti walked over to it and sat at the edge.

"What are you doing in here?" she asked.

Tate's head turned and he began to slowly make his way over to her, still glancing around the room. "I needed the quiet to think."

Okay. So, maybe he was having a mental crisis. Desti relaxed her shoulders and reached out her arms. "Do you want to come sit next to me?"

His gaze snapped in her direction, but he held it onto her with a hint of aggression that lingered in his eyes. He stepped forward, the ground shaking under his shoe.

"What I want right now, is to fuck you until you scream my name in agony," he said firmly.

Woah. Desti couldn't help but let a snort escape her chest. I mean, she loved it when he talked dirty to her, but was now really the best time for this? He was staring as Desti talked to herself in her mind, trying to decipher this…situation, his eyes gleaming with something predatory.

Desti cocked her head to the side and said softly, "I want nothing more than for you to do that…to me." Her gaze flicked up and down his body and then he smirked. "But is now the best time for this?"

Tate closed the space between them until the heat of his body pressed against Desti's core. She glanced up as he shifted his gaze downward, drawing his hand from his pocket and guiding her chin up until she was looking right at him. "We may not have a tomorrow, or even another hour. Why not now?"

There was a slight growl that she heard rumble from his chest as he spoke, and by the look in his eyes, he was dead set on rocking her world tonight. "Uhm…" Desti cleared her throat, thinking of the room beneath their feet with their sleeping friends.

But before Desti could speak, Tate grabbed her chin firmly and lifted her to a standing position as if he had some kind of magical strength and held her gaze. To be honest it kind of shocked Desti, and slightly turned her on to see this aggressive side of him in the bedroom. Each breath he took, he took with power, sounding like a feral animal ready to be let out of his cage.

Desti's breath was shallow and ragged. Tate didn't speak, but the way his gaze raked over her body, she felt as though he were undressing her with his eyes. "Take that off," he demanded, as he nodded his chin toward her shirt. Desti nodded, doing what he asked. Tate had let go of her chin but still kept his body so freaking close.

As Desti lifted her shirt above her head, she felt Tate grip the sides of her waist in a solid hold, pressing the heat of his body into hers.

Woah. Talk about sexual aggression. This was different, not like him, but maybe he was just so frustrated from what they had been through. Desti didn't question it now. She kind of liked the way he was demanding and controlling in the bedroom.

Desti let her body ease, getting into this whole dominant and submissive thing that Tate had going on, and raked her fingers over his abs. She glanced up at him as he started to pull his shirt over his head. Every muscle in his body flexed, catching the glowing candlelight that surrounded the room.

Desti placed a gentle kiss on his bare chest, and she felt him inhale deeply, groaning from her touch. The tips of her fingers gently traced delicate swirls down his body until they got to the hem of his pants. Her fingers played with the buttons until she was able to pull them down.

Now Tate stood before her, hard as a rock, and Desti was now fully into this. She kissed her way slowly down his chiseled abs, pressing the pads of her lips in delicate, sensitive spots, slipping her tongue out as she reached down below.

A low and guttural groan escaped Tate's chest as he tilted his head back. Desti yanked off his underwear, sitting face to face with his erect cock. She grasped the hardness of him with the palm of her hand, stroking him as she still kissed gently around.

"Oh fuck," he growled.

Desti kept going and now was bringing her mouth to the tip of the shaft, but before she could place her mouth onto him, Tate pulled away and grabbed Desti by the throat, slamming her onto the bed.

Holy fuck!

She didn't know if she should be scared or turned on. Kind of both, to be honest. Tate lessened his grip on her throat but still kept it there as his other hand explored her body beneath her clothes.

"You need to take this off," he demanded, reaching for her pants and ripping them from her waist. Desti gasped from both surprise and the pleasure that pulsated between her legs. She had never seen this side of Tate in the bedroom. He was usually always so gentle and romantic, but this side kind of turned her on.

The hand that Tate held at her throat drew back and now was exploring her body, making its way down the curve of her hips and onto her waist. He held the meat of her thighs in his grip as he closed his eyes and inhaled, a pleasurable expression rolling over his face.

Tate flashed Desti a smile and then quickly turned his attention to her, nipping and biting his way to her center. She felt his tongue lick its way down the center of her thighs, getting closer to her core, and Desti gasped, arching her back, inviting his tongue to continue.

She wanted to feel his tongue slip its way onto her throbbing clit. And it was as if he had read her mind because that was exactly what he did. Tate traced his tongue in playful and torturous swirls around the spot that desperately ached for his touch. Her fingers grabbed onto the sheet she lay on as she breathlessly begged, "Please, Tate. I need it."

And then his mouth was on it, sucking and pulling, and Desti practically jumped out of her body as the pleasure that exploded between her legs smacked her in the face. A moan forced its way out of her, but she muffled it with a pillow that was lying next to her head.

Tate continued his exploring as his tongue danced feverously around the pulsating wetness. Desti was gasping between moans, barely able to keep still, and she didn't think it could get any better until she felt Tate slip two of his fingers inside her.

Her moans grew louder and louder, becoming harder to mask beneath the cushiony pillow that she now had squeezed over her mouth. And then just like that, Tate pulled back, leaving Desti's rising climax to fall back down to a dull tingle.

She glanced down at him, and he was standing over her sprawled legs, glaring between them with a wicked look in his eyes. "Tate?" she tried to ask, but as she spoke, Tate snatched Desti's ass cheek into his hand and flipped her completely over, and yanked her hips into him until her face pressed against the mattress.

Tate smacked her ass, firmly holding onto the meat of her cheek, easing the sting that lingered. Desti gasped, not knowing if she was turned on or not. "I couldn't get this out of my head," he groaned. "I've thought about the way you looked, smelled…" His voice was low and guttural. Before Desti could contemplate what he had said, Tate yanked her waist into his, sliding his hard cock into her.

He slid right in, and took no time to savor it, as he began pounding the living daylights of out Desti. She screamed his name, burying her head into the mattress. Tate had told her that he wanted to fuck her until she screamed his name, and she guessed he had gotten what he wanted.

The pleasure was out of this freaking world, cascading her body to a whole other level of ecstasy. The way his cock rammed into her, hitting her just in the right spot, sent a wave of heat to her core and between her legs. At this rate, she was going to cum soon, and she could feel it building. It was growing now, the dull tingle now a full-on rush of pleasure feeling as if she were ready to explode, and as Tate's cock thrust into her again, her entire body shook and quivered from the exploding orgasm that she was experiencing. A literal scream escaped from her as she cried out in pure pleasurable agony—

just like he had said. She thought Tate would simmer down a bit and give her a moment to recoup, but kept his momentum, slamming into her with a fierce pressure. Desti tried to move her body away slightly to ease the aggressive pounding she was taking, but then Tate leaned forward while still slamming into her and yanked her head up by her hair.

Okay, now this was going a little too far.

Desti groaned and tried to ask Tate to release her head between her moans, the pain shooting down her neck. "Tate, please let go," she managed to beg.

But Tate didn't let go. He held on firmly and fucked her harder now. Now he was being too rough, and the pleasure was subsiding, being replaced with pain.

"Tate, I said let go." Her voice was more commanding now, but he still didn't listen. Desti tried to move away but Tate had pinned her body down with his other free hand. Fury and rage began to build inside her and now she was full-on bucking her body trying to get away, his cock still pounding into the wetness between her legs.

His grip was tight, but what happened next sent a fear like no other swirling into Desti's core.

"Tate stop!" she cried. But he didn't. The thrust of his body kept pounding her from behind as his hand held her down. She began to cry and writhe, trying to wiggle her body free from his grip, and that was when she heard it…that familiar and sinister voice that haunted Desti in her dreams, and he was *chuckling*.

His grip tightened on her, and she felt the last of his thrusts shove into her as he came. His body quivered, still firmly pressed against her, pinning her down in her own pool of tears.

"Tate, what the fuck!" she cried. "Let me go!" But he didn't loosen his grip on her. He laughed, and that was when Desti realized that the man fucking her wasn't Tate at all. It couldn't be. Tate would never do this to her. He was sweet and romantic and gentle, and whatever this was, was demanding and aggressive, and forceful.

Desti's heart dropped to the floor when she felt the body of Tate press into her, as he leaned over to her ear and whispered, "Surprise."

Desti sucked in a gasp and held it in her chest. *No. This can't be.* She knew this voice. This evilness. Desti began to silently sob, tears running down her cheek as the realization came crashing into her.

This wasn't Tate. She knew that now, and as her mind racked around with endless thoughts, she recoiled into herself when she realized who had just fucked her and was still holding her body pinned, *naked*, against the bed.

The Shadow.

Chapter Seventeen

All Hell Broke Loose

A complete sob broke free from Desti's chest as she cried helplessly pinned on the bed. She felt Tate—the Shadow—lean forward until his mouth just barely kissed the edge of her ear as he whispered, "I couldn't get you out of my head…I wanted to feel myself inside you. It's all I've been thinking about."

Her body recoiled in utter disgust for this *thing* that had ahold of Tate, who had just fucked her senseless. A wave of disgust rushed over her body as she thought about this thing making her cum and using Tate's body to get off. Rage and fury ignited in her chest as she tried to scream but the Shadow had shoved her face into the bed, muffling her cries for help.

She was still naked and so was he, cock still inside her. "I'm going to get dressed now. If you scream, I will kill your friends. Do you understand?" he groaned. Desti nodded her head in a silent cry. The last thing she wanted was for her friends to be hurt. She felt him slip Tate's body away and heard the rustling of him putting his clothes on.

Desti turned around, pulling her knees into her chest to cover her bare body, only her bra was still on. "When did you take him?" she said flatly.

Tate—the Shadow—cast a wicked smile at her. "Here put these on," he said, ignoring her question, tossing her clothes in her lap. Desti obliged and slipped back into her clothes trying to think of how she would be able to help Tate, save her friends, and get out of this mess. She knew she had powers stronger than she originally thought, but Desti didn't know how to fully use them or to what extent that power reached. If the Shadow knew just how powerful she might be, it could make her situation worse. She decided to play into the submissive weak character, for now.

"I want to know when you took Tate."

Tate scoffed; his back still turned toward her. Desti trailed her gaze along the splatter of scars along Tate's back and flanks. He had been through so much torment and pain in his life, and yet he was such a kind and protective soul. Could he hear her? See her? *Feel her?*

She had remembered him describing how it was like not being in control of his body as the Shadow had taken over the first time. Did Tate, the real Tate, have to stand there and feel and watch the Shadow hold her down?

Desti shook her head. Tate was now dressed, and he walked over to Desti, yanking her up by the arm in a firm grip. "You want answers, then you do what I say."

Desti whimpered. She glanced at the window that had a board nailed to it, but tiny beams of moonlight trickled through the withered cracks of the wood. What time was it? Desti didn't have a way to tell time from this room but if she had to guess, it had to have been about one in the morning.

Tate let go of her arm and strode over to a chair that was placed in the shadowy corner. He dragged it across the room, a screeching sound ringing along with it, and placed it in front of the door. What was he doing? Desti cocked her head to the side trying to figure out what he was going to do.

His body moved differently, not like how Tate would walk. Instead of the casual, confident stride, this *Tate* walked with an anger to his step, heavy and demanding. He plopped himself down in the chair, now blocking the door.

Great. Now she was trapped in here with this *thing*. Desti sat back on the bed and held her knees into her chest, heaving deep trembling breaths. "What do you want?" she managed to ask through gritted teeth. A flash of something wicked gleamed across his face before he leaned forward and spoke. "We have plans for you, Escaped One."

Desti was seething. She could practically feel the anger seeping out her pores and rolling into the air, and she knew that the Shadow was loving every second of her torment. He smiled at her occasionally but mostly sat in the chair quietly watching her. Was he going to make her sit here all night?

After a while of silence, Desti found the courage to speak up again, because she just had to know what plans he was talking about. "What plans?" she nodded her chin. "You said you have plans for me. What are they?" Desti had laced her fingers together beneath her knees.

Suddenly, Tate—the Shadow—stood aggressively from the chair and stomped across the room, stopping just right before his body touched the bed. "How dare you speak so freely around me. If it were up to me, I would have ripped your fucking throat out already," he growled.

Desti sucked in her breath at that. Holy shit, he was scary. This was a bad situation. Really bad. She recoiled and leaned back as far as her body could go before bumping her head into the wall behind her. His eyes, devoid of any emotion besides rage, glared at her, and she shrunk into herself even more.

Desti squeaked, trying to ask a question but he threw his hand up to silence her. "He has a plan. I am just following orders. You are lucky your blood is so special, or you would have died long ago," he said flatly.

Desti slipped a glance downward, thinking of her friends down there, sleeping, not knowing what was happening just a floor above them, but she immediately regretted that because the look in Tate's eyes flashed to something more sinister.

"Oh, your friends," he growled, tilting his head. "They have a purpose for this plan. Until then, I won't kill them, but I can't wait until Amaros gives me the free will to rip out all of their throats." He licked his lips as if he were tasting their blood coating his tongue. Desti had to remind herself that the Shadow was a higher demon, *and* that he was a bloodthirsty monster.

Desti tried to get up from the bed, but immediately she regretted that. Tate moved so quickly that he turned into a shadow crossing the floor, grasping her by her throat. Desti choked on her breath as his hand clamped down around her jugular. "You don't fucking move from this bed until I say so, do you understand?" he seethed.

Black spots and stars began to cloud her vision as she started to go in and out, but she just barely managed to nod her head which got him to lessen his grip. Her eyes were only a few inches away from Tate's, but it wasn't him looking back. These eyes were black as coal, swirling with an evilness beneath them, like spilled ink in the deep ocean.

He cracked a wicked smile. "Don't worry. We will be leaving in the morning. That is when the fun will begin."

Oh shit.

That couldn't be good whatever it was. Eventually, his hand retreated, and he went back to sitting in the chair in front of the door, watching Desti with a sinister stare. Desti didn't know what else to do, so she lay down on the bed, curled into a ball, and wept like a baby until blackness engulfed her mind.

Desti woke to the smell of smoke and as she cracked open her eyes, briefly forgetting for a moment where she was, she saw orange flames flickering through the cracks in the wood that boarded the window.

"It's time," that evil voice purred from across the room. She almost forgot what had happened, but that quickly came rushing back to her the moment she heard the Shadow speak through Tate.

Desti didn't speak in fear of being strangled again, or worse…

And then she heard screaming, a high-pitched, glass-breaking scream coming from the basement. Immediately her eyes popped wide open. *Anthony. The others.*

Desti sprung forward without even thinking now as her body lurched forward toward the door, but Tate jammed out his arm and stopped her. "What is happening to them?" she demanded, tears now welling in her eyes. Tate only smiled at her. "I told you that the morning would be when the fun would begin."

She could hear them crying out for help. Tess. Anthony. Kaelen and Seraph, and Brandon. It pained her to her core that she couldn't be there to help them. "Please don't hurt them. Please, I will do anything!" she begged.

Tate didn't seem pleased at her pathetic begging and whimpering. He simply scoffed and said, "Let's go. It's time," grabbing her arm and dragging her down the hall. As Tate was dragging Desti across the house, that was when another demon barged open the basement door with a wad of Kaelen's hair in his hand as he dragged her forward too. She locked her gaze with Desti, meeting her with watery eyes. Desti didn't speak and neither did Kaelen.

It was like a train of torturing higher demons, one by one, yanking her friends—her family—from their hair and to the outside. Silent sobs echoed around the house as Desti was pulled forward. She wasn't prepared for what was to come next because what she saw made the bile in her stomach swirl like a storm into her throat.

Tate kicked the front door off the hinges and that was when she came face to face with what she so desperately dreaded. It was inevitable, and now it was happening, right now, right here. A ghastly gasp caught in her throat as her eyes peered upon the most horrifying scene her mind could never even imagine.

It was the apocalypse.

The end of days.

The rapture…and it was happening right now.

Chapter Eighteen

End of Days

Screaming and torment and pain surrounded Desti at every corner of the city, relinquishing the agonizing cries of the damned and the tortured. Desti thought the city had pretty much been abandoned, but as she gazed upon the fire-lit city, she saw thousands of helpless souls being ripped limb from limb, flesh being torn from their skin, and children being ripped from their dying parents' arms as the city burned in the hellish inferno. Demons slithered their way from the shadows, like cockroaches, and preyed upon any of the people who were left. The thought of Peter crossed her mind and his people. Were they being tortured right now? Were they safe? There were so many people screaming for help, and it caught Desti off guard.

She thought the city was abandoned, but maybe the people were just really good at hiding. But not from this…

Desti staggered back wanting to escape the terror that was before her, but she felt the tight grip of Tate's hand grab her firmly and shove her forward. The heat of his breath caressed her neck as he spoke softly and sinisterly in her ear. "Surprise."

A river of tears streamed down her face as she shook her head back and forth in disbelief. Kaelen was shoved into her back and Desti heard her gasp with horror and then hit the floor as she sobbed. It was instinct; Desti went to cradle Kaelen but that was a bad idea because the next thing she knew, she was being yanked up by her hair. Desti yelped and then was thrown down the front steps and onto the dirt ground.

One by one, her friends shared the same fate, being tossed into this realm of terror, hitting the ground with heavy thuds. She could see the staining of their tears wash away the dirt that caked on their faces. The smell of burning flesh seeped its way into the air, causing Desti to gag.

Kneeled in the dirt, Desti glanced to her right, gazing upon the sorrow and defeat that lingered in her friends' eyes. Anthony slipped a glance at Desti and tried to smile at her. Immediately, her heart melted. After everything that he had been through, he still tried to be so strong for her. No words were spoken but when she met his gaze, she knew he could tell what her eyes were trying to say; *I will get us out of this.*

There was so much chaos happening around her, that she almost forgot that before her stood a group of higher demons, standing alongside Tate. Their bodies were contorted and twisted, some having horns protruding from their skulls, and others looking as if their skin was covered in burnt bark. Their eyes, devoid of anything besides pure evil, stared right through her as she studied their grotesque features. Then her eyes met Tate, and for a second, she forgot he was under the control of the Shadow and smiled at him, but the evilness that held his expression immediately made Desti suck in her breath.

Tate flashed her a smile, but this one was wicked and sinister. He then stepped forward, dangling the small knife that Desti had hidden in her pocket between his fingers. She had forgotten that they all had small weapons, and instinctively she grabbed for it in her pocket, but it was empty.

Shit.

The other demons must have taken her friends' knives as well. There was no way they were going to leave them with something to defend themselves with. Then it hit her, that *she* was a weapon, and her original plan of staying under the radar flew out the window as she thought to herself, *fuck that.*

Desti drew in a large breath and then hardened the lines in her face, focusing on bringing the light within her to the surface. She didn't know what kind of powers she could yield yet besides beaming a ray of light from her hands. Maybe she could do more than that.

The other demons stalked around Desti and her friends as they all kneeled there in the dirt, fire, and tormented souls screaming all around them. They were crying, her friends, their sobs whispering through the ashy gusts of wind that blew through.

Okay, it was now or never. Bring the light to the surface and burn these motherfuckers to the ground. She waited until Tate glanced away, seemingly in some kind of conversation with the other demons, and now was her chance.

A small vibration rattled through her body, starting from her limbs and then centering in her chest. The power grew as she focused on the good things in her life: Tate, Anthony, Tess, Seraph and Kaelen, and Brandon. They had all become a family through all their pain and journeys. It grew intensely until it felt like a burning in her body that so desperately needed to be released, and then her hands began to glow, encased with a translucent white outline. She lifted her hand and aimed it at one of the demons who literally looked like a walking tree trunk, but just as she was about to shoot her angelic power beam from her hand, she felt someone yank her head from behind, pulling her to her feet by her hair.

A slight whimper escaped her throat and immediately her powers retreated back into her body and disappeared.

"I knew you would come back to me," his voice growled. The heat of his breath coated the back of Desti's neck, causing the tiny hairs to spike. She knew that voice. His voice was like venom, striking her with its threats. A sob caught in her throat when she realized who had ahold of her hair, and with a pathetic whimper she breathed, "Amaros."

There was that sinister chuckle that he did. He stalked in circles around her until he stalled, standing right before her in his freshly pressed suit, flashing her with his wicked smile. "Hello, Desti…or should I call you The Escaped One?"

Desti growled and then spat on the ground at his feet. "Fuck you." To her left, she peered through the tangled mess of hair that hung in her face, glancing at her sobbing and defeated friends next to her, and then her gaze drifted toward Tate, longing to see anything of *him* left in the blackness of his eyes. But there was nothing but pure wicked evil lingering in there.

"Why Amaros? Why not leave us alone?"

Amaros craned his head back and bellowed a laugh deep from his chest in mockery. "You think I was going to just let you all go? Why do you think I sent your friends back here at this time?"

So, Desti's suspicions were right. Amaros did send them back to the time before the Era of the Damned in a calculated manner. He wanted them to suffer the same torment that their ancestors had. As realization came crashing into her, Desti let her sobs escape her chest in an agonizing cry.

"We were never really free, were we?" she questioned. To her left, Kaelen had started crying as one of the demons grabbed her firmly by her shoulders and began to lift her to her feet. Immediately, Desti's heart started to slam in her chest, eyes wide, as she feared that she would never see Kaelen again.

The sound of Amaros's voice grasped her attention back to him for a moment as he replied, "You were always smart,

Desti. I'll give you that." He circled her as he continued. "Your friends were never really free, and you were going to share the same fate, but *after* I had harnessed your blood…your power." His voice dropped an octave and now was a low guttural growl. "But you ruined what I had planned for you when you stole the Lux from me. You will give it back to me, Desti…or else."

The lines on Amaros's face were hard and etched with rage, a fiery anger burning within the depths of his eyes. She couldn't stand to look at him with such aggression plastered on his face, so, instead, Desti tried to give Anthony and Kaelen a smile of reassurance. She wasn't going to give up. Not yet.

"Don't you look at them," he hissed, snatching Desti's chin in a firm and striking grip. Amaros dug the tips of his nails into her flesh until he drew blood, making her wince from the pain.

"I. Don't. Have. It," Desti growled.

Immediately, Amaros shifted his body and was now only inches away from her face, his hot, musky breath violating her senses as he spoke. "I don't like lies, my Dear. You will give it to me, or else…" he lingered on those last words, savoring the torment it was causing Desti.

The tears came rushing down now, and Desti sobbed, realizing that there was no way out of this situation. "I don't have it. But even if I did, I would never give it to you!" Amaros needed Desti to charge the Lux somehow because he couldn't access the power. His blood was cursed, she remembered him telling her that, and now he wanted to finish what he started.

Amaros seemed to believe Desti that time, clicking his tongue and whispering something into Tate's ear before stomping off toward a wall of flames, and then he just disappeared into the thick, black smoke that clung to the air.

Tate gripped Desti's arm, the rest of the demons followed, grabbing her friends aggressively, and one by one they were dragged away from the house and into the chaos that had ensued in the city.

"Tate where are we going?" she cried.

"Shut up and walk," Tate hissed. Desti prayed that she would be able to reach *her* Tate somehow. He had to be there still, deep within. She brought him to the surface before, and so she could do it again, right? The group was forced into the wall of smoke, and Desti thought they were going to push her right into the flaming inferno, but all of a sudden, she had appeared somewhere else entirely, as if she had just been transported into another dimension.

Chapter Nineteen

The Ruling Realm

Where the Hell are we?

It smelled. The stench of sulfur and tangy blood coated the air, causing Desti to gag a little when she inhaled. As she peered around the room, she realized that she was in some kind of building; it looked as if it had gone through a bomb explosion and then put back together lazily.

Brandon and Seraph were shoved to the ground, and they whimpered once their knees hit the concrete. Kaelen and Anthony were silently glancing around the room, looking as if they were trying to find a way to escape, and Tess was glaring right at the demon that had ahold of her wrist as if she were calculating all the ways that she could rip him apart.

Tate strode his way over to Desti, smiling with an evil grin. He lifted her chin with his finger until she met his gaze and then he said, "I've got something for you…"

Desti sucked in her breath when she saw Tate's lip curl in a sinister smile. Before she could speak up, she felt something clamp down onto her wrist from behind, causing a searing pain to shoot up her arm. Immediately her body hurled forward in a desperate attempt to ease the pain. Through the tears and whimpering, Desti craned her neck back until she was staring at a hideous higher demon, who was flashing its ragged, sharp teeth at her.

"Suprise," he hissed.

Desti glanced down at her wrist which now had a small metal cuff locked onto it, and which seemed to be burning her with some sort of dark magic. She could feel a warm pulsating energy in the cuff, and it felt as if it were sucking her energy right from her body.

"What is this?" she demanded.

"That, my Dear, is how we will keep you under control," a thundering growl said from behind. Desti snapped her attention to that sinister voice, and immediately her stomach dropped to the floor.

The depthless, soulless black eyes were staring right at her, grinning with a displeasing smile plastered along his face.

"Master," she breathed.

After everything that Desti and her friends had been through to escape the clutches of him, now here she was, right back to being his prisoner. Desti could hear the audible gasps and grumbles coming from her friends as the Master appeared in the room like a ghost, and then there was Anthony whimpering in pain as his demon slapped the same metal cuff onto his wrist as well. They were in some kind of building on the top floor, because when Desti tried to glance toward the outside, through a massive hole in the wall, she was glancing down at the burning city. The Master's hooved feet scraped against the concrete as he strode closer to the edge, peering over, and laughing.

"It's music to my ears."

Desti wanted to cry at that. He was gesturing to the horrific screams that were being carried through the wind. Their agonizing pleas for mercy made Desti want to curl into herself and join them. It was torturous listening to that and knowing there was nothing that she could do to save them…or her friends. Not with these cuffs on.

Desti lifted her hands and observed the metal cuff that clung to her wrist and frowned. "What are you doing here?" she asked the Master, but then Amaros stepped into the light, emerging from the shadowy depths, and spoke. "We are the bringers of the apocalypse. The High Kings of Hell, and we will make sure we get to witness this glory."

"It's true then?" Desti heard Seraph whisper from her right. Desti shifted her gaze to him, noticing the look of utter defeat on his face. She locked eyes with him and tried to tell him through her gaze that she would get him out of this. She would get everyone out of this, but now with this cuff on, it was like all her power was locked away somehow.

The Master smirked, twirling his finger in the air and then stroking his chin as he walked closer to Seraph and the others. He peered down on them with his charcoal eyes and said, "I am the ruler of the wicked and the damned and my kingdom lies in Hell and on the Earth. So, yes, Boy…" he hissed. "I am the High King of Hell, and you will do as I say, or else…"

Seraph stiffened and got really quiet, but Desti had to know for herself. She had to know how the Master was ruling the city of Mors, the realm of Hell, *and* being the "mayor" here all at the same time.

"How did you do it?" she pried. He smiled and then glanced at Amaros who also shared the same wicked expression. "My portals allow to me walk through time and space. It's as easy as walking through a door. Ruling my realm of Hell and ruling over the Wastelands was, to me, the same realm."

He plodded across the room in a slow stride and continued. "But I had a plan for coming here. When Amaros told me that you had escaped, I knew there was still a way to make you suffer and get what we wanted, and so, I came back, years before the end of days, and infiltrated this city, making *friends,* and gaining control of the people. And the people of your city are now under the reign of Elijah."

Desti was practically seething, pouring hatred from her pores the moment Elijah's name slipped from his vile lips. Elijah had betrayed his people. He betrayed Desti, tricking her into thinking that he was some kind of prisoner, and then tried to poison her and Tate with demon's blood to control them like slaves.

Tess scoffed and immediately, the Master shot her a deathly glare. He didn't say anything, but his eyes spoke horrors. "You had to do all that just so you could catch Desti. It's pathetic," she hissed. Tess's wild, orange hair blew crazily with the fiery winds and in her eyes, Desti could see the anger that was festering. The Master didn't seem to like her comment too well and yanked her up by her neck, squeezing his claw-like hand around her throat. She heard Tess gasp for air and then was silent as the color on her face changed to blue and then purple.

"Let her go!" Desti screamed.

The Master chucked her to the ground, Tess slamming into the hard, concrete floor, and then growled as he stomped his way over to Desti. "Let's get this over with, shall we?"

Get this over with? What did he mean?

Fear immediately took hold of Desti as this monstrous creature stalked toward her like an angry buffalo. Tate just stood off in the distance, watching sinisterly as Desti and her friends suffered. He had to be in there somewhere. *Please help me*, her eyes begged, but there was nothing in his glare. "Desti," Anthony said, worry in his voice.

"Don't worry. Everything will be okay. I will get us out of this. I promise," she said. To be honest, Desti didn't know what was about to happen. The room was filled with horribly frightening creatures that looked like they wanted to rip her throat out with their teeth, and the world around them was literally burning in Hellfire. It was the end of days, and anything could happen now, but one thing was for certain. Desti would not give up without a fight.

Desti curled into herself and prepared for his titanic body to come crashing into her, punch her, or something, but instead, the Master held out his open palm, whispering in tongue, and a black cloud of smoke shot from his hand and wrapped around Desti until blackness engulfed her, pulling her under until her consciousness faded away as the distant sounds of her friends screaming were the last thing to flutter into the darkness.

A ghastly gasp forced its way into Desti's lungs as she shot up from the ground, the last bit of memories trickling its way into her mind until she regained full consciousness.

Shit.

The last thing she remembered was some kind of dark smoke that the Master shot from his hand, and apparently, it could knock her out cold; good to know, second, her friends were screaming just as she got knocked out.

Desti had obviously been moved to somewhere else entirely; the ground was cold to the touch and the room was no longer half-blown away concrete, instead, it looked as if it were made of marble, but as she tried to stand and walk across the room, something yanked her back, making her lose her balance.

Desti glanced down and blew out a sigh. *Chains.* She was once again chained to a wall. The room was empty, clean, except for a small table at the other end, and on it sat her cross necklace. Desti instinctively grasped at her chest, feeling for her necklace, but it was gone, snatched from her when she was probably knocked unconscious.

Do they know what that does? She thought. If Amaros knew that the necklace held all the power of the Lux, then that would definitely create a problem. As if someone could sense her awakening, faint whistling echoed from around the bend of the wall, growing louder as she could hear footsteps walking toward the room.

Desti threw her body back down in a lifeless position and closed her eyes, pretending to still be asleep, but when the footsteps reached her side, she heard a grunt, and a familiar voice broke her out of her focus.

"Get up. I know you are awake," Tate said flatly.

At first, her instinct was to still play as if she were unconscious, but once Tate nudged her with his foot, she jolted forward in fear of him doing something worse. Tate crouched down, getting eye level with Desti, and smiled.

"There you are," he purred.

Desperation filled her heart, causing it to pound in her throat the moment she gazed upon her love, desperately searching his eyes for reminiscence of him, but there was nothing but emptiness, an evil darkness that clouded the once glimmer that she loved so much.

"You're pathetic. I can see you trying to reach him, but he is gone, darling." Tate stood from where he was and yanked on Desti's chain. "Get up," he demanded.

Desti lurched forward and followed Tate across the room as he took a seat in a wooden chair that sat by a fire. It was as if the words in her mouth disintegrated before she could even speak as if something had caught her throat in a chokehold. Maybe it was the fear of being somewhere new and alone, or maybe it was the fact that the world was ending all around her, but truthfully, when she looked deep within herself, she knew why she couldn't speak up. It was Tate; the lostness in his eyes, the grief that she felt for her love, knowing that his soul was trapped beneath that *thing*.

"Is he still in there?" she finally spoke.

Tate didn't react to her question except for a slight grunt. He turned his chin slightly until Desti saw the side of his face. The stubble on his chin had started to grow in, causing a dark shadow to spread across his smile.

"He's still here, but he is under my control."

Every step she took was slow and careful, the sounds of her boots hitting the marbled floor gave off a distant echo as she crossed the room. "How did you take him…this time?" Desti had to know. How *did* the Shadow take Tate? *When* did this happen and how had she not seen it?

"Do you really think that the Master and I would have kept Peter alive out of the kindest of our hearts?"

Peter? In the midst of all the chaos, Desti had forgotten about Peter and his people briefly. Were they still alive? She closed the space between them, stepping closer with a curiosity burning within her.

"How did Peter have anything to do with this?"

"You stupid girl!" Tate shot from his seat and was now towering over Desti, glaring down into her eyes. "I used him. I used his body. All I needed was for Tate to touch him and he would be mine," he seethed. Suddenly, Tate snatched Desti's jaw in a firm grip and drew her face to his until his breath violated her senses. "I thought I was going to have to wait days, but that bastard gave me what I wanted right away..." His eyes flicked down and then slowly traced up Desti's body until his lip curved into a wicked smile. "I couldn't wait to fuck you, feel you for myself while he was forced to watch through his owns eyes."

Desti yanked her face from his hand and spat in his face. "Fuck you!" The thought of the Shadow touching her, groping her, using Tate's body, and sticking his cock in her, filled her with rage and disgust. She wanted to scream, and honestly, she wanted to rip his throat out. It was a good thing that the Shadow was wearing the love of her life's body like a shield.

But then the thought of her friends rushed her mind, sending her body into a total panic. Her heart ached for Anthony and the others, knowing that they were probably scared and alone. Tears lined her eyes as she drifted into her mind, but then she blinked them away, hardening her face with rage.

"Where are my friends?"

Are they alive? She wanted to say, but held that question in, in fear. Tate smirked and pulled a small dagger from his pocket, flashing its silver. Desti sucked in her breath the moment she saw the dagger in his hands. The last time she was with the Shadow, he had sliced Tate's chest open and tried to kill her. Fear immediately coursed through her veins, pulsating through her beating heart and into her head until she felt fuzzy.

"Your friends are alive, for now. Amaros needs you for something. Your blood is the key to his plan…and your friends, well they have a purpose too."

My blood.

Right. Amaros had spoken of Desti's blood and how it was pure, uncursed, able to connect to the angelic realm, while his blood had been tainted with a curse when he was cast down from heaven and exiled to rule Hell's forsaken realm. Amaros wanted to rule all the realms, control the realm of the angels and walk among the wicked on Earth and in Hell, but he needed her blood to activate the Lux so he could harness its powers. She wondered what he was going to do to her when he found out the Seraphiel, the angel, had taken the Lux back to where it belonged.

Desti shivered knowing that the rage would be indescribable. Her eyes flicked up and noticed that Tate was walking toward her, fast, with the dagger firmly in his grip, and he was smiling an evil smile, closing the space between them quickly.

She flinched.

"Time to start," he purred, and then he grabbed her.

Chapter Twenty

It Has Started

"Tate, please. I know you are in there. Please. You are stronger than this," Desti begged.

She had been dragged out of that marbled room and was now somewhere dark, cold, and haunting. There was a stagnant taste in the air as if it had been closed off for centuries, only to be opened up for a certain purpose. She'd guessed she was that purpose. This room looked so similar to the cell that Amaros had held her in during her captivity in Hell, but there were some minor differences: a stone table set in the center of the room, and blood-stained walls.

Tate slammed Desti to the table and chained her arms too, locking her by her wrists and ankles. Desti thrashed her head, flailing around, trying to break the chains that clung to her skin. It was ice cold and felt like needle pricks along the spots where they touched.

She was alone right now, the only sound that fortunately was being held in this dungeon was her own whimpering, but Desti immediately sucked in her breath when she heard the footsteps of Tate returning.

"It's no use. You won't be able to break out of those," he said flatly. Tate had said that he needed something to start the process, whatever that meant. All Desti knew was that "the process" sounded like something that was going to hurt, and when Desti's gaze flicked down over Tate's body and stalled at his hands, she noticed a flash of silver—a dagger—and that was when she knew that her fears were correct. He was going to hurt her. Maybe even kill her if he gets what he needs.

Shivers crept over her body and under her skin, causing her body to tremble with fear, her heart now slamming against her ribcage. Desti staggered back as Tate crossed the room, flashing that small dagger in his hands and flashing his sinister smile.

"Hold still," he growled, and then he reached for her arm, gripping tightly, pulling her down back onto the stone slab. A cry forced its way from her throat just from the pain from his grip on her arm that was now shooting up to her shoulder. Her eyes widened when she noticed his grip on the dagger was firm and angled.

"What are you going to do with that?" she croaked.

Tate smiled. He raised his hand as if he were preparing to stab Desti, but she flinched and begged, "Please! Don't! I'll do anything." That caused him to take a slight step back and cock his head to the side as his eyes curiously raked over her body.

"Anything?"

Desti saw a gleaming look of evil in his eyes all the way down to his crooked smile. Tate snatched Desti's face with his hand, squeezing her cheeks until they ached and then he drew her face closer to his. Tate hovered his lips just barely over her mouth as he spoke. "You give me what I want, and I will consider finding another way to harness your powers," he purred.

Desti nodded her head, tears lining her eyes. Tate inhaled, his eyes rolling into the back of his head, and then he stuck his tongue out and licked Desti's tears from her cheek. It was wet and hot, and if it wasn't the Shadow doing this to her, she wouldn't have minded, but knowing that this *demon* was violating her, made her want to recoil.

A low, pleasurable groan reverberated from the depths of his chest as if he were getting pleasure from the taste of her fearful tears, the whites of his eyes rolling into the back of his head as he inhaled. The sounds that came from his mouth were nothing short of demonic, sounding like a mixture of growling and hissing.

Tate still had Desti in his firm grip, but he pulled his face away for a moment and studied her. "Do you know what kind of demon I am?" he inquired.

Desti just shook her head slowly, almost scared to know the answer. Tate flashed his teeth and chuckled. "I am the demon of lust…" his lips savored that last syllable. He was now panting, growling, staring her body up and down. "You said you would give me what I wanted, and what I want is to feel your body shake from the pain that his cock will cause you."

Her eyes shot open wide, fear now coursing through her. When she had said anything, she didn't mean *that*, but what could she do? She was chained to a stone table like a dangling piece of temptation ready for him to just take.

Tate had to be in there somewhere. *Please help me. Please break out of his control.* She tried to break Tate out of whatever control the Shadow had over him, peering into his eyes with complete sorrow and brokenness on her face, but there was nothing.

His hand shoved her back down, making her lay flat on her back, and then she felt the chains pull tighter until she couldn't move at all.

"Wait! I didn't know—"

"A deal is a deal, Darling. I want what I've been promised."

A lump caught in her throat, drowning out the cries that would have escaped. Then his touch came, starting at her shoulder as he traced his finger gently down to her wrist. It was as if he were savoring every moment and every sensation as he used Tate's body to explore hers.

"Your skin feels like silk," he purred, inhaling. "You smell of fear and desire…" He inhaled and smiled. "your body still wants his touch. I can smell it." And as the last words passed his lips, he drew his hand over to her thigh, grazing over the hem of her panties. She hated to admit it. Hated to admit the fact that he was right, even though she despised the Shadow, her body reacted differently. It *was* Tate's touch that her body yearned for and was used to, so even though the Shadow was using him, her body only reacted to what it wanted.

Desti couldn't do anything except lie there, being touched by him. Tate stood towering over Desti, and she could see his erect cock, bulging in his pants. He groaned in pleasure as he touched himself, hovering over her.

How the Hell was she going to get out of this? At this point, she wanted to take her chances with the dagger instead of letting *him* have his way with her, but she couldn't move. Her arms and legs were pinned hard and ached from the rusty metal.

She tried to surface her powers, tried for anything, any light so that she could send him flailing across the room, but she only had seconds at best. Tate already had dropped his pants and was now reaching for his underwear.

Desti closed her eyes and tried to focus on the light within her. Bring it to the surface, she told herself. Warmth started to flush throughout her body, but as that was happening, she felt Tate rip off her pants, leaving her lying there in just her underwear and shirt.

His grip on her thighs was firm and forceful as he spread her legs out more. With the warmth that now was pulsating inside, followed a tingle sensation that she felt centering in her chest. This was the same feeling she had when she first learned how to use the Lux to harness her powers. Seraphiel had said that the light was within her, and so maybe she was strong enough to break herself out of this.

She heard Tate groan as he stroked himself, standing before her sprawled-out body. But as the light began to fester, she immediately felt a burning sensation radiate up her arm from the cuff that still clung to her wrist.

She cried out in pain, and that cry for help must have been what the Shadow was waiting for because that was when he took her hips into his grip and thrust himself into her with all the power a higher demon could have.

"No!" she cried. So much pain came from all over; her wrist and arm ached and burned from whatever dark magic the cuff had on her and now her body was being used like a toy, a plaything, for the Shadow. He was the demon of lust, he had said, and so he must have gotten his pleasure from causing sexual pain to his victims.

Desti tried to buck and writhe free from his grip, but he was too strong. He pounded hard into Desti as she cried out for help. Hope almost slipped from her grip, but suddenly, she felt

Tate wince in what seemed to be pain and pull himself away from her.

"Agh—" he groaned as he hurled over and gripped his head.

Did she do that? Did her powers somehow cause him pain? Desti tried to lift her head to see what was happening but the only thing she could see was Tate's hunched body on the ground.

Maybe a minute passed and then he shot up so fast that it made Desti jump. In his eyes, there was a look of pure sorrow and fear. He stepped to her, quickly.

"Desti!"

"Tate? Is it really you?" she cried.

Tate leaned over her and stroked her hair as he let a stream of tears flow down his face. "I'm so sorry, my love. I am so sorry that I couldn't stop him—"

Before Tate could finish, he winced as if he were in pain and gritted his teeth. "We have to hurry. I can feel him fighting to take back his control."

Tate hurried around the corner of the room and returned with a set of metal keys. He unlocked Desti from the restraints that were on her ankles and wrists and pulled Desti's pants back up from her ankles. Desti slipped into her clothing and stood.

"You need to find Anthony and the others. They are not safe. Do you hear me? He is going to hurt them." Tate had gripped Desti's shoulders in a panic, locking his fearful gaze onto her.

"What about my cuff?" she held up her wrist. Tate's face fell and a defeated look came over him. "Your cuff is laced with dark magic. You can't take it off unless you—"

"Agh!" Tate dropped to the ground and was now curled into a ball.

"Tate! I need you. Please fight him and come with me. I can't save the others without you," she cried.

Through gritted teeth, he spoke, "Desti, go! I'm losing my control. You need to find them. You and Anthony are the keys to stopping this."

Desti didn't know where she was or where her friends were, but the moments she heard the Shadow's voice start to fight its way to the surface, she took off running, glancing back only once as she left the love of her life behind in the clutches of the demon.

Chapter Twenty One

Lost

Was this Hell?

Or was this Hell on Earth? Desti couldn't tell where she was, because everything around her was scorched, burnt to ash, and withered to dust. A charcoal-like mist clung to the ground and distant howls echoed from afar. She had run from a cave and was now in some kind of wasteland. Desti had made sure that the Shadow didn't follow where she went. The muscles in her legs hissed in protest as she tried to take one more step; she had run far enough to where she felt like she was safe from him, but now as she gazed upon this dead and decaying land, she wondered what other things could be lurking in the darkness, waiting to snatch her up.

Was this the wastelands back at home? Or was she still in Peter's city? And how on Earth was she supposed to find her friends? There was a relentless storm crashing through her mind; waves of anger, fear, and sorrow twisting together like a raging sea, and as she stood there gazing upon the brittle, oppressive wasteland, she fell to her knees and clenched her fist to her chest, bellowing out a bloodcurdling scream.

There was a point at which everything would become too much to bear, fraying a person's nerves until they ultimately snapped. Was this hers? The gravel beneath her knees burned from the relentless heat that the blazing sun cast down, but she didn't care at this point. Every time she thought that she was closer to an answer to solving her problem, it felt like she had taken one step back.

Thoughts of her friends rushed into her mind, flushing out the despair that tried to linger, and for once, she smiled, wiping away the tears lining her eyes.

Anthony—her sweet young boy that saved her more than she saved him. A boy filled with such strength and kindness, despite all the pain and torment he had endured.

Tess—her wild, free friend. Desti had grown fond of her over her time spent with Tess and had concluded that she was in fact quite a great person to be around when she wasn't poisoned with demon blood.

Then Tate melded into her mind with such warmth and passion that it was almost too much to bear. It had felt as if her heart had cracked in two, knowing that Tate was trapped beneath that evil *thing*. What if she would never feel the way his fingers felt, gliding over her skin like silk again, or when he would whisper sweet nothings in her ear, or feel the electric pulse the moment his lips would touch hers with such incredible gentleness and passion. He was her person. Her true love. She knew that now…what love truly felt like, because when she was without him, it felt like someone had ripped half her soul away from her body, leaving her just an empty shell.

The darkened sky, thick and ominous, clouded above her until the last bit of rays of the sun were shrouded in a blanket of a gray, misty haze, and without warning, the heavens opened up, relenting a downpour of rain, a relentless torrent, lashing into Desti's skin like needles, but as she lifted her trembling hands to her face, that was when she realized…

This isn't rain. A stream of thick, crimson red coated her hands and trickled down her arms, and that was when it hit her. It wasn't raining water.

It was raining blood.

It really was happening. The end of days. Desti had remembered learning about the signs that led to the apocalypse: Earth-shattering storms, famine, disease…blood rain. Her hands were trembling as she gazed upon her crimson-soaked fingers. Frantic, Desti darted her head in all directions, trying to see anything that would give her hope to finding her way back to her friends, or at least back to civilization, but the walls of tangy blood were too think for her eyes to peer through, and so she curled into herself and waited out the hellish storm.

After hours of torment, this foreboding curtain of red eventually parted, and with it blasted through rays of light. Desti lay there, blood-soaked, defeated, and hopeless, but seeing this little bit of sunshine gave her a tiny spark of hope to keep going. Was this Seraphiel, the angel who watched over her? Did he offer her help in her moment of despair?

As Desti lifted from her knees, she brushed away as much gravel and blood as she could, her skin forever tinted with reminiscences of what had fallen from the sky. Now that the blood had stopped pouring down, Desti could see for miles along the wasteland that she gazed upon.

Then, a thought crossed her mind. Could her angelic powers give her a way to find her friends? She had never thought of her powers doing anything besides blasting beams of heavenly lights from her palms, but maybe she could do more than harm with it.

"Okay, just breathe," she told herself. Focus. Inhale. Desti closed her eyes and softened her breathing until the only sound she could hear was the wind whistling through its breeze. A slight buzzing feeling festered in her chest, and eventually spread out to the tips of her fingers like a flowing electric current. Without thinking, Desti lifted her hands, and that was when she felt it. A pull. It was difficult to explain, but it was as if there was an invisible rope tied to her wrist, and as she opened her eyes, arms stretched out wide, she felt something pull her arms in a direction toward the horizon.

Is this the way? She thought.

Ahead was a vast, open land that looked as if it were a part of Hell. She still didn't know where or when she was, because when Hell had spilled onto Erath, it had eradicated the beauty that once blanketed the land, leaving it to look exactly how Amaros and the Master wanted it to—terrifying.

One step.

Two steps.

Before she knew it, Desti was following the invisible pull that was guiding her. She couldn't explain it, but she knew that she had to follow it. Deep down, her body could feel that it wanted to go where the energy led her.

Please take me home.

Please take me to my friends.

Tate—in the brief moment of his escaping the clutches of the shadow—had told Desti that her friends were in grave danger and that she had to help them. She just hoped that this was where she was headed.

Every step Desti took now was torment, her thighs screaming in agony from exhaustion. Desti had walked, what seemed like, hours now, following this invisible pull, but as she gazed upon her surroundings, things began to look all too familiar, sending a rush of dread to course through her veins.

Ahead, among the harsh, brittle land, stood a sharp-tipped mountain, surrounded by a jagged canyon that seemed to stretch on forever. Desti had spent enough time out here to know what her eyes had fallen upon. A slight whimper caught in her throat as she swallowed down a sob, eyes lining with tears, knowing where she had stumbled to.

She would recognize this place anywhere. This was where she had first saved Tate. This was where she had so many agonizing memories that she had to shove way down just to be able to get through her day because when she traced the edges of the stone that etched the sky, that was no doubt, the very place that she had so desperately tried to escape.

Before her, towering up to the clouds, just like Amaro's castle, stood Rotten's Crude, or what Desti referred to it now as the Master's Chambers. It was all too much now. Desti dropped to her knees in defeat, slack-shouldered, and sobbed as she let the tears stream down her blood-stained face. The tips of her fingers dug into the palms of her hands causing a slight pain to shoot to her wrist, but she didn't give a damn about pain right now, because nothing could compare to the torment that was ravishing through her at this very moment.

A moment.

This was a moment of utter despair, but in her dark and clouded mind, a whisper unraveled its way through her self-doubt and pity, causing her eyes to shoot wide open.

Find her.

"What?" Desti softly spoke. Find who? Was she hearing her own voice? No. Desti shook her head, thinking that she might be going crazy, but then the voice, louder this time, spoke clearly into her mind.

'Find her,' the voice demanded.

Find who? But as that last thought trickled away from her mind, she felt the pull deeper now, as if it were pulling from the center of her core. Reluctantly, Desti took a step forward, following this pull, but eventually gave into it, and started her path toward the forbidden Wastelands.

Dusk was soon enveloping the horizon, casting an eerie shade of purple and blue along the canyon, and with that, the faint sound of hisses and growls trailed behind, for Desti knew what nightfall meant in the city of Mors, or anywhere in this time.

It meant demons. It meant death.

It meant run.

Chapter Twenty Two

The Wastelands

"Oh shit!" Desti yelled as a vicious demon lunged toward her with its jagged teeth. She dodged it, barely, and tuck-and-rolled to the side.

Night was now in full effect, and Desti was merely helpless without any kind of weapon. All of her weapons had either been lost or taken from her, and the only thing she had managed to salvage on her treacherous adventure was a sharp, pointed rock that she now held firmly within her grasp.

Its leathery lips curled back in a snarl as it flashed its teeth. They were pointed to the tip and dripping with venom. One bite from this thing and Desti would be good as dead.

Thump. Thump. Thump. Thump.

Her heart was slamming against her ribcage as total fear and adrenaline were kicking in. This was a fight-or-die kind of moment, and Desti didn't plan on dying anytime soon. She blew out a huff of ragged breath, and cocked her neck to the side, eyeing this hideous creature up and down, looking for any vulnerable spots where she could spill its blood.

Its stomach was bulbous and pulsating like a beating heart and the skin kept shifting from black leathery textures to a darker green scaly texture. It sure was fascinating. As the demon lurched its body back, preparing another attack, Desti saw it coming and swiftly tumbled out of the way, but not before jamming the tip of her pointed rock into that pulsating stomach.

It hissed in pain and retreated slightly, but that only seemed to piss it off more, because when the thing lifted its head and glared at her, its eyes rolled back into a hard and frightening stare as it snarled, flicking its tongue around in the air. It was too fast before Desti could react, and before she knew it, a crack of thundering sound exploded in her head followed by her body flailing into the air and then slamming into the side of the canyon wall.

All of the air ejected from her lungs from the initial hit, and now her vision was shifting through waves of blackness.

Don't you dare pass out, she told herself.

Desti knew that if her body succumbed to the darkness, that would be the end for her, and there was no way that she was going to let herself die at the hands of this *thing*. The pointed rock was still in her grip, but her arms were weak now and she could barely lift without hissing in pain. In the depths of the shadows, a silhouette, grotesque, hideous, titanic, came plodding toward her with a hunger that she could sense in the air.

From its throat, ripped a cacophonous growl that seemed to wake the entire wasteland as it tilted its head back in its final kill call. She knew that the demon thought it had her, that it thought there was no escape, and because of its illusion of victory, Desti noticed a weakness now—a distraction.

A noise.

All Desti needed was just one small sliver of time to escape and that noise was her way out of this mess. As the demon shifted its glare toward the vast unknown, hissing and growling at something that her eyes were not capable of seeing, she forced her body to stand, knees aching and burning, as she took off running toward any direction that got her far away from that thing.

It wasn't long before the wind carried its cry of fury through the air, and she knew that it was chasing her now. Every heavy, ragged breath forced its way into her lungs as she continued sprinting into the darkness, the only sliver of light trickling down from the glow of the moon that hid behind the shroud of misty clouds.

The ground started to rumble beneath her feet. She could feel it. Hear it. The demon getting closer. Her tiny, little legs were no match for that beast of a creature, and Desti knew that she was out of options, but as the distance between them was closing in, she had one final thought of hope that could save her at this moment.

My powers.

But quickly a frown snatched that curve of a smile from her face as she remembered that Amaros and the Master had slapped a magical cuff to her wrist. Desti reached for the cuff, its cold metal shell feeling like ice against her skin. The last time she tried to use her powers, it had caused a searing pain to shoot up her arm and made her body feel physically sick. But she had to try, because if she didn't then she would be good as dead.

Seraphiel had told her that the angelic light yielded within her blood, her veins, and maybe she could still shoot that beam of light from her hands in a moment of survival. She hadn't had long, with Peter's people, to practice the strength and depth of her powers, but it didn't hurt to try.

Through the running, through the gasping for air, Desti pushed herself to look deep within and focus on bringing her light to the surface. She dropped her razored rock and balled her hands into fists.

Come on. Breathe. Think…love. Think happiness.

Then she felt it, a warm rushing sensation that spread all throughout her body and into her fingertips, and as she lifted her hands, there was a faint glow about her skin, a power that she could feel coursing through her veins, but as that power grew, so did the radiating pain that she felt from the cuff.

Desti winced. It hurt, but maybe she could push through it. Through her steady and shallow breaths, Desti tried to welcome the pain and turn it into something else, and eventually, it felt as if that pain had melded into her skin, only giving her powers more strength at this moment.

The curve of her smile twitched in a small victory and then she halted, turned around, and held out her palm. There it was, tumbling down the darkness like a monster in your nightmares, but this monster was very real. Yes. Desti sucked in her breath and festered all that power that was now coursing through her into her palm as a vibrant, blinding white light shot like a laser beam, straight at the deathly silhouette. The cuff was electrified, zapping Desti around her wrist, but she ignored that electric pulse and kept her mind set on one thing—kill this demon.

There wasn't even a second that the demon had to scream or hiss before its body exploded into the air, its meaty chunks of skin falling from the sky like a torrential downpour of blood and rain. She stood frozen for a moment, complete shock had ahold of her body as she lifted her trembling, bloody arms up and in front of her face.

"Holy shit," she breathed.

Realization crashed into her. She was a full-on demon-killing weapon now, and it was the first time in all her miserable life that she felt that maybe, just maybe, she really could be the one to save the world. She was the daughter of an angel, born into the land of the dark and wicked, brought up to live in a life of torment and suffering, but maybe all of that was necessary to make her who she was now, at this moment—a complete fucking badass.

There must have been some kind of scent of power that clung to Desti because the rest of her time wandering the darkness of the night, not a single demon dared to come close to her, only their distant howls circled around, but nonetheless seemed more of cries of help than of hunger.

Orange and pink splayed across the horizon with beautiful artistry as the sun started to rise, and Desti tilted her head, admiring the beauty that lay before her. Even in a world of darkness, even in a world of death and torment, the Earth never gave up its hope of one day returning to the beauty it once was, and this sunrise was a reminder of that.

In her small victory of survival, the painful thought of her friends and Tate had been pushed out of her mind, but now, as she wandered the Wastelands, all that guilt came crashing back into her.

Where were they now? Were they safe? Scared?

Desti let a single tear form in the corner of her eye until it fell down her cheek. She promised Anthony that she would keep him safe, and now look, he was a prisoner of Amaros and the Master, and they knew about his powers. Who knew what kind of suffering they were making him endure? Desti went to grab at her cross necklace but flinched as she remembered that it was taken, lying somewhere with that lust demon that now had Tate under its control.

Without it on her, she felt an emptiness linger in her heart. It was a gift from Ms. Joan, the crazy lady who lived at the edge of Mors. The lady who the town feared, but Desti grew to know a soft side to Joan and became fond of her friendship.

How did she die? She thought. Even after death, Ms. Joan had looked out for Desti, gifted her a relic that could yield her angelic powers to something that could eradicate the world of the death and decay, and free the slaves that suffered here, and as this last thought slowly trickled out of her mind, something in the distance snagged her attention.

Before her, a thick, gray blanket of ash and ruin lay in the distance; a reminder of the horrors that she had to escape from, the people that she had to leave behind. The smell of burnt ash and rotting bodies swirled in the breeze, causing Desti to gag at the horrid, pungent smell. Desti's breath caught in her throat as she tried not to drop to her knees and cry from the scene before her.

The camp, once a lively haven of shelter and safety, was now reduced to a smoldering ruin, a scene of utter devastation. Blackened beams jutted out of the charred earth-like skeletal fingers reaching toward the sky, remnants of structures that had been consumed by the flames. A suffocating warmth clung to Desti's skin as the heat in the air lingered with a heavy presence, and a single droplet of sweat beaded on her brow, gliding down her worn and sorrowful face. Here and there, small embers still glowed dimly, flickering in the soft, dying light of the day, stubbornly refusing to extinguish completely.

This was the scene of death. This was the scene of all the people she had to leave behind. It was as if someone had jabbed a knife into her heart because there was a literal ache in her chest as she gazed upon this scene. It was her fault, and she had to abandon everyone who lived here. Desti kept her pace slow and steady, taking a careful stride forward as she drew herself closer to the Resistance.

"Hello!" she called out.

How much time had passed since the attack on the Resistance? Because as Desti glanced around, analyzing the scene, it seemed that it had only been maybe a day since Elijah brought the Master's horde of demons to annihilate his people.

Desti scoffed. How could she have been so stupid to fall for his tricks? Elijah had completely fooled her into thinking that the entire time, Tess was the one who she should have had her suspicions about, but it was in fact a ploy to keep the attention off him; him helping her look through Tess's tent for anything to solidify Desti's suspicions, him bringing Desti to the same cave that he had Anthony imprisoned in…

Desti stopped for a moment, shallow breaths hitching in her chest. What if she had followed him into the cave that night? Would she have been trapped in there along with Anthony? The thought of how close Desti had come to a different reality struck her like a whip.

A gust of wind blew heavy from behind, blowing tendrils of her hair around like ribbons in a current. Desti lifted her gaze back to the camp in front of her and continued to walk forward, and every step closer she got, the more she felt as if she were shrinking into herself.

Silence hung over the scene, broken only by the occasional crackle of dying embers as if the very land was holding its breath in the aftermath of the destruction. It was a sight that spoke of loss and ruin, a stark reminder of how quickly everything could be taken away.

Chapter Twenty Three

Rise From the Ashes

The smell was a violating sensation of decaying and burnt flesh, along with the charcoal smell of the flame-engulfed tents.

This was not how Desti thought the Resistance would have looked like when she escaped from here, but as she stood at the backside of the camp, she couldn't help but feel guilty, responsible for all the death that happened—bodies, scorched to a crisp lay splayed across the ground like some sick decoration, blood coated every surface in striking splatters, the smell of pungent, tangy iron clung to the air, and as Desti tried to inhale, it soon became almost unbearable to breath.

A sob escaped from Desti's chest as her eyes studied her surroundings. There was no holding back right now, walking through this scene. *I did this*, she thought. Then thoughts of the brief friendships that she had made at the Resistance fluttered into her mind: Clara, Tilly, Matt, and so many others. *Were they all dead now?* She couldn't save them and that was something that Desti would carry the weight of for the rest of her life.

Suddenly, a slight and distant cry for help snapped Desti from her soul-wrecking thoughts. Her eyes popped wide open now and she hurried forward, stepping over the piles of desolation.

"Hello!" she called.

The thought of a demon coming out here lingered in the back of her mind. She knew that the higher demons could and would come out during the day, so, she kept her eyes sharp, looking all around for any signs of threats, but this place seemed to be deserted.

"Help," a faint voice cried.

Desti sucked in a breath and stopped in her tracks, gazing at the land until she saw something move in her peripheral. If Desti had to guess, she was standing in the spot where Tess and all of her friends would fight those demons in that cave for sport.

Desti scoffed, shaking her head at the memory. Elijah had everyone so blinded by what was really happening, fooled by the illusion that they were going to make a difference in the world. *"Train to learn how to kill the demons,"* he had said, *"and once you are good enough, we will take back what is ours."*

How could all of these people not have known or had their suspicions? But then Desti thought about how easily Tate started to turn into something she didn't recognize. The demon blood had him under its spell too, and if she hadn't been around, if her angelic powers hadn't diluted the potency of the poison coursing through him, who knows what would have happened.

Tears began to well in her eyes at the thought of Tate—her beautiful soulmate, a man with so much love and loyalty that she couldn't have asked for a better friend. Desti lifted her hands and closed her eyes, imagining grazing her fingers along the ridges of his abs, the soft velvety feeling of his skin under her fingertips, and the way his lips pressed against hers with such gentleness, felt so right. Desti lifted her finger to her lips, touching softly as she thought about her last kiss with Tate, and then a fiery rage began to build in her at the thought of how she had lost him to the Shadow.

"I can't think of this right now. I need to focus," she told herself. Desti blinked away the remaining tears and refocused on what was happening now—that cry for help. She began walking toward the rustling that was happening in the distance. It was difficult to see exactly what it was at first but as her steps drew her closer, Desti almost choked on her own gasp.

Hands to her mouth, Desti stood there frozen for a moment in pure disbelief of what she was seeing…*who* she was seeing. Even though this person had caused so much grief and pain and resentment to ravish her, Desti couldn't help but burst out into tears.

"Mom?" she cried.

Her voice croaked as a gut-wrenching sob tore from her chest, sprinting forward with her arms wide open.

"Oh my God, Mom. I can't believe it…what happened to you?"

"Desti," her mother softly spoke. She was covered head to toe in a black silt, faint stains of dried blood coated her skin and as Desti's eyes grazed along her mother's defeated body, she noticed scars too—new scars.

"Who did this to you?" Desti began uniting the rope that held her mother prisoner, attached to some kind of wooden beam. The fibers were hoarse and thick, and even though the tips of her fingers hissed in pain at trying to untie the rope, she ignored it and pushed through the pain.

"Your father, he…" her voice fell to a soft whisper. She was too weak at this moment and Desti knew she needed to get her somewhere safe. If her mother was tied up here, then that only meant that whoever did this to her would be back soon.

"Shhh, Mom, don't speak. I'm going to get you somewhere safe. Come on."

As the last bit of ropes fell to the ground, Desti's Mother's body slumped forward, Desti catching her within her arms. All around was a wasteland, a now distant memory of the Resistance that once stood. To her right, was the way to the Master's Chambers, and to her left was where she had just come from. There was nowhere truly safe out here in the Wastelands, and the only place that Desti could think of right this moment was the cave where she had found Anthony.

"Come on. I know where to go for now." Desti held her mother's arm over her shoulder and dragged her along to the back side of the camp, leaving the burnt and charred, ashy remains behind them. Desti was looking for the markings along the wall and the slight hole that was almost too small to see.

After a few minutes of walking, Desti stopped in her tracks. "There. It's right there." The demonic runes that were etched into the side of the canyon were still there, and as Desti grazed her fingers over them, she couldn't help but shiver at the thoughts it forced into her mind—Anthony's fragile and beaten body, him so desperate for sunlight, a young broken soul. Desti covered her mouth, forcing a sob down that was trying to come out. This place was a brutal and horrible place that had only brought so much pain to the sweet boy that she loved, but now, it was going to be a place that would give her shelter.

With one deep breath, Desti pulled her mother through the opening and was now seeking refuge in Anthony's torture chambers.

"Here Mom, drink this," Desti softly spoke as she handed her mother some water that she had found in a nearby stream. Water was scarce here, but she remembered that Anthony found a small trickle of water in the backside of the cave, and luckily, it was still there. After doing her best to wash away the blood and dirt from her body, Desti had spent the entire day and night holding her mom as she went in and out of consciousness. At one point, she could have sworn that her mother stopped breathing but was relieved when her chest began to rise and fall in shallow breaths again.

It was a weird sensation for Desti to care for her mother like this when her entire life, Desti's mom was so absent to her abuse and pain. All she had wanted was for her own mom to hold her while she cried from the beatings that she had endured, but as Desti felt the frail body of her mom slump into her arms, that resentment and anger slowly started to fade.

"Thank you, sweety." Blood-encrusted fingers grasped the small, hollow stone that Desti used as a cup, and took a sip of the water that balanced within it.

"You were in and out all night long. I didn't know if you were going to make it." Desti tilted her head in an annalistic way, studying the cuts and bruises more closely. "Mom, what happened to you? What happened after I left?"

Desti's mother—Evie—set her water down and took in a sharp breath, wincing from the pain, and placed her hand over Desti's. An expression of grief washed over Evie's face for a moment, a silence that seemed to scream at the horrid memories that her mother was about to speak about. "After you left, everything changed." Desti listened silently, leaning closer as she continued. "Ms. Clyde, she was more than just a teacher, Sweety. She was one of those secret spies sent by the Master embedded into the population.

"A Cambion," Desti breathed. Evie just nodded, Desti's mind going back to when she and Tate used to joke about Ms. Clyde being half-demon.

"When you went missing, she came to your father and offered him something. Your father had been talking about sacrificing you. He knew your birthday was coming up and knew that his opportunity would soon fade. Ms. Clyde had heard from Tate's father about his interest and offered both of them the rewards if they could find you and bring you to the Master."

'So, that was how Dad made it out to the Wastelands unharmed. He had the demons working for him. How come Ms. Clyde didn't come herself?"

"Ms. Clyde runs this town and must stay at her post. Your father went off to find you and Tate. He must have met that kid, the one with the tattoos…" Desti knew that her mom was talking about Elijah. "I must say that I never expected your father to team up with him or the Master. When I heard that he had found you…" Evie's voice whimpered. Desti reached out her hand and placed it on her arm, but something within her was building.

"Why didn't you stop him, Mom? Why didn't you *ever* stop him?" Tears were now streaming down both of their faces as Desti met her mother's gaze in a fury. Evie glanced away as if she couldn't bear to see the pain that lingered in Desti's eyes.

"I'm sorry, Sweetie. I…your father made sure that I wouldn't be a problem. He was too loyal to the Master and the way of this world and so, he would buy demon blood at the market from some seller. Now that the poison is starting to wear off, I remember…I remember everything and how I did *nothing* to save you. I'm so sorry."

The heart-wrenching cries of Desti's mother were amplified by the unforgiving, cold stone walls. That was the cry of a grieving mother. Desti knew she was grieving the loss of her daughter's innocence, the loss of her daughter's childhood, at the very hands that were supposed to protect her, but this world was a cruel and unloving world and Desti had to remind herself of that at times.

"I thought you didn't love me. I thought that you just didn't care that dad would…hurt me." Desti traced her fingers along the faint scars, reminders of the torment her father would put her through.

"Oh, Honey, I love you very much. I love you so much. I am so sorry that I couldn't have been there for you." As Desti's mom finished that last word, Desti leaped forward into her mother's arms, embracing her in a long and overdue hug. All the pain and trauma that Desti fought so hard to keep hidden was finally fizzling away from the touch of her mother's arms around her.

Desti pulled back, glossy-eyed, and asked, "Did you know? About me being Nephilim." Silence stilled in the air at this moment. Evie straightened at the word Nephilim like it was some kind of wound that caused her pain. She opened her mouth to speak, and after a long pause, finally got the words to come to life.

"Who told you that you were Nephilim?"

"It's a long story Mom, but Amaros did, he is—"

"The high king of Hell? Desti, Sweetie, how on Earth did you end up with him?"

That was when Desti took the time to tell her mother about her treacherous journey through Hell and her experience in the Resistance. She spoke of her friends, of Anthony, of Tate, and how they had gone back to the beginning of the Era of the Dammed, and as Desti finished telling the horrible tale of the torment she had endured, Desti's mom couldn't speak, silenced by the unwavering shock of it all.

Now that she had her mom back, there was only one thing that she could do now, and that was to find her friends.

Chapter Twenty Four

A New Journey

"So, after I left, Dad went searching for me? And had locked you in the house?"

Evie just nodded as she continued forward. The dry air and sweltering heat were a brutal reminder of just how bad the Earth had become since the time before. In every direction, the land was ashy and decaying, not a single vibrant color peeked through, and that got Desti thinking back to the forest that she and Tate had first stumbled upon. It was so lively and beautiful, so untouched from corruption and destruction, and she thought that there must be a way to save it, to save everything back then.

Evie and Desti had been walking for a few hours now. After stopping by one of Elijah's tents to snag some of his water stash, they both made the decision that getting back to the time before the Era of the Damned was where and when they needed to be. Desti could feel something inside her body growing with intensity, her powers just waiting to be released, and she knew that Seraphiel was right. She could be the key to saving the world.

Evie broke the silence. "Your father was furious about your disappearance. He smashed almost everything in the house, screaming that you ruined his plans to gain power and protection. He had been sneaking off quite a lot to that forsaken market, buying God knows what, and then he took off, but not before chaining me to my bed."

"Mom, I'm so sorry…" Desti tried to speak but her words fizzled into an echo on her lips. For the first time, Desti saw emotion swirling in her mother's eyes, sadness, and guilt, all blending together like a relentless storm crashing through her mind.

"Sweetie, I am the one who should be sorry. I should have found a way to be there for you and protect you."

"You were being *poisoned*. I saw firsthand what that demon blood does to people, and you had no control over the effects it had on you." Desti's voice hitched in her chest before she continued, "And I am sorry that I didn't notice what was happening to you all those years. I could have helped you—"

"Don't Sweety," Evie interrupted. Desti glanced over to her mother with glossy eyes, meeting her gaze in an unwavering stare. It was like looking into a mirror and seeing yourself, your *real* self, for the first time, raw and vulnerable.

They both had lived and endured so much in their lives and had to carry that pain all alone, but now, they were here, and they had each other.

"So, after your father had left me, it wasn't long before one of those higher demons came for me. They broke through the front door and snatched me from my room claiming that the Master wanted me." Evie held up her arm, exposing a burn mark laced across her skin in the shape of a hand. Desti had heard of some demons being able to burn you just by their touch, and looking at the proof sent a knot in her gut.

Desti gulped and took her mother's hand as she continued forward. They were coming up to Rotten's Crude, the Master's chambers, and with every step that brought her closer to this hell hole, Desti found herself wanting to shrink and cower away. She turned her head and said, "When Dad found me, we were out here with my friends, and he was with Elijah and the Master's demons. I couldn't believe that everything was connected like that; that the man that I thought I had saved from the Master ended up being secretly evil and somehow had found his way to Daddy, both of them working for the Master... Two evil men who had such an impact on my life."

"So, they through you into a Hell portal?" It was almost as if speaking those words was painful for her mother as she had to think about her own daughter being sacrificed to Hell, and then that was when a thought popped into Desti's head at this moment—her friends, her *marked* friends. They bore the mark of the king of Hell, forever imprisoned under his control. How on Earth was she going to break that curse?

Desti only nodded as she relived the terror that had coursed through her the moment the Master flung her body into that fiery pit, the flames swallowing her up like it couldn't wait to taste the fear running through her, and that fear was now resurfacing, knowing that that was her only way back to the time before the Era of the Damned.

Desti thought this through, and to get back to her friends, she knew that she would have to venture into Hell again, through the terrifying terrain, fighting off the demons that lurked within the shadows, breaking into Amaros's castle and using his portal to jump back in time.

Easy, right?

Desti scoffed at her plan. It seemed impossible, but there was no other way. She had to do it. "This is it," Evie breathed.

Towering up to the sky, touching the swirling dark clouds that shrouded above, was the cave system that Desti hated so much, the very place that had caused so much torment and suffering. She sucked in a deep breath and squeezed her mother's hand tightly, shifting her gaze until she met her mother's eyes.

"Are you ready?" Desti asked.

Evie nodded and took the first step into the darkness that lingered before them. One step into the unknown, but Desti knew what was waiting for her through the veil of darkness—the start of the prophecy, the beginning of her story, and if

Seraphiel was right, this was when Desti would begin her war with the evil of this world, and she didn't plan on losing.

Since blasting that demon with her angel light beam, Desti had discovered a new and useful gift—a flashlight. There was a suffocating blackness that seemed to swallow all the light from the outside, but as Desti and her mother ventured farther, she didn't have to fear becoming victim to the shadowy depths of the cave, because, within her palm, there was now a gentle glow emitting from her.

Faint, shimmering beams of white danced across the cavern walls as Desti continued forward. She could see clearly what surrounded her; sharp, serrated ceilings, rocky, uneven terrain, and small enclosed spaces, as she moved through with careful steps. It seemed that every hour, her powers were growing stronger, and this new light was coming in real handy.

"I can't believe it," Evie whispered, her voice trickling away like the fading echoes of the drops of water dripping from the walls.

"What? That I have a ball of light emitting from my hand?" Desti joked. Evie chuckled but shook her head. "No, that you really have the power of the angels within you. I never told you about your true father."

Desti's breath hitched at the word *true father*. He must have been an angel, but her mind yearned to know how on Earth her mother ended up with him. She cocked her head to the side, glancing toward her mom as she continued forward and asked, "Did you know what he was when you met him?"

Evie shook her head. "Not at first, no. He looked human and I had met him when I was young, right before I was forced to marry your father. Your father was always an angry man, and I didn't want to be with him, so I would sneak out at night while he would sleep, and one night I ran into this beautiful man, almost as if he were waiting for me…" Evie paused for a moment, recounting her memories. "Anyway, we fell in love, but I knew that us being together was forbidden, I loved him, and so he promised me that one day he would come back for me. I hadn't seen him since, then I found out I was pregnant with you. I kept it a secret all these years, but your father started to grow suspicious. I—"

"Shh!" Desti ducked behind a large bolder and pulled her mom down with her. Her heart was now slamming in her chest as she listened to the sound of something coming, something big.

Echoes of hisses and growls bounced around the room like a furious storm, and as they grew louder, Desti found her body shaking in terror. So many terrible memories haunted her about this place, and she knew that demons still probably lurked within this cave system. She should have known that she was bound to run into them along her journey. Desti closed her hand, vanishing the light from her palm, and now she sat there in total darkness.

They didn't have any weapons to defend themselves. Desti hoped that it was a lesser demon because if were anything more, she knew that she was going to be in some deep shit.

Suddenly, she could hear them, the howling voices all around her, close enough that she could have sworn its breath was pressing against the back of her head, but Desti didn't move, didn't breathe, as she waited for them to leave, praying that the demons wouldn't hear or smell her.

Within less than a minute, the presence of the room shifted; no more oppressive weight or decaying stench trailed through the air, instead, it felt as if whatever forces were holding her body down had finally let go.

Desti sucked in a breath and coughed. She held up her palm and emitted her light again, bright enough so that she could see her mother's face. "That was a close one," she said, but as Desti's lips slipped that last word, she hurled over and groaned, holding her arm as a pain shot up to her shoulder.

"Sweetie. What's happening?"

Desti was quiet for a moment. The cuff that she was wearing was causing a pain to shoot up her arm, but it wasn't unbearable, just slightly painful; Desti had been through so much worse, so, she pushed through the pain that radiated through her and kept her white light from going out.

"It's nothing, Mom. I'm fine."

Evie's eyes were wide open and filled with terror. Desti wondered if she had ever been in the Master's chambers before, or if she had always stayed a prisoner of her father, trapped in that half-broken house of theirs.

"Do you think they heard us?" Evie's voice quivered.

"No. We wouldn't be sitting here talking if they did. Come on, we need to hurry. Let's go." Desti stood, brushed off the dirt that clung to her pants, and held out her hand, waiting for her mother to take it. Evie was hesitant at first but then slipped her fingers into Desti's palm and pulled herself forward.

"Do you know your way around here?" she asked.

The Master's chambers were something that the people of Mors never dared to speak of, a horror story that was meant to frighten the people into submission. No one was actually supposed to see the inside of this cave and live, but Desti had survived here, more than once. She scoffed at the thought of that. She shouldn't know her way around this maze of a cave, but now that she had walked these halls on more than one occasion, there were passageways and things that lurked within that were familiar to her. So, yes, she did know her way around.

A slight smirk pulled at the corner of her mouth before she replied, "Yes, now follow me and stay quiet."

Chapter Twenty Five

The Master's Chambers

After that close call with those demons, Desti wanted to make sure to be extra quiet and extra careful when venturing through this cave system and to do that, she had to tread very slowly.

One tiny step forward after another, careful not to trip over loose pebbles and rocks, calming her breathing so that an echo doesn't travel down the cavern halls, and the constant holding of her mother's hand, to ensure that she also doesn't slip up and make too much noise. Desti had pulled her mother far within Rotten's Crude now, and now she was seeing something that looked familiar, sending a gut-wrenching horror through her.

Desti gasped.

She had stumbled upon the same ledge that she had first laid eyes on the Master; the same room in which she watched his contorted, half-demon body rip a man limb from limb, eating the meat from his bones until the white of the marrow was all that was left, but this view was one hundred times worse, because as she gazed upon the Master's torture chambers, it wasn't a random man she was seeing, but in fact, what lay in front of her, were some familiar faces she once knew.

Desti gasped and pulled her mother down to the ground, heavily breathing in a moment of terror. Evie immediately cupped her hands to Desti's cheek and gazed into her eyes, trying to calm Desti's breathing. She lifted her finger to her mouth and nodded.

Desti understood. *Be quiet. They will hear you*, was what her mother's eyes were telling her. Desti slowed her breathing until it fizzled into shallow, ragged breaths. In her mother's eyes, she could see that there was a deep worry in them, but not the horror that Desti knew lingered within her own.

She must not have seen what Desti saw—the blood. The flesh hanging from those tortured bodies. The terrified faces that were frozen into their expressions. Desti gathered herself and gave Evie a hard look before she guided her chin up and over the ledge to see for herself, and as she did so, Evie almost collapsed at what was down there.

Hundreds of bodies, young and old, scattered the ground like a pool of blood and flesh. They all appeared to be dead, by the way their necks and limbs bent and contorted in unusual ways. Crimson red soaked into the porous floor and trickled its way down the walls as if it had been raining blood, and then it pooled in the center, encasing around the stone table of torture. Rotten, pungent odors whirled around in the air, violating her senses with every breath. It took all the strength within Desti to not gag and puke from how horrid the smell was.

This was the smell of rotting corpses. This was the smell of spilled, innocent blood. But the worst part of it all was the sheer enjoyment Desti could see on the faces of the demons below.

Higher demons.

Desti had seen enough in Hell now that she could tell which was which. These demons—humanoid—gathered around the stone table in the center, gnawing away at a piece of someone's leg and torso. Their razored teeth ripped through the flesh as easily as a heated knife would cut through a cow's hide. Just the very sight of these vile creatures sent a fear rushing through her like she didn't know existed, and as she peered over to her mother, eyes glossed and wide with terror, she knew that the feeling was mutual.

It probably wasn't a good idea to use her angelic light in this moment, Desti knew that now, and so she closed her hand around her light, flushing away the white until the only light now was from the flickering torches in the distance. Their garbled voices spoke in tongue as they indulged in the flesh of the innocent, laughing even, as if this were just a normal day to them.

Fury and disgust clashed in her stomach as she watched them, but nothing could prepare her for the shock of what she saw next.

"I have our next offering," a familiar voice growled. The demons, in a unanimous howl, all laughed and growled as Elijah pulled a woman forward, a chain wrapped around her neck. Her fiery red hair stuck to her face, caked on with her fading tears and dirt. Desti knew that face. She had met her briefly once, and then just occasionally saw her around the Resistance, but Desti was too preoccupied back then to engage with making friends.

Immediately Desti ducked down and pulled her mom close. "I know her. And him," she whisper-screamed. "That guy, his name is Elijah. I saved him, or so I thought, from this place, and he led me to the Resistance. That woman with the red hair, her name is Rebecca."

"How is Elijah working with those demons?" her mom questioned. Desti wanted to scream at just the thought of how he had given himself up to the Master; how he struck a deal in order to gain power rather than fight to protect his people, but she kept that urge down for now. "Once a desperate prisoner, he made a deal with the Master, in exchange for power here, and protection from the demons. He is the one who gave us up and caused so many to die," Desti continued, "Rebecca, I met her briefly. She was a fantastic fighter and would practice fighting the demons almost every day. We need to help her."

An ear-pitching scream ripped through the air like lighting shattering glass, causing Desti and Evie to both jump back in terror. It was Rebecca. All Desti could see was her fiery hair peeking through the bodies of the demons.

What were they doing? Desti tried to see, but their bodies surrounded Rebecca; whatever it was, Desti knew deep down that something bad was about to happen. In her mind, a storm of emotions clashed through her relentlessly—*help her...No, it will get you killed...you will regret not helping her if she dies...*

The yearning in her heart to save Rebecca pulled Desti forward, but the logic in her mind held her down, knowing that it could probably get everyone killed, but as she glanced to her mother, seeing the desperation pouring from her eyes, Desti knew which choice she had to make.

This was going to hurt. Whatever dark magic was laced within this cuff that clung to her wrist was already starting to ache and burn as Desti tried to fester up as much of her power as she could. It was growing stronger day by day, so maybe if she could control it enough, she could get Rebecca out of there. Evie placed her hand on Desti's and shared a soft smile.

"We have to help her," she softly spoke.

Desti nodded, concentrating on her light within, and that was when she felt it gathering in the palm of her hands, flushing through her body like a river of flowing electricity, but with it came an agonizing pain searing up her arm. Desti winced and hurled forward, grabbing her arm with the cuff.

Through barred teeth, she groaned, "It hurts. I don't know if I can." She wanted to be strong, but this pain was intense and the stronger Desti grew, the more the pain grew with her.

"Can you share the pain, Sweetheart? I can take some from you," Evie suggested. That thought had never occurred to her. *Could* she share her pain? Maybe even her power? Through the pain and agony, Desti focused her attention now on their interlaced fingers, sending her mind and energy to the tips of her fingers, praying that her mother would be able to take some of this power and pain.

It was like trying to break glass with your mind. At first, it felt like nothing had changed, and as the minutes continued on, Desti could feel her body getting weaker. She wanted to give up, but suddenly a faint cry escaped her mother's throat.

Evie hurled forward and groaned, grasping her stomach as if she were trying to claw away at something from the inside.

"Mom? Are you—"

"Keep going. It's working," she interrupted.

Desti obliged, sending her energy and whatever dark magic that coursed through her to her mother in a steady flow, and finally, the pain in her own body was now starting to ease, but what Desti didn't expect was for Evie to also begin to develop a glowing light around her hands.

She gasped and let go.

"Mom your hands…they are glowing."

And as Desti trailed away from that last word, Evie lifted her shaking hands to her face in almost disbelief, glancing over at Desti with wide, unbelieving eyes. It was possible then. She could share her powers. This meant that Desti could give all her friends a fighting chance at beating the Master. Beating Amaros, until they were free from their blood-thirsty hunger.

"How do I use it?" Evie asked. She held out her hands as if they were something not a part of her body, shaking, probably from the slight pain that now radiated under her skin.

"I just open my palm, aim, and think of white light. It seems to grow more powerful if I think of something happy, and good in my life." There was really no time to spare. No time to truly test out the strength that coursed through both of them, because, in the distance, the screams grew louder—a wailing of pure terror echoed around, and if Desti didn't do something *now*, Rebecca was going to be dead.

"You ready?" Desti asked. Evie nodded her head and held out her now glowing palms. "Ready," she replied.

They emerged from the depths of the shadows and surged forward as they prepared to kill every last one of those blood-thirsty fuckers, because there was another blood-thirsty entity walking this Earth now, and she was ready to take back what was hers.

This Earth was hers, and the blood of the damned and wicked was going to be spilled to get it back.

Chapter Twenty Six

A New Friend

A brilliant beam of white shot through the cavern air like a whip, striking one of the demons from behind, but this demon didn't explode like the one out in the Wastelands, no, this one instead hissed with pure rage as it staggered back.

Rebecca was let go and dropped to the ground, her limp body lying contorted over some jagged rocks. She seemed to be unconscious—*please be unconscious*, Desti thought. The higher demons scattered like roaches, dispersing into the dark veil of the cave, but she could hear them; hissing, growling, even laughing, as their rough and terrifying voices echoed around her.

'Escaped One.'

'We have found her.'

'I can smell your fear, Child.'

Their voices were nothing like anything that Desti could describe. It felt as if their words were more like an entity than a sound, caressing her body until she felt violated.

"He will be pleased to have found you. He has been looking for you," one of the demons spoke out loud. Desti felt the back of her mother press against her. They were surrounded, stuck on that ledge with no way to escape, and all she wanted to do at this moment was to run, but as her gaze shifted to the lifeless body lying below her, she couldn't bring herself to leave Rebecca behind.

"Mom…we need to do this together, quickly. We move as a unit, understood?" Desti felt her mother shift her body, and she knew that was her mom's way of saying yes. It was one quick drop-down, about five feet, until they would be stepping into the torture chamber, and then about another twenty feet to get to Rebecca.

This was possible, Desti tried to tell herself. "Ready?"

"Go!"

Desti tucked and rolled and flung herself over that ledge so fast that she almost thought she was going to fall. Evie was right behind her with the same swiftness and now they both barreled toward Rebecca.

That was when the first attack struck her down into the harsh terrain of the cave. It felt as if she had been struck with a sword, or something jagged and serrated because when she touched her hand to her side, there was a pool of warm, red liquid now coating her hand. Three gashes laced her skin, easily sliced away with one hit.

Desti stopped running and was hunched over, clutching the side of her body in anger. "Shit, it got me."

Evie stopped and retreated, placing her back to Desti's. They were in the center now, standing right next to the table of torture, and now Desti watched as her own blood mixed with the reminiscence of the previously spilled.

"You foolish human. You think you are strong enough to defeat me?" it hissed.

A cacophonous echo of laughter ripped through the room in mockery. They thought she was weak, merely a human, but maybe she could use that to her advantage. Did they know that she could heal faster than others? The blood of the Nephilim carried healing properties, and it was already taking its effect. Gushing blood no longer poured from the deep gashes that laced her side; instead, a trickle of red was all that was left from the quickly healing wounds.

"I think you forget who I am. *What* I am, and I am not afraid of you." Desti lifted her hands, ignoring the radiating pain from her magic-enlaced cuff, and like an exploding star in the atmosphere, her light struck through the air in tendrils of pure power. The room lit up. The shadows were cast away, and now Desti could see where these creatures were hiding.

As she gazed upon their leathery skin, sharpened claws, and twisted faces, a wave of repulsion and disgust hit her hard in the face. They were hideous as they were frightening, but in the depths of their black, pit-like eyes, she could see something that hid beneath their furrowed brows—fear.

Desti flashed the demon to her left a wicked smile and shot a beam of light at it so fast that it didn't have time to react. The light exploded around it, then turned into an almost liquid state until it surrounded the demon's titanic body. It was drowning. Drowning in the holiness that encased it, and through the sheer surface of her power, she could see the demon's body start to crack and burn from the inside out.

But suddenly, something smacked Desti across the face, causing her to drop her arm and lose focus. The demon fell to the ground, growling in pain, but it wasn't dead, no. Desti was knocked off focus before she could fully kill that thing. When she turned around, that was when she saw two more of these vile creatures, standing before her, smiling.

Evie was right next to her, holding up her hand, but it seemed as though her power wasn't as strong as Desti's. The demons stood in the way of getting to Rebecca and in the way of the exit. Beyond that opening toward the back of the cave chamber was where the fiery portal to Hell was, and even though it terrified her to her core, she knew that that was her only way back to the time before, where her friends were.

"She thinks she can defeat us," one of them hissed.

"I can smell your fear, girl. You don't fool us."

Quickly, Desti dared to slip a glance at the demon she shot to the ground, and thankfully it was still recovering. For now, she only had to worry about the two standing in front of her; their eyes were laced with hunger, a desire for revenge and blood.

Desti closed her fists and screamed, "Go!" Evie ducked and rolled and within a heartbeat, Desti was already barreling her fists into the face of the demon to her right, cracking its jaw with a strength unknown to any human; she knew it was from the light within her.

It hit the ground but then the second one lunged forward, swiping its claws toward her neck. Just barely did it miss the flesh of her skin, coming only centimeters away from slitting her throat wide open. Thank God she pulled back in time. Evie had run over to Rebecca and was trying to shake her awake, and now Desti was surrounded by the two demons as they shook their heads, building with an evil rage.

"You think I am weak, but I am not. I have defeated your kind before and I can do it again," Desti spat.

"You think escaping is defeating? You cannot defeat us. We are immortal you fool." Maybe they were immortal, but Desti had immortal blood running through her veins—Nephilim blood, and if the legends were true, then the blood of the holy, the power of the angels could wipe away the demons of this Earth.

As Desti was about to blow another attack, a wall of dread crashed into her when she felt the sharp hands of something grasp ahold of her arms. Desti bucked and thrashed but it only dug its claws in deeper.

"Let me go!"

"See," the demon hissed. "You are weak, pathetic. An easy kill to say the least."

"I'm going to rip your throat out for what you did to me, Escaped One," its voice pressed into her ear. Desti sucked in her breath. But then Desti did something that it probably wouldn't be expecting; she bucked her head back, smashing the back of her head into its face—she heard a crack and a hiss before it let go.

Now was her chance to escape and kill these things. She dropped to the floor and pushed out her hands and belted out a scream, blasting a light so powerful that she felt the ground shake with her fury. It knocked into their bodies like a wall crashing into them and forced them all to the ground.

Desti stood and lifted her hands, the white light flowed up and followed the motion of her arms like a pool of flowing water, but this was no water, this was liquified holy energy, and as she waved her hands down, the liquid glow thrashed onto the ground of the cave, encasing it until all the darkness had been swallowed up in a sea of ethereal light. Desti sucked her fingers into a fist and that was when the liquified light suddenly petrified into something solid, trapping the demons' frozen bodies of terror underneath.

"Holy shit," she breathed. This was a newfound power—an awesome power.

She ran forward and dropped down next to Rebecca who was still lying on the ground. "Is she breathing?" Desti's voice quivered.

Evie glanced back and nodded. "She is breathing, but she seems weak. Can you help her?" Desti lifted her hands, the faint shimmering of her light still lingered slightly as it was fading away, and the ache in her arm was now fading with it.

Could she heal Rebecca? Like how she could heal herself? From what Desti could gather, Rebecca had been hurt badly; deep gashes decorated her arm, almost as if they were part of some ritual, and the meat of her thigh had been torn from what Desti could only think to be the teeth of the demons. They were about to eat her…

"I'm going to try something." Desti held out her palms and placed them on Rebecca's chest; she could feel the faint rise and fall of her shallow breathing, but it was growing weaker with every passing second. Rebecca was dying, and if she couldn't do something to save her, Rebecca would be dead within minutes.

She closed her eyes and focused her attention on the power at her fingertips, imagining it flowing from her and into the beautiful red-headed woman who lay before her. In her mind, she prayed, prayed to Seraphiel that he would hear her and help her heal her friend—yes friend. Rebecca was Desti's friend, even if she barely knew her. Desti didn't want her to die and between all the praying in her mind, Desti must have let out a cry because her mother had placed her hand on her shoulder and leaned into her.

Both of them hunched over the lifeless form of Rebecca, praying in soft whispers for her recovery. The cuff on Desti's wrist was starting to burn, and Desti could hear whimpering coming from her mother too; they were both feeling the pain, but also sending their power into her wounds.

Rebecca's color suddenly shifted from a soft gray to a more of a pink complexion. The gashes on her arms began to retreat, disappearing before her eyes, and the chunk missing from her thigh soon closed up.

Gasping like her life depended on it, Rebecca shot forward, clutching her chest as she took in her surroundings, and then her gaze shifted to Desti until she met her eyes, asking, "What the fuck just happened?"

Chapter Twenty Seven

A New Light

"So, you both were being held prisoner by Elijah?" Desti asked both Rebecca and her mother.

Evie and Rebecca shared a quick glance before Rebecca stepped forward and spoke. "I saw your mom a couple of days after the attack on the Resistance. Elijah and some man had brought her in and chained her up. They kept her hidden from the rest of us though."

Evie just stood silently in the background, but Desti was curious and couldn't help but pry. "What man?" Evie made a slight noise of discomfort and cleared her throat. "It was your father."

"Okay, so Dad and Elijah were the ones who attacked the Resistance? And what happened to you?" Desti was now asking

Rebecca. Rebecca had probably been up at the front when the demons attacked. Desti remembered the feeling of helplessness that crippled her as she endured hearing the screams of her friends crying out in desperation. She couldn't help them back then and it still killed her to think about it.

"Elijah killed most of the strong ones; the men, mostly, and then herded us like cattle waiting to be slaughtered. He used us for his army of demons. We were their playthings, their food, and sometimes he would throw one of us through this portal. Said that we would meet our demise down there." Rebecca peered over the abyssal portal of fire; her features illuminated by the flickering flames.

Rebecca seemed mostly shocked by it all as she continued. "The craziest part was seeing Elijah standing with those creatures. He came rushing in a sea of black, and when I looked at him, it wasn't the Elijah I once knew anymore. His eyes were dark and twisted, evil. Something changed him and that was when I knew that there was nothing I could do in that moment."

Rebecca stepped away from the portal to Hell and was now standing next to Evie. "Thank you for saving me, Desti. And you too, Evie." A moment of silence enveloped the room as the three of them peered around, taking in their surroundings. More demons could be coming, the Master or Elijah could be coming, and Desti knew that she had to hurry back to her friends.

This room brought back a sense of dread that Desti couldn't bear to feel. This was the very room her father had thrown her to the Master, the very room she watched each one of her friends get thrown into this flaming portal, and now she was going to have to jump through it all over again. A blasting heat wave emitted from the Hell portal, making it almost unbearable to be around. Desti remembered the sensation when she was thrown in, feeling as if she burning under the scorching sun.

"Will it hurt?" Evie asked.

Desti looked back at her mother's worried face and then to Rebecca's, whose face was unreadable, and sighed. "It will not feel pleasant, but we will be okay." She held out her hand and waited for her mother to take it, then Evie held out hers for Rebecca. They stood over the abyssal portal, together, and with one last glance over, Desti asked, "Ready?" and then she stepped forward, letting the orange flames engulf her.

First, Desti hit the ground, smacking her face into the burning gravel she remembered all too well. She groaned and rubbed her head as she pulled herself to her feet. The fiery portal hung just a few feet above the ground, and as Desti tried to peek inside, that was when her mother smacked her body hard, followed by Rebecca.

"Fuck, that hurt," Rebecca grumbled.

"Mom, are you okay? Let me help you." Desti ran forward and helped her mother stand and brush the dirt from her face and arms. Desti had forgotten that there was a perpetual daylight that shrouded the land, making the heat unrelenting. Once everyone was standing, Desti began to take in her surroundings.

"We need to move quietly and quickly. The lesser demons roam this part, and they will come running in hordes to eat you if they detect that you are here." Desti's mind drifted back to the moment that Tate had saved her from the sea of demons that tried to chase her. The softness of his lips pressed against hers almost lingered still as she recounted his embrace. Desti lifted her fingers to her mouth, missing the touch of him. Was he okay? It killed Desti to think that he was trapped, and she could do nothing about it, but thinking of Tate right now would only make her journey more difficult, so she shook her head and refocused.

Ahead was a land of decay and rot, scorched, withered trees stood crooked and contorted like a forest of jagged thorns. Desti could see the dark forest where she and her friends almost fell victim to the hunger of its bloodthirsty trap.

"Where are we going, Desti?" Evie asked from behind. She had bent down to grab a handle full of pebbles, letting them fall through her fingers like a waterfall spilling over an edge; the particles of sand twisted with the scorching wind that blew through. Evie glanced up with big eyes and offered a soft, encouraging smile.

Desti placed her hands on her hips and drew in a breath, searching every angle of her surroundings, and sighed. Just ahead was the forest of death and there was no way Desti was going back in there, and behind her, was a cliff that seemed to have no end, touching the sky above the glooming clouds, and to her left was the mountainside, and cave where Tate had brought her before. The only new location and path that she hadn't taken was right.

Her gaze shifted that way, taking in what was before her—a vast, intimidating land. In the sky, shadowed figures flew through the smog-filled clouds; they were *huge*, and Desti knew they must have been some kind of demon, and most certainly probably fed on the blood of the innocent, but the land did seem to be somewhat open.

This way was the only option in her mind, and so she lifted her finger and pointed in that direction, toward the decayed plains, and said, "We go that way."

Rebecca arched her brow and asked, "Are you sure?"

No. Desti was not sure about anything down here. This land was alive in a way that she could not explain; it fed on your fear, adapted to it, creating your own tailored, personalized tormenting hell.

"It's the only way I haven't taken before and we can't go through there, I barely made it out of there last time." Desti had pointed to the forest and scoffed. "We should hurry before someone finds us."

Desti began walking the path to the plains, keeping a careful eye on those "birds" in the sky. Evie and Rebecca leaped forward to catch up and matched her pace.

"Why do think someone will find us?"

Desti hadn't fully told her mother about how she escaped Tate *and* that he was probably tearing their world apart looking for her, or that fact that he was demon-possessed, possessed by a higher demon—the demon of lust. A wave of repulsion flushed through her as she recounted that creature using Tate's body to pin her down, the way his touch just felt so…wrong. She couldn't explain it, but her body knew the difference between the caress of the person who loves you versus the touch of something more sinister. But maybe now was a good time to mention to both her mother and Rebecca that they were probably being hunted.

Desti sighed and pushed away those awful thoughts that kept trying to resurface and stopped for a moment. "Rebecca, do you remember my friend Tate?" Desti was staring at her now, never realizing before the beautiful specks of gold that laced her irises.

Rebecca tilted her head as if she were thinking for a brief moment and replied, "Yes, of course. I remember seeing him train with Matt and Clara." Her voice quivered at the names of her lost friends.

"When we were trapped down here, he was possessed by one of the high king's demons. It wore his body like a suit…" Desti gulped. It was difficult to think about. Speak about, but then she continued. "Somehow, I blasted it out of his body, right before we escaped, and when we had jumped back in time, I thought that was going to be the end of that, but the Shadow found him again and took his body. Before I found my mother, and you, he was holding me prisoner somewhere out in the Wastelands, but I escaped. I know he is after me. That demon is drawn to me and maybe it's feeding off him somehow, using his love for me as a way to detect where I am because he always seems to catch up to me."

Rebecca just blinked and then Desti realized that Rebecca hadn't heard the whole backstory of what Desti had gone through. "You went to the past?" was all she asked.

She couldn't help it, but Desti let out a laugh. It was insane to think about everything that happened just so not long ago. "Yes, we did. The portal is hidden in the high king's castle. That is why I brought you to Hell because that is our way out of here."

Desti held out her hand and waited for Rebecca to take it. "Come on. I will tell you everything that happened up until I found you." She slipped her fingers into Desti's and began to walk forward, the orange and yellow glow of the perpetual sky outlining their silhouettes as the three of them ventured toward the horizon.

Chapter Twenty Eight

The Plains

"Oh my God, I don't think I can make it any farther," Rebecca cried, dropping to her knees.

The path on which they started from was now a mere speck in the distance; even the forest of death was a distant memory now. Rebecca's once lively, vibrant hair was now dull and clung to her sweat-coated cheeks, then Desti's gaze shifted to her mother who wore the same expression of defeat.

"I'm sorry but we can't stop. It isn't safe." Desti glanced up at the demon birds in the sky, keeping a careful eye on their position. She'd noticed that they had followed her the entire way as if they were waiting for her to drop dead. Desti ran forward and snaked her arms under Rebecca's and lifted her to her feet. "We can't stop. We are being hunted." Desti's eyes shifted up to the sky and then Rebecca did the same.

"If we stop now, those things will come down here and eat us. They have been following us this entire time."

Evie walked forward, looking almost as bad as Rebecca, but still offered some help and took one of Rebecca's arms and laced it around her neck. "Come on, I'll help you."

Together, the three of them dragged their tired feet—just one step in front of the other, Desti kept telling herself. One more step.

"So, tell me. What was your favorite thing about being in the time before?" Rebecca tried to ask between ragged breaths. Anything to keep her mind from the sheer exhaustion that was probably crippling her body. Desti frowned, knowing that Rebecca was trying to keep her mind occupied from the discomfort she was probably feeling. First, she shared a smile with her mother as they stumbled forward, and then said, "I think my favorite thing was the forest. I had never seen so much green in my life. The water was the purest I had ever tasted and the smells from the flowers were like nothing I could describe."

Desti didn't realize it at first, but she found herself smiling from the memory of her time in the forest before she had stumbled upon the true nature of the world back then. It was at its end of days now, and Desti had to remind herself that.

"It sounds wonderful. I don't think I have ever seen true grass, let alone an entire forest."

"Yeah, it took my breath away the moment I saw it for the first time. Our world was beautiful." Desti shifted her gaze toward Rebecca and smiled. "Don't worry, I will make sure that you get to see it with your own eyes."

Before Rebecca could respond, a shrill of terror ripped the air as Evie was yanked up by her shoulders from the claws of one of those demon birds. "Mom!" Desti screamed. She had dropped Rebecca on the ground and lunged for her mother's foot. It was almost too far away to reach but somehow Desti was able to grab ahold of her shoe and anchor herself to the ground, wedging her foot between two medium-sized boulders.

It felt as if Desti were playing tug-of-war with her mother and this creature of Hell, and as Desti dared to meet the creature's gaze, she immediately regretted it the moment it locked eyes on her. This *thing* was far more than just a bird from Hell. She could have sworn it curved the muscles around its jagged teeth into a sharp smile.

'*Escaped One,*' it hissed into her mind. This thing knew who she was, and if that was the case, then there must be more of these creatures out here hunting her. Did Amaros know that she was back in Hell, heading right toward his castle?

"Let her go!" she demanded. It was like a mixture of a squawk and a cackle of mockery as the beast opened its mouth and laughed. Pure rage boiled in her chest at the demon trying to take her mom. Evie was screaming an ear-pitched scream as the sharp talons of this demon dug into the flesh of her shoulders. Desti could see a stream of red soak the top of her shirt.

Swiftly, Desti glanced back for a second at Rebecca who was lying pretty much lifeless on the ground. For now, Rebecca was fine and was going to have to wait, because right now, Desti needed to save her mom.

Still gripping onto her mother's foot with her left hand, Desti used her other hand to look for something she could use to pry away the demon's grip. All around her was just an endless wasteland of rot and decay; nothing useful was scattered along the ground.

It was becoming more difficult to fight the strength of this demon. Desti felt her hand growing weaker as the seconds passed, but the thought of losing her mom—*now*—ignited something inside of her.

Desti did something that even she wouldn't have expected, unleashing her foot from the security of the boulders, taking ahold of the talons of the demon, and pulling herself up. It flapped its leathery wings with might, blasting Rebecca with a wave of dusty wind, and pulled Desti far up into the sky.

Desti took her mother's hands, placed them around the ankles of the beast, and said, "Don't let go. Okay?"

She was soaring high above now, and she could see the entire realm of Amaro's Hell from up here. His castle scraped the eerie sky like a razor tip, but she needed to focus. Still flapping its wings, the demon started snapping its snout at Desti, trying to take a bite out of her. She kept climbing, using its thick scaled skin as a way to leverage her weight and pull herself up.

Suddenly, Desti took hold of the side of its wing and used the momentum of its movement to swing her body up and over the demon until she was now sitting on its back.

"Who's got who now, you disgusting beast?"

This definitely pissed it off. Desti felt its body drop and now she was freefalling, and this demon did a nosedive in the air. Evie screamed with terror ripping through her, but Desti didn't let out a peep. She was planning for it to do this. Over the past few days, Desti had been thinking about what kind of powers she possessed, ones undiscovered and hidden within her, and so she was counting on this moment to bring them to the surface.

It had to work.

The ground was coming up fast and as Desti started to get her body ready to yield some angelic light, that familiar and awful pain burned up her arm from the cuff that was clamped on her wrist. They were now only fifty feet or so until they met the hard surface beneath them, and so, Desti swung her body back down, dangling herself from its leg, and took ahold of her mother with her other arm.

They shared a quick glance before Desti ignited a burning white flame from her hand, melting the demon's legs from her touch. As Desti burned the demon's leg off, it let go of Evie's shoulder and dropped its grip. They had seconds before it would be too late.

"When I saw grab this, you grab."

She reached for the bottom of the wing—the part that connected it to its back—and ripped it clean off, shoving herself and her mother from its back. "Grab this!" she yelled, and Evie listened as Desti shoved one end of the demon's wing into her mother's hand and took the opposite side into her own.

The wing was massive, canopying out like a giant sail caught in the wind, and as Desti and her mother held onto the edges of the wing, they glided down to the ground until they hit with a heavy thud.

All the air expelled from Desti's chest the moment she hit the ground, but she wasn't complaining. It was better than splattering like how her little friend did after she ripped its wing off.

"Holy shit, Desti," Rebecca called from the distance. She was now on her knees, leaning against a boulder, but in her eyes, the look of utter surprise consumed them. Desti rolled to her side and coughed. She groaned and then sat up, reaching for Evie.

"Mom? Are you okay?" Evie was curled in a ball, covered in gravel and scrapes, but she was alive. She was shaking and reached her hand out and grabbed Desti's. "You saved me," her frail voice cried.

"Of course I did. I would never let something take you."

Evie pushed herself off the ground and leaped into Desti's arms, embracing her as if it were the first time a mother got to hug her child. "Oh Sweetie, thank you. I am so sorry." The sound of her voice in her ear sent a feeling of comfort through her. Finally, she had her mom.

"Are you going to tell me what the fuck that was?"

Desti laughed as she walked over toward Rebecca who had a smile plastered on her face. "You are a literal badass, do you know that?"

"Come on, I think you might have hit your head when I dropped you."

Rebecca was okay. Evie was okay. Desti was okay. She had just killed a demon with her bare hands, letting free an all-new power and hunger. If she can do this, then breaking into Amaro's castle should be a piece of cake, right?

But still, that demon's voice wouldn't leave her mind. *Escaped One.* Which meant that it knew who she was, and if it did, then maybe Amaros knew where she was lurking. Would he send Elijah after her? Tate? The Master? All of whom probably couldn't wait to capture her for their own personal torment.

Elijah must have been furious when he returned to the camp to find Evie and Rebecca gone. And Tate—the Shadow— was after her too, after she had escaped him. All of them seemed to want power, but more importantly, they all seemed especially interested in *her* power.

But they didn't know what was coming. They didn't know the fury that had been sparked inside of her, because Desti was going to stop at nothing to take back her friends. To make them pay for what they did, and when she was finished with them, she was going to take back the world, because no creature of Hell should ever roam the Earth again.

Chapter Twenty Nine

The Castle

The obsidian that the castle was etched from gleamed under the bleak, blood-red sky in an unnatural luster that reflected the hellish flames licking its base. Jagged spires pierced the sky, dripping molten flames from the tip as if drawing blood from the source.

"This place is *huge.*" Rebecca stood hunched, bracing herself on her knees as she drew in a large breath. Desti felt just about the same—tired. Beaten. Dirty. The journey to even make it to Amaro's castle was treacherous and unforgiving.

After Desti had slaughtered that winged demon, she thought that the rest of the journey was going to be easy, but she soon found herself falling into another realm of terror. Evie almost collapsed at her feet the moment Desti and Rebecca stopped to gaze upon the monolith structure.

Despite the terror and madness that the castle exuded, there was a strange, dark allure to it. A power that beckoned her forward, daring her to confront whatever lay within its walls, and as Desti gazed upon it, she could feel the weight of the journey ahead—a sense that this castle was not just a place, but a final, ultimate challenge where the true nature of her strength would be tested.

"How did you get through this the last time? It looks like those thorns go all the way around the castle." Evie was making an observation. Yes, the dreaded labyrinth of deadly, poisoned thorns still encased the castle in a protective circle. It was merely a suspicion but now that Desti was coming up on the *other side*— the side she hadn't seen before—her suspicion was now a reality.

The wall of vines and thorns stood about fifteen feet high and seemed to go on forever. Just from her previous experience, she knew that it would be pointless to try to find an opening, or even a path, for that matter. And there were probably demons guarding the inner parts of this labyrinth just as they had done the last time, slithering their way out of the depths of the shadows, snatching her friends up one by one.

Not again. She had a new plan to get inside.

"We cut through the vines using its own thorns, and made our own pathway," Desti replied, but she never broke her gaze as she stared at this towering wall. Evie made a sound that sounded like relief and Rebecca was just pacing back and forth as she took in her surroundings.

"Will that work this time?" Evie asked. Desti shook her head. "I don't know but we almost didn't make it last time, and when we had made it through, that was when we were captured. They came from nowhere and took us out one by one."

"Well then, what do you propose we do to get through?" Rebecca interjected. Her furious, red hair blew in loose tendrils as the blasting Hell winds picked up their speed. She looked like a warrior standing among the horizon, covered in blood and dirt, wearing a face of vengeance.

"Last time, I didn't have my powers, and I think that now, I should try to use them."

Desti held out her hand and said, "Stand back," before refocusing her position and aiming toward the wall of vines. The metal cuff on her wrist ached with dark magic coursing through her, trying to stop whatever power she was festering to her surface, but she ignored it.

"Breathe," she told herself. "Focus." Something positive. Something loving. Those were the kind of thoughts that brought her the most power, made her the strongest. And as Desti closed her eyes and brought those thoughts to the surface, she felt it—the warm sensation of pure power coursing through her body. It flooded her. Cascaded through every nerve until the tips of her fingers were electrified with her light, and when Desti opened her eyes and glanced down at her open palms, she noticed that she was *glowing*, as if she were an angel plucked right from Heaven.

She heard Rebecca and her mother gasp in unison as this ethereal white light encased around her body, and when she aimed the palms of her hands at the wall of vines, her light flew from her fingers and smacked into it, almost melting away the poisoned thorns that twisted their way around the castle.

As if they could feel pain, she heard a hissing sound as she watched the wall wither away to dust. Desti released her pose and brought her hands to her side, wide-eyed in disbelief at what she had just done.

"Desti, Holy shit," Rebecca said while limping over to her. Evie just stood in the distance looking as if she were in shock and disbelief, but before she could call her mother's name, she was embraced into Rebecca's arms. "I can't believe you just did that. That was amazing." Rebecca pulled away and smiled. This was the first time Desti had seen a genuine smile on Rebecca's face. This world did that to people. It broke them down, tore away any happiness they held onto until they were consumed with their own suffering, wearing the expression like a mask.

Before Desti could speak, she heard her mother gasp. "Look," she breathed. Desti pulled away from Rebecca's embrace and glanced to where her mother was pointing, and that was when that good, happy feeling left her body, being replaced by total fear.

"Shit."

Desti traced her eyes along the charred, cracked ground that snaked its way forward and that was when a new nightmare emerged from the shadows. She didn't miss that smile, or that smug face of his. Amaros stepped forward, dressed in a finely pressed suit, keeping his hands in his pockets.

"Oh, Escaped One. That's what my demons have been calling you," he purred. "My. My. You sure are a fascinating one. Who knew that you could yield so much power, and it seems as though my cuff was no match for you." Amaros slipped a glance at the cuff on Desti's wrist but quickly brought his gaze back with a deadly stare.

She was paralyzed. Stuck in her own perpetual hell that was now ravishing her. His demons must have tipped him off that she was coming. "I see you brought some friends. I do believe Elijah was looking for you two." Amaros tsked and wagged his finger, he then pointed his finger at Rebecca and with the slightest flick of his hand, he pulled her forward with some invisible force.

She gasped and not even a heartbeat later was in the arms of him. She was trembling and Amaros was drinking in her fear.

"Let her go. Let all of them go and I will do what you want." Desti wasn't sure if she even believed herself, but it was the only leverage she had over him. He wanted her blood. Her power. She could use that to her advantage.

"So quick to make a deal with the devil again, aren't you? Are you sure you are willing to go down that route again?" Desti just shifted her gaze to her mother, her eyes beckoning Desti to say no, but Desti knew that she had no choice, if her friends were to live.

"I want my friends set free; I want Tate to have his freedom back, and I want you to take your nasty creatures of Hell and go back where you belong." Evie stepped forward, and Desti knew she was reaching for her, but Amaros lifted his other hand so fast that she didn't see it coming and with his dark force, yanked Evie up by the hollow of her neck.

"Stop it! Let her go!" Her mother's face had drained of its blood, turning a purple-blue color. "Please let her go," she begged. Amaros didn't seem pleased with her begging, but he lessened his grip and tossed her aside like trash.

"I should kill you right now."

"You'll never get what you want Amaros. The angels foretold of this prophecy and there is nothing you can do about it." Evie glanced up through the strands of hair that hung freely in her face and smiled a wicked smile at Amaros.

Does she know him? By the look of pure hatred that was burning within her eyes, Desti would assume so. She wanted to rush forward and hold her mother. She wanted answers to all of the questions that burned into her mind, but Desti only stood there in silence.

Rebecca whimpered in pain as Amaros tightened his grip on her. After what seemed like an eternity glaring into his depthless eyes, he snickered and answered, "No deal." Before Desti had a chance to react, Amaros lifted his arm and disappeared into a cloud of black smoke, taking Rebecca with him.

"No!" Desti ran forward but nothing was there now. They were gone. "No! He can't do this again! I was going to save them all," she cried. Tears slid down her cheek, but as she knelt on the burning gravel, something unearthly snatched her sorrows from her throat.

Hissing.

Desti slowly shifted her head toward the castle and that was when they emerged from the shadows—an army of demons stepped forward, each and every one of them with a hunger for her blood lingering in their eyes, and Desti could only get out one word before they came barreling toward her.

She glanced back to her mother who was still lying on the ground and screamed, "Run!"

Chapter Thirty

The Horde

The horde.

A wall of black; a sea of monsters; an army of demons were now chasing Desti and Evie into the wastelands of Hell. Just from a quick glance back, she could see their snouts pulled back into a snarl, revealing their sharpened, jagged teeth. Some dripped saliva, others seemed to ooze venom. Either way, if any of those creatures caught her, she would be dead.

"Where do we go?" Her mother cried out as she ran forward. Desti could tell her body was struggling by the way it was limping. She was too. God knew she had been through Hell and back—literally.

But as Desti scoped her surroundings, she couldn't help but feel an overwhelming sense of dread, as there was nothing around to offer safety. Behind her was Amaros's castle, to her left and right was just an endless plain of withered, decayed land, littered with skeletal remains of lost souls, and ahead, well this was something new and Desti wasn't sure how she felt about heading there yet.

She had no choice but to go straight, to keep running forward, but something emerged from the horizon that almost made Desti stop in her tracks. "What is that?" Evie yelled breathlessly as she pushed forward.

It was a burning lake of molten, bubbling lava, engulfing the surrounding land in its fury. Desti remembered learning about the Lake of Fire, the place where the lost souls of Hell were trapped. You were banished to the Lake of Fire for the most heinous of sins committed. It was a place where your torment and suffering were endless, feeding it with your agonizing cries for mercy as if it were a living creature.

"We can't go in there!" Desti called out.

"Where do we go?" Evie was running with all her might and Desti glanced back just as Evie did. The horde was catching up to them; she could practically feel the heat of their breath reach out and touch her. Tears began to well in Desti's eyes. "I don't know! I don't know where to go."

She had to do something. Use her powers, but how? What could she do at this moment to get her out of this situation?

Think Desti. Think.

Desti thought back to the Holy book. What it had said about the power of the Lux. *He who shall yield the powers of the angels shall cast away the demons from Earth and banish them to Hell,* or something like that. Desti knew it had mentioned the Lux had power over the demons in a way that she probably hadn't access yet, but did that mean that she could control other elements of Hell?

She had to try. Or else she would be dead.

Desti reached out her hand, screaming from the searing pain that the cuff was emitting, and lifted her arm as a flash of white exploded from her hand and shot into the Lake of Fire. The lava rose into a towering wall of orange flames, moving with the momentum of her hand, but before she thrashed that wall of lava into the horde of demons, she screamed to her mother, "Go that way!"

Evie, mouth gaped open, just nodded and ran as fast as she could, ducking to her left and out of the way of Desti's newest weapon. The moment her mother was in safe proximity, Desti hurtled that sea of lava into the horde of demons that were thrashing toward her, drowning them in their own misery and pain.

Their dark silhouettes were sucked up into its raging fury and Desti could hear their hissing and screeching as their bodies were melted. And when the wave of lava retreated back into its pit, there was nothing left on the ground to indicate that an army had just been chasing her, nothing at all.

This was a moment of clarity for her. She was the one to be feared here, not the other way around, because she could yield the light of the angels now, she could control the elements of Hell, and now it was time to go get her friends back.

"Mom!"

Desti ran for her mother who was standing frozen in shock. "Mom, are you okay?" When Desti placed her hand on Evie's shoulder, she winced, her gaze lost into something that Desti didn't recognize.

"It's okay. I'm here. We are safe now."

Evie's eyes shifted and once they met Desti's, she could see the moment her mother came back to her. "Oh Sweetie, what was that? How did you do that?" Evie embraced her with a hug and then pulled away, more questions than answers now burning in her eyes.

"I don't know. It just came to me. I think I know why Amaros has taken all my friends. To use them as leverage to get to me. It's his last chance at controlling me, which means we need to hit him by surprise."

Desti knew that her journey was coming to an end. Amaros knew it. The Master knew it. She knew it. There was a war coming, the war to end the end of days, to eradicate the Hell that ravished the land, and to restore what was once lost. She was the key, the answer to it all, and she just hoped that she wasn't in over her head.

"If I am going to do this, I need to get this stupid thing off. Can you take that rock and try to smash it?" Desti had her arms splayed out on a flattened boulder, readying herself for the pain that was to come.

Evie held a large stone between her hands and angled just above the cuff on Desti's wrist. "I don't know if this is a good idea. What if I hurt you?"

"I can't take this pain anymore. I'm getting stronger. My powers are growing, and so is the pain of this cuff. Please. I can feel it holding me back. If we want to win this war and save my friends, I *need* to get it off."

There was a part of the cuff that seemed vulnerable, where the two sides clicked together. Desti knew that if she could hit it just right, it would crack open. "I'm ready," she said, gritting her teeth.

Evie held up the heavy stone and blew out a huge breath before bringing it down onto Desti's wrist with all her might. A scream so loud, so ear-pitching, ripped from Desti's chest, as Evie smashed into her wrist. A bone-shattering pain engulfed her senses and made her dizzy.

"Oh, I'm sorry." Evie dropped the rock and studied Desti's now *very* broken wrist. "It didn't work. I can't believe I let you talk me into doing this."

Through the pain and the tears, Desti cut her off. "Stop. Help me get it off." With Desti's wrist now hanging loosely, even as painful as it might be, she now knew that she could slip her hand away from the cuff. "Pull it off me."

Evie stared blankly at Desti for a moment but then nodded and grabbed her wrist and the cuff gently. She tugged and guided the cuff down her arm and pulled until Desti's wrist was free from the enchanted metal. Evie chucked the cuff into oblivion and returned her attention to Desti.

"It worked," she cried.

Desti scoffed, and even though her arm seared with pain, she managed to crack a smirk. "I didn't think I was going to get it off by breaking my wrist, but…"

"Will you be able to heal it?" Evie cut her off.

That's right. Desti did heal faster than normal humans, and now that her powers were growing exponentially, now that the cuff was off, she probably would be healed in no time. She could already feel the light inside her at work as the searing pain began to fade.

"It's healing. Now let's go inside this castle."

There she was again, standing before the castle that had caused her so much pain and sorrow. Too many agonizing memories were brought to the surface as she gazed upon its towering beauty. There was no more labyrinth to protect it from her getting inside; she had destroyed that with the flick of her wrist, and now his army of demons was gone too.

Desti wondered if Amaros knew that she was still alive and about to enter his home. Or was he too preoccupied with taking over the world? Evie was silent as she traced the edges of the walls, gazing up to the tips of the jagged spires that pierced the sky. In her eyes, there was a hazing fear.

"What's it like in there?" she asked.

Desti didn't know how to answer that. What was it like? It was like your worst nightmare coming to life, like being trapped in a perpetual Hell. Every corner of this place radiated evil and if you weren't careful, it would consume you.

"Just stay close to me. Don't go anywhere alone. Our goal is to get to the portal and get back to my friends."

"How do you know he has them there still?"

"I can just feel it. Something inside me is telling me that we need to jump back to the time before. He was using them there. That is where this will all end." Desti held out her hand and offered her mom a soft smile. Reluctantly, Evie took her hand and followed as Desti took her first step through the threshold of Amaros's castle.

Chapter Thirty One

Inside

Desti didn't know what she expected to see the moment she walked through those doors—to be captured by some entity waiting to snatch her up, to be struck dead, or to stumble upon the horrors that had tormented her before, but instead, his castle was…empty. Quiet.

It was massive.

The vast entry hall snaked around, disappearing into the shadows, marble walls stretched impossibly high, disappearing into a void of darkness, and there was an oppressive weight lingering in the air—a feeling of despair that crept its way around the room, suffocating Desti with every shallow breath she took.

"I wasn't expecting this," her mother's voice echoed. Evie stepped forward and peered around the room in a silent curiosity. "What were you expecting?"

"I don't know. Maybe like a throne made of bones, and fire." Desti laughed. She had had the same thought about what the inside of a High King of Hell's castle would look like, but no, it wasn't some terrifying building, in fact, it was quite the opposite.

"It's…beautiful, actually."

Desti nodded her head. This place did have a classy appeal to it, but she knew that there were places in this castle that were where nightmares came from. Her mind swirled around the memories of her time in the arena, being trapped on that battlefield, thinking that she was going to die. Or the dungeon in which she had lost her sanity, being held captive while she waited for her life to end. This place brought out the worst in her, pulling those horrible emotions to the surface.

Maybe Amaros wanted her to feel this way and knew that being inside this castle would do so. It was the complete opposite of what she felt when she was in Heaven, or when the light of the angels coursed through her. This place weakened her; diminished her light.

"Come on, let's hurry. I don't like being in here."

It was like a maze, but Desti had seen enough to navigate her way around and not get lost in some alternate dimension. Some of the doors were pathways to places of nightmares; places that would swallow you up and feed off your soul, and so she avoided walking through any rooms that she didn't recognize.

Despite being in Hell, the air that filled the room was cold, freezing actually. Maybe it was just another way to make the souls of this place suffer. Desti curled her fingers into her arms and hugged her chest, blowing out a sigh.

"It's so cold."

Her mother was holding her arms, rubbing up and down, trying to create heat from the friction. They had ventured down the endless hall, and eventually, it cornered into another section of the castle.

"I think we are close," Desti softly spoke. Something felt off. Wrong. The silence that stilled in the air was overwhelming, and this was *too* easy of a mission. She threw out her arm and stopped her mother from walking any farther, shooting her a glare of worry.

"What's wrong?"

"This doesn't feel right. Why would we just be able to walk straight to it? ...It's a trap." Desti's voice echoed around and when the last echo faded that was when the hairs on her neck spiked as she heard a familiar sound.

The first thing that Desti noticed was the small, silver necklace that now dangled at the hollow of his neck. Desti sucked in her breath. It was like seeing a ghost of someone you love, knowing that they weren't really there, because when her eyes met Tate's, it wasn't him staring back at her, no. It was the glare of something evil that lurked within him.

The Shadow.

"How did you find me?" she breathed.

Tate played with the necklace that hung around his neck, taunting her, and smiled knowing that she yearned to get it back. The gleam of his skin was like sunlight gilding honey. He was perfection to her, and it killed her knowing that his soul was lost somewhere in the darkness.

"I didn't know the kind of power this little necklace had until I put it on. Turns out I am able to do a lot with it."

He was wearing the necklace that Seraphiel gave her. That Ms. Joan had saved for her. It was a beacon to connect Desti to the angelic realm *and* was more powerful than the Lux. If he knew just how powerful that necklace was, she wouldn't stand a chance at getting it back, so, she had to play cool.

Desti stiffened and took a step forward. "It's just a necklace. It was a gift from an old friend. May I have it back?" It took everything in Desti not to lace her words with venom. God knew she wanted to destroy the Shadow, but in order to get her necklace back, she had to keep him leveled.

"Why don't you tell me what this necklace does, and then I might consider letting you have it."

Desti knew that was a lie. Demons were creatures of the dark and the wicked. Lies were a way of existing for them, twisting and contorting their reality to feed their evil hunger. It would be foolish to give him such a gift. Desti kept her face unreadable and brought herself closer, so close she could now see the golden specks in the irises of his jade eyes.

He had to be in there somewhere. *Please see me. Please come back to me.*

"Why don't you tell me how you found me first." Desti didn't dare slip a glance at her mother now. Evie had stood quietly off in the corner and hadn't grasped the attention of Tate yet, and that was how she wanted to keep it.

She watched as his fingers dangled the charm and twirled it around. "It's like a radio when I wear this. I can sometimes seep into your thoughts, feel where you are. I could sense you through its power."

The light of the angels was more than just energy. It was a power so advanced that the human mind couldn't comprehend it. She knew that from the moment she had met Seraphiel. Something about that encounter changed her, filled her with this innate knowledge of the heavens, and so she knew now that her necklace was tethered to her soul, just as the Shadow was tethered to Hell.

Tate snickered, offering Desti a playful smirk. "Oh baby, can't you see that we are connected now? You are mine. I consume the pain and sins of the damned. I am the demon of lust, and I wear your lover like a suit. Your body craves his touch, but your soul rejects the demon inside. But you are too late my Dear, because I have had you. I have claimed you as mine forever."

Flashes of the Shadow holding her down, using Tate's body to thrust himself inside her, made her knees buckle under the crippling feeling of hopelessness that rushed through her.

What did that mean that he had claimed her? Would she be able to banish him from Tate? Behind her, she heard her mother gasp. That was not something a mother should hear.

"I will never be yours," she spat.

There was a wicked look that played in his eyes as he said, "If you want this, then you'll have to play by my rules."

The necklace was the key to everything. She needed it to save her friends. The world. But to subject herself as his slave…

She shook her head. There had to be a better way, but maybe if she just pretended long enough to gain his trust, she could figure out a way to free Tate from the Shadow and get her necklace back. Glossy-eyed, Desti glanced back at her mom giving her a sorrowful stare. It said, *I'm sorry.*

Desti gritted her teeth. "Fine. I am yours and I will do what you say." There he was, that primal beast that hid under the beauty of her best friend. He couldn't hide behind those eyes. The eyes were the window to the soul and shall reveal the true self that was within. And she saw him alright; he was dark and vile, a soul-sucking, lusting demon, but he had a weakness—his desire to have her as his, and she was going to use that to her advantage.

"I want to know where my friends are," Desti said flatly.

Tate had lured her and Evie to a section of the castle where he was to keep his victims. She thought she was going to another dungeon, but when he had brought her to a room, with a bed, her heart almost fell to the floor.

"Are you still going on about your friends? There is no reason to worry. You aren't ever going to see them again."

Desti bit her lip to keep herself from screaming some kind of insult at him. Tinges of blood coated her tongue. She watched as he took a seat in a chair across the room, not even slipping a glance at her mother who was perched on the bed, watching.

"Your friends are with Amaros and the Master. You and your mother shall remain here with me in Hell."

"What is going to happen to them?" Desti was almost too frightened to ask. Tate crossed his leg over his knee and leaned back into the chair.

"They have their purpose. Amaros and the Master will bring forth the rulers of Hell, continuing their reign on the Earth."

"And you?" Desti asked.

Tate narrowed his brow as if he didn't understand her question. "Will you be ruling the Earth with them?" He scoffed and leaned forward. "No, darling. I will be the new ruler of Hell, king of all the realms of the damned. There will be no more need for them to rule down here when they can have the freedom to walk the Earth."

"If the Master is ruling by Amaros's side, then who is going to see over the Wastelands?"

Without a higher demon in charge, all the lesser demons would have free control to do what they please. *Eat* who they please. It would be total chaos. When she brought her gaze back to Tate, he was smiling at her. Not a playful smile, no. This was the kind of smile that struck fear into her heart.

"Elijah will be taking over your pathetic city and your pathetic Wastelands. The true future will begin in the past. The three kings shall rise from the flames and create a new Hell on your planet."

As if her world wasn't already terrible, the three kings of Hell wanted to make it even more tormenting…wait. He said *three* kings.

Who was the third?

But Desti didn't have to think about that, because she remembered the stories growing up, about the devil and how he ruled the land of flames and death. The third king, the most powerful king, had to be him. Which meant that Desti was now way in over her head. This was going to need a very extensive thought-out plan, if she was going to take down not only Amaros and the Master, *and* their army of demons, but now also, the devil himself.

She didn't let the fear show on her face. That would only give him what he wanted, but as Desti studied his features some more, a thought flashed into her mind as her eyes flicked to the shining silver dangling from his neck. *If the necklace was so powerful, then how come Amaros hadn't taken it from him yet?* She needed to get that necklace back, but for now, she was going to lay low and play by his rules—that was until she figured out a way to banish that demon from Tate and rip his soul seam from seam.

She wanted the Shadow to suffer. She yearned to hear his screams rip through the air, and in this moment, silently, she promised herself she would do just that.

It had been a week now, acting as the Shadow's own personal slave. Desti had nearly scrubbed every inch of this part of the castle until her fingers were numb and raw, and when Tate wasn't ordering her to get on her knees to scrub away the tiniest speck of dirt, he made her perform other duties while down below. And to her demise, her wrist was now prisoner to another, magically charmed cuff. But this cuff felt stronger, hurt more. Tate had slapped it on her the moment he had his chance to. There was now a constant ache that radiated through her arm, and Desti had to work extra hard at keeping her light at bay.

Evie had been transferred to her own room, not too far away from the room that Desti had to share with Tate and every day, Desti tried to reach his soul that was locked away down in there, but the more she tried to pull him to the surface, the more it seemed he was slipping deeper into the abyss.

"Have you thought of a way to get us out of here?" Evie whispered to Desti while she helped clean up the living corridor. The short answer was yes; there was a way that Desti and Evie could probably escape, but the chance that she may never see Tate again, she may never get the chance to free his soul if she left him, ultimately was the anchor that kept her obeying this twisted new life of hers.

Desti nodded. "I know where the portal is, but I won't leave here without Tate." She continued fluffing the pillows that were sprawled on the embroidered couch and moved her way over to a table to clean up residue from the previous night's *festivities*. The Shadow took pleasure in indulging in sinful acts, and every day, she was made to clean up the evidence.

"Sweetie, Tate is lost in there. You may never be able to get him ba—"

Before Evie could finish that sentence, Desti shot her mother a deathly glare. Evie sucked in her breath and gulped down that word. "Don't you say that. He is in there. I can feel it. He broke free before, just for a moment. That was how I was able to escape him before I found you." Desti's eyes were pleading, begging for her mother to believe her.

Yes, she could easily take her mother and sneak away in the midst of the night, but leaving Tate behind would be like abandoning him to the darkness of Hell. She'd rather suffer with him for eternity than do that.

"Can't you use your light on him?"

"I wouldn't do that. I don't want to hurt him. I am too powerful now, plus, he found a way to amp up this cuff's charm. I can barely make a ball of light from my palm now." Desti held up her empty hand and dropped it just as quickly. "I need to find the key to unlock this cuff, and I will continue to try to find a way to get Tate back to the surface. I know there is a way."

Before Evie could respond, she straightened and nodded her head to what stood behind Desti. Desti's breath hitched as the air in the room turned frigid, a looming, dark presence filled the space around her, and before she could turn around, the heat of Tate's breath pressed into her ear. "Come with me," he growled.

Desti nodded, not breaking her glare with her mother. Evie's face had the look of utter sorrow, but Desti didn't linger on the devastation that was plastered on her mother's face. She was too preoccupied with what mattered more—seducing the demon of lust, just enough so that he lost his focus, and then bringing her beloved back to her.

The tips of his fingers trailed the throbbing veins in her neck until they stopped just above her breasts. His other hand glided down her other arm until he was pulling her away to follow him.

It was time for another session with this demon, and she was dammed sure going to use this to her advantage. Now was her time to get Tate back. Tate led Desti out into a vast hallway, laden with elegant drapes and red velvet carpets. *So cliché*, Desti thought.

"Are you bringing me to your room?" she asked, trying to hide any sharpness in her tone. Tate glanced back, face sharp and angled. His eyes were just as vicious. "Not right now. I need to do something. It has been requested by Amaros."

Desti stopped dead in her tracks and pulled away. "What does Amaros want? I thought that he left you to this realm to do as you please."

Tate snatched her arm back into his grip and closed the space between them until the heat of his rising chest lingered over her body. "He is still my master. I must do what he requires, and his patience has been running thin."

"What does he *require*?" Desti was practically seething at this point.

"Did you forget that you have a purpose in his plan? He needs your blood, Darling. Without it, he won't be able to keep his reign up there forever. With your blood, you may be able to purify his and end his curse."

"And then he would hold the power of Heaven. No one would be able to beat him…" Desti's voice fizzled away, and her mind went off to a distant thought. If Amaros was able to consume Desti's power—her blood—then he would be impossible to kill. She would never be able to save her friends, or the world from the demons.

This was bad. Really bad. Tate pulled her farther down the hall until her eyes noticed a familiar stone pathway.

Desti tried to rip her wrist free of his grip, but Tate was too strong with the Shadow lingering within him. "No!" She growled. "You can't have my blood. You can't have anything from me."

Tate only laughed, and said, "I can have whatever I want from you. You are *mine*."

"I belong to no one, you disgusting demon," she seethed. "I'll find a way to destroy you, and I promise demon, I will make you suffer."

"Such wild imagination. You're going to need that to keep your sanity. Welcome to your new home, *Darling*." Tate said while shoving her into a cell. The metal door slammed shut before Desti was able to reach for him, and the last thing she saw before being left alone was the faintest of smirks pulling at the corner of his lip. And then he walked away, being engulfed by the shadows of the dungeon halls.

A sob ripped from her chest as Desti dropped to her knees, sulking in her utter defeat. How on Earth was she supposed to get herself out of this? Desti had almost forgotten about what Amaros had mentioned to her—that her blood was the key to purifying his own; to break his curse so that he may control all the realms.

Thoughts of what he was going to do to her violated her mind, crashing around like a furious storm. Her knees ached from kneeling on the sharp gravel beneath her, but she didn't pay any attention to the discomfort it caused her. Desti was too lost in drowning worries that flooded her body.

It was the same cell that Amaros had confined her in. The same trickle of water, mocking her with its taunting echoes. The same shallow puddle of muddy water that offered her a reflection of the defeat that laced her face.

She was a prisoner again.

Tears gathered. A salty stream of sorrow ran down her cheek, and as she sat there, and kneeled on the ground, the thought of her mother crept into her mind. All her life, her mom had been subjected to being a slave, poisoned by her own partner, and forced to obey as she watched her daughter suffer at the hands of him. The horror it must have caused her…

Desti shook her head, not allowing herself to sulk anymore. "No," she told herself. "I won't let this defeat me. I can't."

There was no telling what "time" it was down here. Time was an illusion in Hell, passing through existence like a river carving its path through stone—slow, relentless, and unstoppable. For all Desti knew, years could have passed on the surface of the Earth; her friends could be long gone, and then, what was the point of fighting this battle?

Think. It felt as if the world was against her, taking away any bit of hope that emerged from her, but then a thought gave her one last bit of strength to cling to the diminishing hope.

Her necklace.

She remembered that Tate had taken it from her, and then she had seen the shining silver wrapped around the hollow of his neck. If she could somehow get that back, then maybe it would be the key to breaking her out of this cuff and saving Tate's soul.

Exhaustion from the day had finally caught up to her body, pulling her mind into darkness. Desti didn't want to sleep, not when she must plan a way to escape, but she would be no good without a good rest, so she let her body loosen and closed her eyes until silence and nothingness were all that existed.

Chapter Thirty Two

Plaything

"Get up," Tate growled from the hallway.

Desti peered through the cracks in her eyes, pulling her mind back to this depressing reality, but when she traced her eyes and met Tate's…

"Woah…"

The usual finely silken shirt was nowhere in sight; in its place—nothing. Desti found herself gazing a little too long at Tate's exposed torso. He was only wearing black slacks. Everything else was simply…not there.

The warm flickering of the torchlight caught the contour of his chiseled abs, his skin glossed over as if someone had rubbed oil all over him. Desti bit her bottom lip, caught in a hungry daze at this sight. Each ridge of his abs stood out like carved marble, narrowing down to his waist. How could she not get lost admiring the artistry of such perfection, but Desti shook her head and reminded herself that this wasn't her Tate. No. This was a vile, evil entity, using her lover's skin like a mask.

"Like what you see?" he taunted.

Desti crossed her arms over her chest and scoffed. "Not while *you* occupy his body." The jingling of keys set in motion an echo of clanging. She couldn't help but to suck in her breath in excitement to leave this cell.

"It's time. Come," he demanded. Desti stood but then something held her body still. "Where are you taking me? Where is my mother?"

"So, many questions. Amaros is growing impatient. If you want your mother to live, you do as I say." Tate held out his hand and yanked Desti forward the moment her fingers slipped into his. Being tugged down this hallway brought back the worst of memories to her, and here she was again, living through the same horror.

"Where is she?"

"For now, she is fine. I have her on cleaning duty Told her that I was going to fetch you."

"You say that as if I am your pet," Desti sneered.

"Aren't you?"

Fury was building in her chest, and if she didn't have a goal in mind, she would have exploded from the rage that was built up inside, but Desti gritted her teeth and ignored his rude remarks.

"I'm no one's pet, *demon.*"

Tate glanced back slightly, and briefly, Desti caught a glimpse of his golden and green eyes, a magical swirl of colors that used to be filled with so much love and hopefulness. It broke her heart to now see those eyes devoid of any compassion, and instead, replaced with pure evil hatred.

"You said that Amaros was impatient. Impatient about what?" The moment Desti finished that sentence, she remembered her conversation from yesterday. *He wants your blood*; a voice spoke in her mind. Desti's eyes grew big at the realization that she was walking to her inevitable torture and death. If she panicked, it would make things worse, he would feed off her fear and probably start the torturing early.

There must be a way out of this. Think. Think.

His fingers wrapped around hers in a furious grip, pulling her forward through the darkness. Desti had been through this hallway before, and she knew that there was a bend coming up soon, and after that, the room she was dreading. As Desti racked her brain on ways to get out of this mess, her mind kept coming back to a simple thought.

Her necklace.

It hung from Tate's neck in a taunting fashion, but if she could distract him, maybe she would be able to snatch it from him. Free herself. A bright light now appeared from around the corner and ahead stood a red door. She knew what was behind that door—her death. Her suffering. Her end.

"Wait!" Desti halted, pulling her arm back.

A low, guttural growl escaped his throat as he slowly turned around, mouth in a snarl. "What is it?" he hissed

Desti relaxed her shoulders, and even put on the faintest of smiles. She knew how to put on a façade when she needed to, and this demon was the demon of lust. Surely, she would be able to seduce him until she could get her hands on that necklace.

"I've been thinking about…" she traced her fingers along the ridges of his abs, slowly, seductively, and continued. "Our time together." She brought her other hand to his chest and shoved him against the stone wall, pressing her body onto his. She glanced up, praying that she would see lust lingering in his eyes, but they were stone cold.

"I want it. I need it. I can't keep going pretending that my body doesn't crave your touch. His touch." Desti had lifted herself on her tiptoes, her breath softly caressing the hallow of Tate's neck, and with a sigh of relief, she heard a pleasurable groan escape from him.

As fast as lighting, his hand was now wrapped around her neck, closing in on her throbbing pulse. Now she was the one pinned to the wall. In his eyes, something changed. Something primal, hungry, emerged to the surface and that was the moment she knew that her plan was working.

"Oh, I'll make you beg for it, *Pet*." He grazed his tongue over her throbbing vein, licking the sweat that had glossed her skin. Desti moaned, half from her act, but half because her body *did* crave Tate's touch, and it was hard not to enjoy the sensation of his tongue on her body.

She wrapped her fingers into his midnight hair, pulling him closer until she felt the tips of his teeth graze her skin. His breath warm and demanding in her ear as he spoke, "I'll have you right here before I spill your blood."

Desti lifted her chin until she met his gaze with hooded eyes, she leaned in as if she were going in for a desperate kiss, but the moment his lips touched hers, she bit down hard until she tasted the sweet coppery taste of blood.

Tate staggered back and let go of her. "You bitch!" In less than a heartbeat, her face had met the wrath of the back of his hand as he slapped her to the ground. "I'm going to fucking kill you, and I will make sure you feel suffering while I take your life," he spat.

Desti was curled on the ground, not because she was weak, no. Because she had something that she needed to hide. He must not have noticed in the moment of pain and surprise that Desti had clutched onto her necklace, yanking it clean off him when he threw her to the ground. And now, she had something that could hopefully break the spell on her cuff.

It was known in her world that angelic power triumphed over the demonic realm. Holy light drowned out the dark, as the blazing sun would do to a shadow, and so she took the cross of her necklace and placed it on her cuff, whispering a prayer to her angel Seraphiel, praying that he would free her from her bindings. That he would bless her with her true powers. It was a long stretch, but she had hope.

Pain seared the back of her neck as Tate yanked her up by the roots of her hair, bellowing out a vicious scream. She kicked and clawed trying to free herself from his grip, but he was too strong. In the chaos of it all, she hadn't noticed that her cuff had fallen off until she heard the loud clanging of the metal scrapping the stone reverberate around her.

Silence enveloped. Everything went still. And as Tate slowly turned her around to face him, she knew the first thing he saw was her wicked smile. Fury sparked in his eyes. And before he could react, Desti thrust out both of her palms, blasting her glorious white light into Tate's chest.

She screamed in unison with him as the splitting of the Shadow's soul came undone. It was like a dream, or a nightmare, unfolding before her. A dark looming shadow clung to Tate's body, but she could see her light pushing it out. The struggle was a battle between light and dark. The demon's true self began to emerge from her beloved's body, casting a vicious growl throughout the room.

Desti barred her teeth and held strong. Her love was the key to it all. It was love that grew her powers, and ultimately love that always led her back to him. And now, it was love that was going to destroy this shadowy mother fucker for stealing the only man she cared about.

Tate dropped to the floor and a swirling shadow now hovered above him. She brought her hands up and outward, blasting her light in all corners of the dungeon hall. Before the Shadow was ripped from its seams, she heard its agonizing cries for mercy before it exploded into an ashy powder.

Desti ran forward so fast, dropping to her knees, sobbing, as she placed her hand on Tate. Tears poured from her face, but she didn't care.

"Tate? Please wake up."

Desti shook him, his body lifeless and still. What if her power was too strong? What if it destroyed his soul along with the Shadow? But Desti shook her head. No!

"Please wake up. I love you. I love you," she cried. Her voice was hoarse and raw, just as her soul felt. She had lost so much in her life and just this once, she pleaded for mercy on her suffering. She cried out to Seraphiel to bring Tate back to her. Cried the pain of her loss and begged for mercy.

As Desti sobbed over Tate's slumped body, a soft whimper silenced her from her sorrows. A slight shift in movement. Desti pulled back and gasped. He moved again, and slowly, Tate lifted his head until she met the gaze of those brilliant green eyes, filled with love and remorse.

"Desti?"

There was no holding back. Desti crashed into Tate and embraced him with a crushing hug, crying into his shoulder as the tears splashed onto his bare skin. "I thought I lost you. I thought you were never—"

"Shh," he whispered. "I would never leave you."

Tate had his arms wrapped around her, holding her while they sat entangled in each other's bodies. "I'm so sorry, Desti. For everything. I tried so hard to break his control over me." Now Tate was the one with tears in his eyes. Desti knew he felt guilty for the suffering she had endured by his hands, but they weren't his doings.

"It wasn't you. Don't be sorry. I'm just happy that I have you back." When Desti pulled back, an electric energy fueled the air, swirling around them like a lingering shadow. She didn't break her gaze with Tate, just staring and getting lost in those eyes of his. Moments passed in silence, swept up in the arms of her love when she couldn't hold back anymore.

Desti closed the gap between them, pulling Tate into her in a devastating kiss, their lips meeting in a motion that was both desperate and gentle. His hair was curled into her hands, and her tongue glided into his mouth until she felt the warmth of his dance with hers. This kiss spoke of love. It spoke of promises and unspoken words, of fears laid to rest, and new hopes to be granted.

Chapter Thirty Three

Back to the Beginning

"It's up here," Desti called out.

After Desti and Tate escaped the dungeon, she ran back to find her mother, who was obliviously cleaning the living corridor. Desti had collapsed into her mother's arms and sobbed as she told Evie what had just happened, a running stream of tears coating her face. The comfort of her mother's arms wrapped around her melted away all the sorrows that came exploding to the surface. It was something her body so desperately craved—a mother's touch, love. Evie ran her fingers through Desti's hair until the wailing faded.

Desti pulled back and shifted her attention to Tate who was off to the side, watching with a look of endearment. He must know how much it meant to Desti to have her mother back. To have him back, and now that she had full control of her powers, she knew it was time to go rescue her friends and bring down those who caused them harm. It was time to burn their reign to the ground.

"Mom," Desti softly spoke. But before Desti could speak some more, a screeching echo sounded from down the vast hallway. Her eyes shot wide open, her heart beating too fast. Desti shot a look of worry over at Tate, but his face was stone cold.

Tate stepped forward and pulled Desti and Evie to their feet. "It's the Shadow's army. He must have signaled them somehow before you—"

"Incinerated him?" Desti finished.

Tate nodded. "This place may seem empty, but there are far worse things that lurk in these halls. We must go now before they find us."

Desti knew where they needed to go. It was time to go back to the Era of the Damned. The time before. Thoughts of what she was going to jump into shrouded her mind. Would it be total chaos ensuing? Or would everyone already be dead? It was terrifying that those thoughts could, in fact, turn into reality.

Just one moment at a time, she kept telling herself. It did her no good to dwell on the what-ifs. As the distant howling of furious demons came rolling in louder, she knew there was no more time to spare. Desti grabbed her mother's arm and didn't have to say a word for her to understand that it was time to go.

The three of them took off in the opposite direction, heading toward the place that was going to bring her home.

The portal pulsated, swirling around a black smog that seemed to fill the air with its electric power. The room was empty, except for the fireplace and a small table in the corner—just as she remembered it.

"Is that it?" Evie's voice croaked. Desti let go of her hand and stepped forward. "Yes. It should take us back to the time before. That's where Amaros and the Master have been keeping my friends." When Desti gazed into Evie's eyes, it was a look of utter fear, staring right back at her. She didn't blame her mother. They were in a war, whether they liked it or not, and sometimes war often brought out the worst of emotions.

"Everything will be okay. I promise. Tate and I will do whatever we must to protect you and the others."

Tate was standing over the portal whispering something under a hushed tone, and Desti wondered what he was doing. Before she could ask, he stood and looked up through tousled hair, his cheekbones etched in a sharp and beautiful design. "I had to set it to take us to the time before."

"How did you know it wasn't already set to that time?"

"When the Shadow was inside me, he had changed this portal to take anyone who jumped through to a different realm. A realm of eternal darkness lost with the souls of the damned."

Desti sucked in her breath. "How did you know how to fix it?" Tate offered a soft curve of his lips and held out his hand. "The Shadow may have had access to my thoughts, my memories, but it went both ways. I know everything that it thought, desired, and one of those things being the spell to change the destination of the portal."

There was no more time to wait and ponder, or to sulk in the uncertainties of horrors that could happen. The demons were closing in on them and Desti knew it was time to go. "Won't they just follow us?"

"I've set it so that only a human can pass through this portal. They will be trapped in this realm, where they belong," he growled; Tate's voice dropped an octave to something more primal. Predatory.

Desti stepped to the edge of the swirling black abyss, followed by Evie, and then Tate. Evie was shivering, despite the temperature of the air being sweltering. Desti offered her hand and then slipped her other one into Tate's. "Ready?" Desti called.

Just as the door burst from its hinges, a sea of black, vicious-looking demons came thundering in, but it was too late for them, because Desti, Tate, and Evie had already plunged into the darkness.

Desti would never get used to the terror that rushed her body, every time she jumped through time, through dimensions. It was as if the energy around her, alive and hungry, ripped her soul from her body, piece by piece. But almost as fast as that sensation came, it sucked away just as fast, before her body smacked into the ground.

The air ejected from her lungs, and Desti sat up, gasping to draw air into her lungs. Evie was on the ground, coughing, fingers curled into the dirt beneath her. For a moment, fear shot through her when she didn't see Tate, but then she heard a mumbling groan come from behind her.

"Fuck. I'll never get used to that feeling." Tate was hunched over, gathering himself. Desti returned her attention to her mom. She was shaking. "Mom, are you okay?" Evie drew in a sharp breath and nodded. "I'll be fine. That was just…a lot for my body."

Desti stood and started to take in her surroundings. The breath from her chest almost felt as if it got sucked out as she gazed upon the desolate land. The forest—once vibrant and full of life—was now burnt to ash. The sky was no longer a soft hue of blue and white, instead, this sky reminded her much more like the perpetual smog-coated, orange sky back in Mors. It was almost the color of blood as if the Earth could bleed from its wounds.

As her gaze slowly drifted downward, she found herself staring at the city where she had found shelter. Before, the city was at the brink of the end of its days, but now, it looked as if this city were plucked right from Hell itself.

The once proud and soaring skyline was now a silhouette of jagged, twisted metal and concrete, etching the sky. Glass windows were shattered, and now left only gaping holes in its absence. A thick haze of smoke and dust blotted out the sun, casting over the city with a perpetual orange twilight. Desti stepped forward, holding her breath as she took it all in. Rivers of raging lava snaked through the ruins of the city, casting an eerie, flickering light that made the shadows dance in unnatural ways.

"What happened?" Evie's breath quivered.

"It's the end of days. The Era of the Damned, and we just jumped right in the middle of it," Tate's voice came from behind. He stood next to Desti, taking in the horrifying view as she did. "Do you think we are too late?"

There was silence for a moment. Maybe she was too late. Seeing death sprawled across the land only made her doubt saving her friends, because saving them in *this world was* more like a far-fetched dream.

"It's never too late to save the ones you love."

Tate was right. They were down there somewhere, scared and alone. Desti had to come back to them and break them free of this terrible place, and even though the city was a vast wasteland now, she knew exactly where she would be able to find the Master and Amaros.

Chapter Thirty Four

A New War

A sea of black had enveloped the orange sky, casting down a darkness over the city. Desti glanced up for a moment and noticed the stars, glittering in their brilliance. At least there was something untouched by the hands of Amaros and the Master. A beauty that she could depend on when times got tough.

It took most of the afternoon to venture from the decaying forest and into the city, and the closer Desti got, the more this place reminded her of home. There were familiar and horrifying sounds that lurked in the shadows of the night.

Demons.

Desti knew those howls and hisses anywhere. They were here now, walking among the Earth for the first time, their bloodthirsty hunger desperately calling out for its next victim.

The only sound out in the night was the echoing of their calls. Desti knew that using her light would only draw unnecessary attention to her, and so they traveled through the shadows, the streets only to be illuminated by the moonlight spilling through smog above.

"Should we be out here? Maybe we should wait until morning," Evie whispered. They were crouched behind a building, gaging the distance between where they stood and the building where Amaros and the Master had cozied up.

"If we can just get there," Desti pointed, and continued, "Then we will find them." Evie sighed. Desti was so driven by her hunger to take down Amaros and the Master that her vision of how to go about that was clouded. Danger was no more in her eyes. Tate placed a gentle hand on her shoulder and leaned closely to her ear, his breath brushing against her skin. "If we continue like this, we will get caught. We can find shelter for the night, and first thing in the morning, we will find them."

Tate was right.

Desti gulped down her remarks and nodded. This wasn't defeat. She had to remind herself to take this slow because any wrong step and it would be too late. "You're right. I'm sorry. Let's scope out this building and set up for the night in here."

Luckily for Desti, she didn't have to smash any windows to get into the building. That had already been done. Sparkling shards decorated the ground under the glow of the moonlight. One by one, they stepped through the threshold and into the abandoned building.

Desti used her light once inside so that she could see around her. To her relief, it was empty. No demons lurked, waiting to spill her blood, just a few broken windows and broken furniture.

It looked as if they had stumbled upon an old apartment complex. There was a couch, and toys lying on the ground, as if the family had no time to gather their belongings before fleeing. She'd hoped that whoever they were, that they got away and were safe somewhere.

"Look. There is water," Tate called from the kitchen. He had found cups and water, something that was a scarce delicacy now. Desti's mouth dried at the thought of water. Her body desperately craved the crisp liquid to coat her tongue. Tate handed Desti and her mother a cup and then took a sip.

It was fresh, pure. Untouched by the rot that seemed to follow Amaros wherever he went. "Here, Mom, why don't you lay down?" Desti guided Evie to the couch and tossed a small blanket over her. It wasn't long before exhaustion swept over her face. Desti could tell her mother needed sleep, so she stepped away and nodded her head at Tate.

"Let's go find a room. I'm sure there is a bed somewhere."

Tate set down his cup and followed Desti around the corner and down the hall. This apartment had maybe three rooms max. Desti counted two doors to her left and one to her right. She reached for the first one and stumbled upon a small bedroom, no bigger than the cell that the Shadow had kept her in. For a moment, Desti felt as if the walls were closing in on her as if it were going to suck her in and yank her right back into Hell, but Tate placed his hands over the curve of her hips, and whispered, "It's okay. Let's lay down."

His voice was like velvet. Smooth and demanding. She would do anything for a taste of him. She drew in a breath and stepped in, heading over to a small bed placed in the corner.

"This feels weird," she said.

Tate sat next to Desti and offered a smile. "Why do you say that?" His eyes, his compassion, were back. The depthless, hollow, soul-sucking eyes that once laced his expression were finally gone. She could cry just staring at him, and a tear did slip down her cheek, but not from the look in Tate's eyes. She was crying for the family that once occupied this home.

"This room, *this home*, was once a place where a family felt safe. I can't help but feel as though we are taking something from them by being here."

Tate lifted his hand and brushed her tears away. "You are here to offer this world a chance. A chance to live a normal life and not grow up how we did. You being here is a gift from the angels. You are meant to be here, by my side. We are in this together." In the midst of Tate speaking, Desti leaned forward and pressed her lips onto Tate's.

A gentle, soft kiss.

A kiss that spoke love.

The air in the room seemed to twist around them, turning the energy into something more sensual. Desti pulled away from his touch and melted into his gleaming eyes. "I love you," Desti softly spoke.

"I love you too." Tate looked at Desti as if she were a treasure waiting to be found. A goddess to walk the Earth, and as his gaze raked over the rest of her, well, his gaze then shifted to something more…sensual.

He leveled his stare and took a firm hold on Desti's waist. A not-so-holy sensation rushed to her core, traveling down to the desperate place that ached for his touch between her thighs. Desti's throat constricted in a swallow as she imagined his length…his hardness. It had seemed like an eternity since she had felt his touch. His body, the way it pressed against hers and made her skin melt into his. She didn't know her body could ache so desperately with the absence of him until she was filling that void now. How did she manage being without him? She thought.

This might very well be her last night alive with the one that she loves, because tomorrow when the rays of the sun cast down on this city, a war was coming whether she wanted it to or not. She needed this. Desti needed *him*, just one last time.

Desti drank in his jade and golden eyes, leaning into him, while her hand explored more of his body down below. Desti hovered her lips just above his, her breath caressing his mouth just before he closed the space between them. A hushed moan escaped through her teeth as she took it all in. Their tongues danced together, in a passionate rhythm. A rhythm that craved one another.

Desti leaned Tate back slowly onto the bed until she was able to wrap her thighs around his waist. Even through his pants, she could feel his excitement for her touch beneath her.

No words were spoken, just an unspoken language of love and lust drifted through their gazes, the only sound in the room now was the ragged breaths of passion. His body glistened like a chiseled god under the moonlight, each ridge of his abs was taut and defined, and when she drifted her gaze to his, she could feel the hunger in his eyes undress her before his fingers were able to slip off her clothing.

A small curve tugged at her mouth. Tate's hands explored the curves of her waist, the small of her back, until he dug his fingers in deeper, an eager demand to have her body come closer, and Desti obliged.

Their mouths crashed into each other, no longer able to hold back the sexual energy that had been locked away for so long. It had been so long since she felt his touch like this. So long, since she had heard his ragged gasps escape his chest as he moaned for her. Despite his desperate ravishing of Desti's mouth, Tate managed to slip Desti's clothes off with gentleness, and now she lay there ready to take him in.

Desti leaned herself back and opened her legs, an invitation to the hardness that was hiding beneath his pants. She wanted him to have her in any way he possibly could. It wasn't long before Desti finally got what she wanted, as Tate stood before her, proud and wanting.

He crawled his way over her body, lingering just enough to where his skin just gently brushed against hers. She needed him, desperately. Desti arched her back, beckoning for his body to deliver the pleasure she was craving.

The moment Tate slipped himself inside, it was like a fire exploding within her, a river of ecstasy as his length filled every inch of her. Tate's breath washed over Desti as he thrust himself into her, and even his breath caressing her skin sent a shiver of pleasure to her core.

"Oh, Tate," she cried.

At her cries, he thrust into her harder, faster, as if he were releasing all his built-up rage and frustration that begged to come to the surface. Desti didn't mind, in fact, she pleaded for more. More of him.

She needed a release too. They both had been through so much. So much desperation, so much death, so much grief, and if this was her way of healing, well then, she was going to take him until her body was sore.

Desti clawed her fingers down his back which only made Tate growl in pleasure. "My goddess," he purred. Tate began placing gentle kisses along her neck until his kisses grew with intensity. His teeth grazed her skin just before he nipped at the sensitive spot on her collarbone. Desti wanted to scream his name, but Tate swallowed her moans of pleasure with a hungry kiss.

Pleasure was building. A heating sensation now rushed to her core, trickling down between her thighs, and with every touch of Tate's, it only grew. Her breaths were now ragged and begging, pleading for the sweet release she knew she needed.

"Please," she begged. Her words fizzled into the air, mixing with her cries for him. Tate's body tightened and his grip on her strengthened. She knew he was coming close to his end too, and so she arched herself into him, deepening the pleasure between them.

Only moments until they both would have what they craved. As a wave of exploding, soul-sucking, ecstasy rolled through her body, Desti cried out for Tate, pulling him in tighter as her body quivered from the release. Tate leaned back, and stiffened, groaning, gripping the meat of her thighs as he pulled her body closer with one last thrust.

Tate stayed lying on top of Desti for a moment, drawing in deep breaths of air. She could feel the rise and fall of his chest on her skin. Nothing could have felt more perfect than his touch now, knowing that he was alive. His midnight hair now tousled and messy, hung freely in his face. She pushed it back so that she could get a chance to gaze into his eyes—deep green, with flecks of gold, the most beautiful of irises she had ever seen.

Desti's voice softened, and she cupped her fingers through Tate's, meeting his gaze with her own eyes. "I can't believe that I got you back. I wasn't sure if I would be able to…" Desti felt her voice croak and her eyes began to well.

Tate kissed her fingers and returned his stare to her "The entire time, I was fighting to break free from him. I tried so hard

to speak to you. I am so sorry for the things that I made you d —
"

"You didn't make me do anything. None of that was your fault. You can't blame yourself for the things that he made your body do."

Silence overcame both of them. Maybe they were both pondering on their lives that led up to this moment. Lives that had endured so much torment and suffering. Desti never thought that she would be here, now, readying herself to wage a war on the kings of Hell. She had forgotten for a moment of her newly found powers, the light that hummed throughout her body. She was a weapon. A force to be reckoned with, and the demons of Hell better shake in fear in her presence, because tomorrow, when Desti stormed their land, she was going to reign a new kind of terror over their tortured souls.

She was going to reign the mighty power of the angels, and she'd be damned if she didn't make them scream.

Chapter Thirty Five

War

Desti slipped on her necklace, a symbol of the power she now held, something that once was forbidden in her world. She now wore that power with pride as she stormed her way toward bu lding ahead.

Amaros's building. The Master's building. Probably where so many people had lost their lives or had been subdued to a life of slavery. Desti thought of Peter and his people. Were they captured? Or did they hide like cockroaches beneath the city? Then a more painful thought crossed her mind: Anthony, her sweet young boy who had such a special place in her heart; Tess, her fiery, feisty friend whom she learned had a soft side; Kaelen and Seraph, the power couple who were loyal and loving; Rebecca, her new and kickass friend; and Brandon, her friend who had proven himself loyal over her time of knowing him.

They were her family now, and now, she wasn't even sure they were alive. "Are you okay, sweetie?" Evie asked from a distance, worry hazed into her eyes. Desti smiled, trying to hide her true doubts and worries beneath.

"I'm fine. I have to be." Desti clutched her necklace and gazed ahead. Tate was a few steps in front of them as he cleared a path toward the tower that Desti had briefly been inside.

"Where did all the demons go?" Her mother asked. If Desti remembered correctly, Ms. Clyde taught her about the beginning of the Era of the Dammed. At first, the lesser demons slithered their way from the depths of Hell to prowl upon the Earth. Most of them couldn't bear the sunlight, and so they were probably hiding under the city, in the crevices from which they emerged from.

As for the higher demons, well, they were probably posted around Amaros and the Master. Carefully stationed and ready for a fight. They wouldn't start their reign over the people until destruction and death took over every inch of land.

"I bet the lesser demons only roam the city at night. Since the sun is starting to rise, I would bet that we are safe from *most* of the demons. Desti emphasized the word "most" because that didn't mean that some of them *wouldn't* try to venture out into the world. Evie stiffened as if the mentioning of demons frightened her to her core.

Evie glanced over at Desti with a look in her eyes that screamed worry. "Do you think Rebecca is okay?" Desti gulped. Rebecca was ripped away from her by the hands of her enemies and there was nothing she could have done about it Guilt ravished her, tore away a part of Desti that made her feel normal, and she just hoped that she would be able to make things right.

"I hope she is. And when we free her, and the others, we will have our army of soldiers—the New Resistance—and we will kill every last one of those vile, evil demons, starting with three Kings.

Ah yes. The third King. The Devil himself. Desti hadn't forgotten about him, and she was thankful she hadn't run into the Devil yet, but she wondered how he would appear. Would he have the head of a ram, and hooved feet, snarling back his lips to reveal his sharpened canines? Or would he present himself as Amaros did—sophisticated, suave? Either way, she knew the time was coming. The evil that was seeping into this world was like a virus, spreading across the land and infecting the souls of the innocent. Sure, these people—the leftovers, the ones who didn't make it to heaven—may have not been holy to His standard, but that didn't mean they deserved a life of damnation.

Desti was going to save them. She was going to save everyone.

"Do you see that?" Tate was pointing ahead at a plume of black smoke rising above the towers. "They must be burning something."

Immediately, Desti's heart dropped to her stomach. *Please don't be burning bodies*, she thought. "You don't think—"

"No, I think they are burning something else. If they are, maybe most of them are gathered in the same area. It would be easier to take them out that way."

Desti nodded. Evie looked terrified but smiled when she noticed Desti watching her with worried eyes. Her attention was swiftly stolen when Tate whisper-yelled, "Come on. Follow me."

Tate ducked and took off into the crumbling streets, and Desti and Evie followed carefully behind him. There were distant sounds that seemed to swirl through the air as if the wind were carrying the agonizing cries of the tortured to them. It was a warning of what was to come. Of the promise the demons made to Desti. They were going to make her suffer in ways that she couldn't even imagine. She knew their threats, but Desti had a weapon of her own that would make them beg for mercy.

Entities of the demon realm were no match for heavenly fire—the light of the angels, and Desti's body thrummed with that power. She wondered if Anthony's powers had surfaced like hers, if he had been able to protect himself with it when she couldn't. She could only hope.

"Do you hear that?" Evie whispered. Screaming reverberated down the street, ripping through the air like a jagged arrow. Desti sucked in her breath as she stepped closer to the source of the call.

Tate pressed his body flat against a building and Desti and Evie followed. Whatever that noise was, it was coming from around the corner of the building. Desti watched, wide-eyed, as Tate peered around the bend, but he swiftly jumped back and shook his head. His eyes seemed to be glossed over. Desti narrowed her brows and stepped closer, but Tate silently held out his hand to try to stop her from seeing.

Tate never cried, but here he was, tears lining his eyes. What did he see? Desti swatted his hand away and took a look for herself, but the moment her eyes laid upon the horror that was happening before her, it was like the world came down upon her, crushing her with un-godly sorrow.

There was a woman on her knees; blood coated her hands and clothes as she begged for mercy from two demons. But As Desti got a closer look, she wasn't begging for mercy for herself, but for the young teen, one of the demons had dangling from its claws. This was the cry of a grieving mother. The wailing of someone who had witnessed the worst possible thing imaginable.

She begged the demons to stop, but Desti watched in horror as they took turns taking small bites out of the boy with their teeth. Their faces were like rats—elongated snouts and rows of small, dagger-like teeth. Blood oozed from the wounds, and there were many. Desti's throat tightened, and she could feel herself shutting down. She thought he was dead, but when a slight cry escaped in a gargling plea, Desti froze.

He's alive.

Desti looked back at Tate and by the way he was looking at her, she knew that he knew what she was going to do. Tate shook his head, but Desti could not leave this poor boy to be eaten alive.

The wailing of the mother never stopped, but when Desti emerged down the alley, it was like time froze. "Put him down!" she growled. Rage consumed her. Fury burned within her.

The demons hissed at the sight of Desti, something so close to Holy. The boy dropped to the ground and the mother lunged for her baby boy and clung to him with all her might, sobbing into his chest. There were two of the demons and as Desti got closer, she was now realizing how massive their bodies were, towering at least eleven feet high.

When she met their gazes, it was like looking Death itself in the face. An evil radiated from them like a lingering odor. They stepped away from the mother and her boy, paying no attention because there was a new threat now—her.

"Escaped One," one of the demons hissed. Its tongue shot out like a viper and slithered in the air. It was repulsive.

"You'll make Master very pleased," The one on the left whispered. It was as if their voices were delicate whispers that carried in the wind but were laced with venom. These were no lesser demons, that was for certain.

"I'm not going anywhere with you." Desti opened her palms, emitting a radiating white light from her fingers and as she lifted her hands, it was as if the energy in the air lifted with them. Debris in the alley raised from the ground, crackling as if it were being electrocuted, and along with that debris were the demons right there with it.

Their black, lanky bodies started to burn. Desti could feel their fear coursing through her mind. Her light was seeping into their souls, ripping them apart from the seams. Electric white, jagged cracks began to split on the demons' bodies, and as their screeching reached an octave high enough to break glass, their bodies split in half, as black, tar-like blood, oozed from the fleshy corpses.

Silence was immediate.

Desti sprinted forward toward the mother who just held her son to her chest. He was weak, but still alive. Thank God he was alive. "Here, let me help." Desti reached for the boy, but the mother jerked back with a terrified look burned into her eyes.

"It's okay, I won't hurt you. I want to help him. Please." Desti waited for a nod and then placed her hands on the boy's wounds that laced his stomach. He winced from her touch but then stilled. Desti thought of healing, of love, of fixing all the evil that infected this world, and slowly, his wounds began to close, followed by the color in his face returning back to life.

He gasped for air and shot up from the ground, glancing down at the healed-over scars. "How did you do that?" the woman cried. She looked so worn. So…defeated. Desti couldn't imagine what she must be feeling.

"Look, I am here to help, and I am going to make all of this go away, but I need you to take him as far away as possible, and don't go out after dark. Do you understand me?"

Fear laced the mother's eyes, but she nodded. Desti shooed her away and then turned around. The first eyes that she met were Tate's. He was almost smiling as he stared at her. "Desti…that was amazing. I can't believe…how'd you do that?"

Desti held up her hands and said, "I don't know. I just did. My powers are growing stronger by the day. I can feel it." Evie emerged from around the corner and gasped at the slaughtered bodies of the demons. "Did you do that?" she asked.

Desti nodded. "How?" Desti clutched her necklace and knew that it must have been because she wore this around her neck. It was a gift from the heavens, a siphon that tapped into the true source of the light of the angels. "I just did it. I don't know."

"Come on, we need to keep moving. With powers like that, I don't think we are going to have any problem slaying these mother fuckers." Tate took off toward the true danger, and Desti had a crushing feeling that she was going to face her match down this street.

Her time with the Devil was coming and she was not prepared for what horrors she knew he would bring upon her land.

Chapter Thirty Six

The Building

The air grew thick, an acrid stench of burning filled Desti's nose with every struggling breath. She coughed, trying to expel the gunk that she felt was coating her lungs. Her eyes burned and strained as she tried to peer down the street.

Whatever they were burning, it was creating the most putrid stench. Thick, black plumes rolled down the streets like crashing waves in an angry sea. And the screaming never stopped.

From what Desti could hear, it mostly sounded like men being gathered and tortured. Certainly not her friends' voices. It had taken another hour or so to make it across the city and over to the building that Desti knew the Master and Amaros had cozied up in. She made sure to make mental notes of everything she saw when the opportunities arose, and now that she was standing near it, it was without a doubt the place where she needed to be.

"Do you think they are in there?" Evie quietly asked. She was crouching behind a shattered car; its front looked as if it had been smashed with a sledgehammer. Desti pointed to a male, tall and sophisticated, his jet-black hair slicked back cleanly. Desti scoffed at the sight of him and his *perfection*.

"That one, in the black and gray suit is Amaros. He is one of the kings of Hell." Evie's eyes went big, and she made a grunting sound. "That's a king of Hell?"

"Trust me, Mom. He is dangerous. Try to stay clear of him if you can." Tate was scanning the perimeter of the building, carefully staying just outside of Amaros's view. Desti was waiting for him to report back what he saw. Hopefully, she would be able to get to her friends. Amaros was talking to one of his demons. His minions that did his bidding, and yes, they were terrifying.

Unholy creatures, looking as if they were plucked from a child's worst nightmares. A shiver ran down her spine at the sight of such a vile thing, thinking of the pain those claws could cause. Would they spill her guts on the ground and let the lesser demons lick up the shredded organs as they watched? Desti shook her head. It did her no good imagining these kinds of things.

"Desti," a slight whisper called from the distance.

Desti glanced up and saw Tate's hand wave her over. He was hiding down an alley a little bit closer to the street that Amaros's building was on. Desti pulled Evie over to where Tate was and then crouched until she was hidden behind a pungent-smelling dumpster.

Desti threw her hand over her nose and tried not to gag. "Did you see anything?" she asked. Tate nodded his head, his eyes gleaming with something other than the look of defeat, and this made Desti perk up. He must have good news.

"What did you see?"

Tate drew in a breath and leaned in closer. "They have some kind of camp surrounding the building. They set up a barrier. From what I could see, the higher demons patrol the perimeter, and Amaros's prisoners are all gathered in the front section, over there." Tate pointed to the south side of the city, where the worst of the destruction laid, where fires scorched the sky, and the only thing left of the structures were cracked concrete and shards of metal pipes.

"Of course, it would be over there."

"Are we just going to storm up there and break down their gate?" Evie asked. Desti smiled at her mother, such an innocent and ignorant question. "No, that would be too dangerous. We need a way to sneak in there and destroy them from the inside out. I know the *real* threats hide within that building."

And Desti was right. Amaros, The Master, they both would be somewhere in there, and Desti knew that they were prepared for a war, but she was too. Instinctively, Desti reached for her necklace and held it tight. "Okay, I think I have a plan."

There was a pile of broken concrete slabs, lying right on the back side of the building, the perfect place to hide from sight. Desti was kneeling, peering through the small cracks within the rubble, and was glaring right at a group of demons. "Just as I thought they couldn't get any uglier," she scoffed.

"It looks like a snake mixed with a human," Tate whispered. Tate had a deathly look in his eyes; the kind of look that promised vengeance on those who had crossed him. He turned to look at Desti and said, "I'm going to try to knock that one out before the others notice."

Just as Tate went to stand, Desti snapped her hand onto Tate's wrist, yanking him back down. "Wait." Confusion spread across his face as he looked at her with furrowed brows. "What is it?"

"I forgot about this until now. I can share some of my powers with you. It doesn't last forever, but it will give you some of the strength that I have." This was a crucial part of her plan, and she couldn't believe that it had briefly slipped her mind. She could transfer her light and share it with those who she pleased. Desti held out her open palms and drifted her gaze from Tate and then to her mother. "Take my hands."

Desti cupped her fingers around Tate's and Evie's hands and closed her eyes, imagining herself as a flowing river, as if their bodies were one with hers. She felt it, her light being drawn out from her. It started with a vibration in her head that seemed to slowly travel down to her fingertips, and when she opened her eyes, a dim glow appeared around where they were touching her. Evie inhaled as if she were fueling up from the power that now coursed through her, and Tate did the same, a look of fury now burning within his eyes.

"Do you feel it?" Desti asked.

Tate offered a playful smirk and replied, "Oh, I feel it." Desti leaned forward. "All you have to do is think it, and it will happen. Positive emotions seem to fuel it. They make you stronger."

"What about negative emotions? When Amaros was trying to bring your powers to the surface, he used me as a way to break you, but it worked."

That flash of memory made Desti wince as if it were causing her physical pain to relive that moment. "It worked in a different way. That way drained my energy, my life force, but when I use positive emotions, I can feel my body feeding off it, instead of the other way around."

"So, what is our plan again?" Evie asked. Tate had briefly mentioned his plan on their walk over here. He was going to try to take out the patrolling demons, one by one until it was clear to enter the building. Hopefully, no one would notice.

"Tate will clear the area around the back door, that way we can go inside and search for my friends. Anyone who is not a demon, we help. Do you understand?" Evie nodded, wide-eyed, and brushed her finger through her hair. "Okay. We can do this."

Before Tate ducked off toward the first demon, he planted a swift and gentle kiss on Desti's cheek and smiled. "For good luck," he whispered. And then he was gone. Her heart was slamming in her chest, and if Desti wasn't already kneeling, she thought she might have fallen over from the crippling anxiety. The love of her life, the man that she fought so hard to bring back to her, was now sprinting toward imminent danger, and it terrified her to her core. She didn't want to lose him again and the only thing that kept her from breaking was knowing that he now held a little piece of her within him.

With the power of his love, she knew that he would be able to yield otherworldly energy, and those demons better run for their damned lives.

Suddenly, a downpour of rain dumped over the city, as if the heavens we mourning from the clouds above. The sunlight was now shrouded with dark, heavy clouds, and crackling lightning that struck the city in blasts of fury.

Desti and her mother clung to each other as they nervously tracked Tate's movement. Most of the patrolling demons were up at the front, and only two seemed to walk this side of the building; their long, lanky legs scraped against the ground with every step. This sight was nothing short of nightmarish. Desti gasped.

"Look." She pointed. "He broke through the gate. Evie squinted her eyes and when she got a look at Tate she didn't take her eyes off him. "Do you think he knows what he is doing?" she asked.

Tate had been through so much in his life, and even though he suffered, that suffering molded him into something fierce, someone that should be feared, and when he had to protect the ones that he loved, well, you better watch out, because he will stop at nothing until he destroys whatever comes in his way. Desti had no doubt that he couldn't handle himself.

Desti watched as Tate lifted his hand, a dim glow surrounding his body, as he snuck up behind the first demon, appearing straight from the bushes in a surprise attack. Tate went to attack the old-fashioned way, with his bare hands. He wrapped his arms around the demon's neck and straddled his back from behind and twisted until Desti heard the snap. The titanic body thumped to the ground, and Tate jumped off, clearing it before anyone else would notice.

Desti's hair clung to her face and neck as the rain dropped down on her relentlessly. This must have been a gift from the heavens, a gift from Seraphiel, because, without it, she knew someone would have definitely seen him moving against the shadows. Another demon was now striding its way back that way and Tate moved flat against the wall. It looked like he was waiting for it to turn the corner.

Tate lifted his hand and the moment the demon turned the corner, he shot a ball of light right at the demon's face, blasting it with a miniature explosion of power. The demon dropped to the ground, clawing at its face, but Tate was like a predator, striking the demon so fast that it didn't have time to cry out for help.

He looked like a freaking god standing over the bodies of the things he killed, the ripple of his muscles flexing with even the slightest shift of movement. Desti drank in every inch of him as he made his way back toward her.

She blinked. Tate was waving his hand. "Come on," he whispered. Desti and her mother shared a look and then ran toward him. He was holding open a cut-out section of the fence so that they could duck through it. "Tate, that was amazing." His chest was rising and falling rapidly. Clearly an indication that he was still in warrior mode. "There are three more up at the front, but I can't get to them. Too many eyes. Let's go inside. Based on their movements, I don't think they will notice these two are missing for at least another thirty minutes."

That wasn't long. Thirty minutes to find her friends, bring them to safety and destroy all these evil motherfuckers. "I don't know what we are going to find through that door, but just remember that we are stronger together. We should be feared because we can kill them. We stick together no matter what."

Time froze for a moment, and when Desti gazed into the eyes of the two people that she loved, she took in a shallow, ragged breath and laugh-cried. Desti pulled her mother into her embrace first and cried into her should. "I forgive you, Mom." Desti felt the tension in Evie's body wash away from her in this moment, and then pulled away to turn toward Tate. "After this is all over, I want a wedding. Like how the people in the time before celebrated."

Tate huffed out a laugh, holding Desti's hands, and said, "That sounds great, but isn't it the man who is supposed to ask the woman to marry him?" Desti smiled. "Then you better ask me when this is over."

Another crack of lightning struck the area around them, casting a brilliant light over the shadows of the land. Maybe it was Seraphiel trying to tell her to hurry up. Desti sucked in a large breath and shoved open the metal door and walked into the darkness, ready to save her friends, even if she had to die trying.

Chapter Thirty Seven

A New Darkness

Desti had been shivering from being wet and out under the cold rain, but the moment she walked inside this building, it was like she had been transported into another realm.

"It's so warm in here," she whispered. It was almost too warm, too close to how it felt like being in Hell. She knew that the demons weren't far. If it weren't for Desti's growing powers, they would be venturing into the pitch darkness, but instead, she was able to cast a soft hue of white to illuminate the path before her.

They were inside a large hallway. One that seemed to stretch endlessly with no turn. "What are we looking for?" Evie softly spoke. Tate shifted his gaze to look back over his shoulder for a moment, his sharp features highlighted under her gentle light. He was beautifully handsome. Perfect in her eyes, and when her eyes traced every detail down his body, Desti had to bite her lip to refrain from jumping on him. Even in the most primal state of survival, looking at his perfection sent a heat to her center like nothing else could.

"First, let's find a door," she replied, snapping herself out of her desires. Tate continued forward and she and her mother followed, carefully stepping with ease, making sure not to make any blaring sounds.

"I see a door up here." Tate had ventured far enough that his body was swallowed up by the shadows, but it wasn't long before she had caught up to him. There he stood, before a towering metal door, just beckoning him to open it. Hesitation filled the room, spilling into every surrounding crack and empty space. Desti could feel it within her as much as she felt it seeping off her mother and Tate.

Behind this door could certainly mean walking into your imminent death, or it could mean stepping through the threshold into another realm. Who knew what she was going to find on the other side? But there was only one way to find out. Tate had the palm of his hand gently pressed against the metal, and Desti closed the space between them and placed her palm next to his. She glanced over and offered a smile. "Together."

"Together."

They shoved it open, and stepped forward, gasping, as terror enveloped their souls.

A foul, sweet, and coppery odor violated Desti as she stepped into the room. This smell was all too familiar; she had inhaled the aroma of death too many times not to know that she was smelling blood. Any hope that may have lingered within someone must have vanished because Desti could feel the despair in the room as if it were a living entity feeding off the suffering of tormented souls. This was what Hell was like. It was more than just a place. It was a state of being; trapped in a perpetual torment in your own mind, losing your sanity seam by seam.

Desti instantly reached for Tate's hand and squeezed it tight. Her light wasn't needed anymore now that she could see from a wall of orange flames that stretched around the perimeter. Desti clutched her necklace with her free hand and took in the horror that was before her.

As if being a scene plucked right from Hell, Desti was gazing upon what seemed to be a slaughter room. Her throat swelled as she tried to gulp down her sorrows, but no strength could hold back the tears that she was shedding.

Bodies laden the ground, soaking in their own pool of blood. But these bodies were shredded, torn into bits and pieces, some missing heads, others only missing an arm or a leg, but Desti had to hold her hand over her mouth to silence a sob that forced its way to the surface when she gazed upon small bodies piled in the corner. *Children's* bodies.

Desti staggered back and almost fell backward, and she would have if it weren't for her mother catching her. Desti looked back, no longer able to hide the tears that welled in her eyes and noticed the same mirrored expression lingering on her mother's face. This was a place of utter horror, but what did she expect when walking into the king of Hell's realm?

Desti scanned the area for any familiar faces, begging, praying that she wouldn't see her friends lying along the trail of rotting corpses. There were sharp metals hanging along the walls, stained with dried blood. This must be where the higher demons took out their torment and prepared for their meals.

Evie whimpered and clutched her chest as she doubled over in a sob. Tate appeared by her side and held her until her sobs faded into a silent cry. "I can't beli—"

She couldn't finish. The pain was too raw, too strong to speak. Desti knew because she felt it too, the crushing weight of sorrow on her chest as if someone had reached inside of her and ripped out her heart. It ached in a way that she didn't know was possible as she gazed upon so much death.

"I don't see them," Tate whispered. Desti carefully stepped over the bodies of the dead until she made her way to the other side of the room where Tate was standing. He had his hand arrested in motion, reaching for another door. What other horrors waited to greet her on the other side? She thought.

"Do you think they are alive?" Desti didn't want to imagine her friends succumbing to this terrible fate as these people had. Memories of them never faded from her mind. She always found herself holding onto the idea that they were still alive, waiting for her to save them. Desti wondered if Anthony was scared. She desperately wanted to wrap her arms around him, breathe in his scent, and tell him that everything would be okay.

Soon, she told herself.

Soon she would be able to tell that to all her friends. She drew in a breath and nodded toward Tate. "Let's go." Tate shoved open the door and Desti ran through, disappearing into another room of terror.

There was a lingering presence in the room that hung over Desti like a weight, the feeling of despair, grief, and sorrow, swirling around her like a sinful storm. What was this? It was as if this room had taken the worst memories and feelings that she had hidden deep within her and forced them to the surface. It was unbearable, the way that she wanted to give up. The fact that the thought of just ending this all would take her pain away.

Desti clutched her chest as if the pain had turned physical and kneeled on the ground. A gut-wrenching sob ripped from her chest as she cried with all her might. It seemed this room had the same effect on anyone who entered because when she slipped a glance to her side, she saw Tate and her mother cowering in the same desperate position. Evie cried tears of regret, tears of guilt, and Tate was crying tears of sorrow. She knew that this place was feeding off the worst parts of them and using it to crack their sanity. And this was drowning out her light. She felt her powers retreating from the overwhelming sensation of disparity. Any longer in this room and she might die right here on the floor. All hope for survival was diminished into nothingness and at this moment, all Desti cared about was bringing an end to her suffering. She found a rusty knife lying on the ground and snatched it within her grip, holding it so tightly, that her knuckles turned the color of bone.

She could end this suffering. End it all and finally be done with this life of torment. Desti held the knife to her chest until she felt the sharp pointed tip pierce the surface layer of her skin. She drew in a large breath, preparing for her final end, taking one last look at the people she loved. Their eyes gleamed with the same sorrow, and they just nodded their heads, as if waiting for her to plunge the knife into her heart so that they could meet the same fate.

And so, Desti huffed out what she thought would be her last breath of air and tightened, a sharp pain ripped through her skin, the knife only making it a few centimeters, until something snapped her mind back to clarity.

'No!' A deep voice demanded. She must have been the only one to hear it. Desti dropped the knife to the ground and clutched the small wound on her chest, blinking. "Did you hear that?" Desti seemed to be somewhat back to a normal state of mind. Evie didn't answer; her eyes were set on the dagger that now lay in front of her. She reached for it with trembling and wanting hands, but Desti slapped the knife across the room.

"Mom! No. This room is making us want to—"

Desti couldn't finish. She had to act quickly because when she glanced to her left, her heart almost stopped as she was witnessing Tate about to meet the same fate. "Tate!" Desti lunged for him and snatched a knife from his grip. He only glanced over with hooded, hazed eyes, as if he were in a trance. "Tate, listen to me. This feeling isn't real. We are in a trance. Wake up!"

Desti slapped Tate across the face, and something flashed in his eyes. He blinked. Desti cupped her hands on the sides of his face and began to beg. "Please don't lose yourself to this. I am right here with you. I love you and I need you."

She thought his mind had gone too far into the abyssal depths of sorrow, but when she felt him slip his fingers into hers, her breath hitched in her chest. "Desti?" Tate pulled her into his chest and drew in a large, ragged breath as he held onto her tightly.

"We need to get out of this room. Where is my mom?" Desti pulled back and saw her mother hunched over just staring at the floor. She was still lost in her mind. "Help me." Desti ran over to Evie and lifted her up as Tate got the other side of her. "Is there another door?"

Desti scoped the area and noticed another door hidden in the back corner. She wasn't sure what lurked behind, but she knew that if she didn't get out of this room soon, she would be just another dead body on the floor. Whatever waited for them on the other side, they would face it together.

Chapter Thirty Eight

Endless

It was another damned hallway, shrouded in a shadow depthless stretch. Desti peered to her left and then to her right, and it just seemed to go on forever. She sighed and pushed her back against the wall to steady herself.

"What was that back there?" Evie asked breathlessly. Her mother was now sitting on the ground, shaking, just staring off into the darkness that loomed around. Desti placed a hand on her mother's shoulder and leaned in. "That was evil. The most powerful evil I have ever felt." She glanced around, and continued, "This place feels like it is feeding off our misery. I can feel myself getting weaker every minute being in here."

"Do you think Amaros was able to break his curse? Gain is full power back?" Tate asked. He was still standing—still shirtless, pacing around the room. His taut muscles rippled slightly with his movements, and under Desti's angelic glow, he looked like a warrior standing before her with gilded abs. He was covered in dirt and blood, and yet, the very sight of him brought Desti back to a more primal state. She needed to stay focused.

Desti blinked and looked away. "Come on. We need to keep moving." She stood and held out her hand so that Evie would take it. Her mother seemed reluctant at first, almost crippled by the after-effect of that last room she had endured. Desti lowered her voice to a soft whisper and said, "Mom, I know it's scary, but we can't stay here. They will notice that their guards are dead soon and they will come looking for us. If we want a chance at winning this war, we need to keep moving."

"Come on Mrs. Anderson, I will watch your back." Tate held out his hand and offered a sweet smile. She nodded and stood as Tate helped her up. "It looks like there is no end to this hallway," Evie said.

She was right. This hallway must have some kind of charm cast over it because when Desti gazed down it, it was seemingly a depthless void. But maybe this was just a trick to her mind. This place…this building was the epitome of Hell, sulking in a shroud of evil in every corner, so why would this hallway look normal?

"It's a trick," Desti gasped.

"What?"

"Tate, we are seeing what they want us to see. This place is feeding off our misery, and the more we fall into its trap, the more we seem to get lost, but what if we could pierce this façade and see what truly was before us?"

"It makes sense. I've seen some crazy stuff that the Master and Amaros were able to do in Hell. But how do we break the charm?"

"Angelic light is more powerful than the darkness of Hell. The Holy book mentions that *my* light can cast the demons back into their realm. I have to be able to break it. Just let me focus." Desti closed her eyes, and at first, she wasn't sure what she was supposed to do—call out to the angels? To God? Did she even need to pray anymore? Desti cleared her mind and tried to shove away the evil presence that she felt was trying to cloud her, and then she just began to think of nothing.

Nothing at first. A clear, blank slate, and once her mind had forced the negativity away, that was when she invited her light to come to the surface. Desti wasn't sure what she was doing or if it was even working but she kept her mind focused, calling forth the light of the angels into her body and demanding it to flow through her veins.

I am light. I am holy. I am—

Tate drew in a shuddering breath and Desti then cracked open her eyes to see what caused that reaction from him. Suddenly, as if the walls were melting under the heat of a fire, they started to drip away, revealing a different reality underneath. Desti's light was no longer just in her mind; it was all around her, encasing her body in soft, delicate hues. It was like the midnight sky had rained down thousands of stars, her light unfurling like a beacon, dissolving the shadows in its wake.

No more evil magic loomed, no. Now Desti saw what really was surrounding her, and this hallway was much smaller than it appeared to be. "Woah, that was weird." She lifted her chin to gaze upon the last bit of her light chasing away the dark until the room was left quite…normal, save for the fact that it still looked as if it were in the aftermath of an explosion. There was a thick layer of dirt caked into the ground and the wallpaper was peeling away, exposing the plain stucco that hid beneath it.

The hallway only had a handful of doors, and the carpets that clung to the ground were an off shade of green. It reminded Desti of the color of puke. "I almost liked it better the other way," Evie scowled.

Desti snorted and then glanced at Tate. His face was set in a hard line, ready for trouble if it were to arise. "Which way?" she asked. Tate softened his stare when he met Desti's gaze and pointed his chin toward the farthest door down the hall. "I think we should go through that door."

"Why that one?"

"Look." Tate pointed down, and along the stained-green carpet, were splatters of blood trailing all the way to that door. "Someone was dragged that way."

Immediately, Desti's heart sank, her stomach twisting in knots. It was painful to think of her friends that she had left behind to be prisoners to such horrid creatures. Was that their blood? Were they okay? It pained her every waking second knowing that this could very well be a torturing fate of theirs. Tate must have seen the look in her eyes before she could blink away her tears because he reached for her hand and held it tight. "Desti, it's not their blood. Okay?"

"How do you know it's not theirs? The last time Amaros had Anthony, he was—" Desti choked on a sob and leaned forward, bracing herself on her knees. She couldn't finish that sentence. It was too painful. The last time Amaros had Anthony he was torturing him to try to bring his powers to the surface. Amaros didn't know that torture only damaged the soul and in return damaged the light within him. Anthony would get weaker and weaker until there was nothing left.

Desti thought of the scars that trailed along Anthony's body, the story that they told. He had spent years being tortured, used like some animal for Elijah's sick, twisted seances. Amaros probably was using Anthony in that way. If he had a way to yield Anthony's powers into his weapons, then there was no doubt in Desti's mind that that was what he was doing.

Desti gritted her teeth, setting her jaw in a hard line. "We just need to keep moving then. And when I find that motherfucker who hurt our friends, I am going to rip his throat out." She pushed past Tate and called out, "Come on. We can't waste any more time."

Desti shoved through the door without any thought in her mind. She was now clouded with rage, and this rage was building. She could feel the fire that had lit within her, and she was burning bright. The next thing she knew, she had ventured into a stairwell, steep concrete steps spiraling up at least five stories, and spiraling down below to somewhere darker—a basement.

But there was a small sliver of light flickering from the bottom of the stairwell, followed by a distant echo of screams. She held her breath and stiffened when she heard these cries for help. These were the cries of tortured souls, of someone being ripped apart. She had heard it before when stumbling upon the Master's chambers, watching him devour an innocent man, limb from limb until he choked on his own blood, and just as her mind was able to push away that horrid memory, a sweet, tangy aroma violated her senses.

Blood.

So much that it had traveled up the stairwell. Desti could feel the heat of Tate standing behind her; he placed his hands gently around her waist as if trying to keep her steady. Desti had to clutch the railing just so she wouldn't fall because it felt as if her knees were going to buckle under her fear. She felt him lean closer until his lips lingered above her ear. "Hold my hand. Stay close." He pressed a gentle kiss to her cheek and took her hand stepping past her, following the trail of blood that led down below.

Desti swiftly glanced back. Evie was right on her tail with an expression of pure fear etched into her eyes. This room, this place, was a weight of evil, crushing your sanity, crushing your strength the longer you stood inside. Desti had to remind herself that Evie must be feeling the weight of the darkness seeping into her soul. "Here, Mom, take my hand."

Evie slipped her fingers into Desti's and the three of them strode forward toward the sliver of light. The screaming stopped abruptly, which meant that either the torturing had stopped, *or* the person had finally succumbed to their death.

Please don't be my friends, Desti silently pleaded. She wasn't sure how she would react if she had to witness the blood of her own friends pooling on the ground. It would wreck every part of her soul.

Tate was now standing at the door trying to peer through the crack that was slightly ajar. Flickers of shadows passed over the light as if someone were walking by. Tate pressed his back against the wall and shook his head. His face was unreadable; he had always been so good at hiding his emotions. It was something Desti admired about her handsome warrior—his strength to overcome even the darkest of times. He met her gaze for a moment through his tousled hair, a hint of worry now gleaming in his eyes. If whatever he saw caused his expression to shift so abruptly, Desti didn't want to know what was happening on the other side of this door.

If whatever was beyond the threshold didn't kill her, then the slamming of her heart against her chest just might. The pounding was so hard, so fast, she could hear it thrumming in her ears. Fight or flight. Her body was in survival mode now, and she was ready to fight.

Evie gripped her hand. Desti drew in one last breath before following Tate through as he opened the door. Immediately Desti dropped to her knees and screamed.

Chapter Thirty Nine

The Devil

The putrid stench hit first—thick, metallic, and suffocating, a blend of smoke and burnt flesh that clung to the air like a second skin. Curtains of freshly carved skin hung from the ceiling as if a way to extend the suffering of the deceased. Desti heard Evie gasp and choke on her own gut-wrenching sob as she stumbled into the back of her. Tate was the only one who hadn't shrieked from the sight of what was in there, but his face did shift as if he were experiencing pain.

In the dim red glow cast by flickering torches, shadowy figures writhed in agony, their twisted bodies contorted in ways no human should bend, but as Desti gazed a little bit longer at the scene that was unfolding before her, she realized that they were…*alive.*

Along the blood-caked walls, lying in a pool of blood and feces, were her friends: Anthony, Tess, Kaelen, Seraph, and Brandon. Desti blew out an exhale, not realizing how much tension she had been holding in, but the moment she gazed upon her friends—alive—it was like a weight had dropped from her body. "Tate," she breathed.

"I see them."

Evie lingered like a shadow, quietly staying just behind Desti, not making a sound. "Where are the demons? I heard screaming." Desti glanced at Tate with curious eyes, but he shook his head. "They must have stepped out for a moment, which means we probably don't have long. We should hurry and get them."

Tate went to step forward, but something twisted in Desti, causing her to stay where she was. She reached out her hand, grabbed his arm, and said, "Wait." Something didn't feel right. A looming presence, an evilness hovered in the air with its oppressive weight, and just before Desti had a chance to speak, something yanked her body forward with an invisible force.

Desti shrieked. Before she knew it, she was in the arms of something big. Its skin was like the skin of a reptile, rough and scaly, rippling down into sharp tips, and it was the color of old blood—deep brown with a hint of red. Massive arms wrapped around her and the claw-like fingertips dug into her skin as she was held in place. She could feel hot, musky breath caressing her back with every heavy exhale this thing did. She had never felt so much fear in her life and the longer she stayed there, trapped within the arms of this creature, the more she could feel her light squandering inside.

"Tate," her voice whimpered. A desperate cry for help. But the only voice that responded sent a river of chills down her neck. "At last," it spoke, its voice deep and guttural as if speaking with a hundred different tones of rage and fury. Desti silenced. There was no denying it now. She knew who had her within his grasp. The one king who she had desperately wished she'd never meet, but it was undeniable now. Desti could feel his power radiating off him like an oncoming storm. It was the devil, and he had finally caught her.

She felt the weight of his presence linger over her ear; his mouth touched her skin, and his tongue licked the sweat from her cheek before speaking again. The devil's voice dripped with amusement, a dark, velvety tone that filled the room like smoke. "Did you really think that I wouldn't find you, sooner or later?"

He pulled her in closer, suffocating Desti with his presence, the air crackling with the evil that poured off from him. "Oh, I've been watching you, *Escaped One*, fed off your fear every time you slipped from my grasp. But here you are now, falling right into my trap. No more running. No more hiding. You belong to *me*." The devil spun Desti around so that he was now glaring down at her with his jet-black eyes.

He leaned in, his grin widening, revealing jagged, bloodthirsty teeth. "And this time, there's no escape. I'll make sure of that." His eyes burned with an unholy fire as he whispered, "Welcome to your eternal Hell."

Her voice was paralyzed, ripped from her chest before the shrill of terror could touch her lips, but that didn't stop Desti's body from feeling the panic coursing through her. Every inch of her body buzzed with fear, coating her essence and seeping into her soul. The devil was here. The look in Tate's eyes broke Desti's heart—longing mixed with fury, his fists bawled up tightly at his side, and Evie—Desti's poor mother—only gazed upon her with eyes of that of a grieving mother.

"What do you want?" Desti asked through gritted teeth. There was a pause, a moment of silence before the devil's tone shifted to something more primal. Predatory. "You," he growled. "Your blood." The devil pressed his mouth against Desti's ear, caressing her bare neck with his hot breath before speaking again. "I want your power."

She swallowed down a sob and didn't bother to try to blink away her tears as they poured down her cheek. So close. Her friends were *right there*, and she was so close to being able to break them out of this Hell hole, and now, Desti found herself a prisoner as much as them. The tips of his claw-like fingers dug in deeper, causing a searing pain to shoot through her, and in a moment of desperation, she fought back. Desti writhed and arched her back in a sheer panic, causing the devil's grip to temporarily slip. Desti dropped to the floor and the devil hissed in protest but before he snatched her back up, Desti started to pray.

"Seraphiel!" She begged for her angel to hear her, her sob now turning up an octave as the river of guilt and sorrow came flooding out of her. Then there was a chuckle, deep in mockery, coming from behind. The devil was laughing at her suffering, no longer attempting to yank her up in his grip, instead, he was now simply enjoying her suffering, as if he were watching her cries for help for amusement. "He won't answer you. You are tainted. Unpure. Certainly not worthy of *His* realm!" the devil seemed to be festering some anger because when he spoke of the angel, she could hear an undertone of a growl hiding beneath the surface of his voice.

He was wrong. With every part of her soul, Desti knew that the devil was wrong about her. She wasn't tainted; she was strong. A survivor. Desti reached for her cross necklace around her neck and said a silent prayer to her angel before a rage began to fester within her as well. He may be the devil, but she was a daughter of the angels, pure and full of their light, and if she believed it, her light could shroud the wickedness of Hell. She just needed to believe in herself.

"You are wrong about me. I am worthy." A fire burned within her, a light, coursing through every nerve in her body until it hummed with her true power. Desti kicked the devil's massive body with her foot as hard as she could, catching him off guard, and sent him flying into the wall behind him. The crashing of his body smashing into the wall must have been loud enough to wake her friends because they began to lift their heads as if coming out of a trance. "Tate! Grab them!" Every second counted. She knew the devil was going to come at her with everything he had, and so, if she could just get her friends outside…

"Desti?" Anthony called from below. Desti had to hold back a sob as she peered into the eyes of her sweet boy. "Oh my God! Anthony!" She lunged for him and scooped his frail body into her arms before whisking him away from where he lay. Tate was hurtling full speed toward her, toward her friends who still needed help. "Get them out!"

Desti watched as Tate threw Kaelen half over his shoulder, took Seraph's arms, and dangled them around his neck. He was whispering something to them, and she saw their heads move up and down.

Good. They are alive.

"Anthony. How do I get out of here?" Anthony was weak. She could feel it by the way his body struggled to do the faintest of moves, but nonetheless, he tried. She felt Anthony lift his arm and point toward the back end of the room, and so, that was where she ran.

"Tate! Back there. Go! Mom, grab the others and go!"

Desti didn't have time to think. She didn't have time to react. It was only survival in this moment, because the devil was coming, and he was going to rain down his fury with everything he's got. It wasn't even a minute before a rumbling began to shake the walls, as if the building itself was screaming with rage.

Pieces of the ceiling cracked and crashed onto the ground, parts of the floor split in two, and a growl so loud, so horrifying, pierced through the air and wrapped its way around her. Desti gasped from the terror it caused but didn't let that slow her down. Tate had shoved through the door and when he did, a blast of light shone through the crack.

He made it outside.

Desti cocked her head, immediately confused about how they were able to see the outside from the basement, but she had to remind herself that dark magic was at play here, and weird things happened in its presence.

She could have cried tears of joy for making it out of that soul-sucking place; making it out with her friends, but this feeling didn't last long. The moment she stepped through the threshold, her breath left her body as she gazed upon a new threat.

"Well, well, well. Looks like you found your friends after all."

Desti, Evie, and Tate stepped out from the shadows and into the sunlight that shone through the shroud of angry clouds above and almost dropped to their knees, her friends still hanging onto them with what little strength they had left. At least she got them out of there but now it seemed she may have just run into another trap.

Amaros stood before her, the Master as well, and then the devil came striding toward them, gleaming with rage, never breaking his gaze on Desti. The three kings of Hell, standing together, looking as if they wanted to rip her throat out.

Fear paralyzed Desti, her throat constricting so that her voice came out as a mere squeak. She tried to speak, but it was no use, the words wouldn't come. What would she say anyway? There was no use begging; no use for pleading for mercy, and that's what they wanted. They wanted to *feel* her suffering; *hear* her suffering as she cried out to them, and she would be damned to give them that satisfaction before meeting her end.

Under the blazing sun, standing in the destruction of this town, a war was now coming. A war of good and evil, and the only thing she and her friends could do was give this battle everything they've got. The future of humanity rested in Desti's hands, and now, it was her time to let her light shine.

Chapter Forty

Battle to the End

If Desti wasn't wearing shoes, the scorched gravel beneath her feet would have burned the flesh right from her body. She could feel the wave of heat radiating upward as the cracked ground baked under the blazing sun.

In this sea of doom, Desti was a shining light. Suddenly, the ground began to shake, splitting in half as a raging fire blasted from the depths of Hell that hid beneath her. Desti gasped and fell backward, pulling her friends down with her. She met the gaze of her friends and saw the fear that lingered in their eyes. She knew by the way that they looked at her that they thought this was the end; this was the way that they would finally die. "It's okay. We can do—"

"Silly girl. You still think that you have what it takes to defeat us? The three kings of Hell! You are no match for us, for our power is stronger than ever thanks to your little friend." Amaros flashed a wicked smile as his eyes gleamed toward Anthony. Desti sucked in her breath, knowing that Amaros had tortured Anthony to use his blood. He was Nephilim too, just as she was, and Amaros thought that Anthony's blood would end his curse too. It was a nightmare swirling around her reality, but this nightmare was very real. Desti tried to look upon Anthony, but he bowed his head as if he were ashamed to be seen.

"I'm going to kill you," Desti seethed, standing back on her feet. She swiftly glanced back, relieved to see that her friends were also not afraid to stand back up.

The Master snarled and took a step forward. "I can't wait to taste your flesh; hear your screams as I eat you alive."

"You lay one fucking hand on her and I swear I will rip your heart out with my bare hands." Tate had shoved his arm out and took a step in front of Desti, his face set in a hard line. There was only the predator in him in this moment, and he was going to do everything he could to protect her. She knew that. Her powers probably wouldn't last much longer for Tate and Evie, which meant that if they wanted a chance to kill these demons, they needed to do it quickly.

"Tate," Desti whispered. His gaze shot over to her briefly with an arched brow. "Remember what I shared with you. With my mom. You need to use it now." Tate's eyes brightened and he lifted his chin as if he knew what she was talking about.

"Enough! I want to end this." Amaros let out a gnarly snarl and lifted his hands above his head. The moment he snapped his fingers, a black plume of smoke emerged from the ground, and with it came a sea of demons clawing their way from the fiery depths. Desti had to take a step back as horror rose through her, bile burning the back of her throat. Everyone screamed in the midst of the chaos, and her friends seemed to drop to the ground.

Tess, Kaelen, and Seraph all doubled over in pain and hit the ground, curling into a ball. Their agonizing screams ripped through the air, and that was when realization descended on her. She had forgotten about their marks. That their souls had been claimed by the devil, and now it seemed he was using his power over them to wage this war.

They were fighting whatever magic he had gripping their souls, but then the screaming stopped, and they all stood, baring their teeth at Desti. Tess let out a snarl, and Desti thought she actually saw foam seeping from her mouth, like a rabid animal. Seraph and Kaelen both had a look in their eyes that made Desti flinch with fear. Whatever humanity they clung on to was now finally a distant memory, washed away by the evil grip that the devil had over them. Evie looked horrified and confused as she turned to gaze at Desti.

Before Desti could reply, the deep, guttural voice of the devil snatched her attention. "Did you forget that their souls are *mine*? They were a gift from the rulers of your realm, and now I am claiming their souls." The devil tilted his chin, and that was the moment that chaos ensued. Tess lunged first, clawing, and biting her way toward Brandon who was kneeling on the ground. He yelped in terror and staggered back before she was able to slash her fingers at him.

Thank God Tess didn't have a weapon on her, but that didn't mean she wasn't a killing machine. Desti slipped her gaze toward Tate, and he was already shoving Evie into a corner off in the distance, away from the danger. He went to hurtle forward, to grab Brandon, but that was when he was hit with a brutal force from his left.

"Tate!" Desti ran forward to help him, but Kaelen had blocked her and was now running for her, looking like she was going to rip out her throat. Desti threw her arm up to prepare for the hit as Kaelen came barreling into her with full force, knocking Desti to the ground. Desti was on her back trying to hold Kaelen off, but she was snapping at her as if she were trying to take a bite from her skin. Just as she thought this moment couldn't get any worse, an echo of snarls and hisses stole her attention for a heartbeat of a moment.

Desti slowly shifted her attention to her right and gasped as she was now staring into the eyes of three lesser demons. By the way their bodies stood on all fours, and their elongated snouts protruded with jagged teeth, she knew what she was facing.

"Hellhounds make a great army, don't you think?" Amaros's voice slithered throughout the air. Desti was too preoccupied with not dying to pay any attention to him speaking; she was still trying to keep Kaelen from eating her alive. "Kaelen! Please!" It was a chaotic storm of rage and evil, attacking from every corner. These hellhounds stared aggressively, as if waiting for their cue to attack. Maybe they would if she ran. The thought of their massive jaws ripping her limb from limb tore away at her courage inside.

Kaelen belted out a blood-curdling scream, drooling from the mouth, eyes rolling back into her head. Her lips were curved back in a snarl, flashing her hungry teeth.

It was no use. She was gone. Her eyes were nothing more than a black, depthless pit now, but still, Desti couldn't hurt her. She was her friend, and it was her fault Kaelen was in this situation. Desti used all the strength she had to kick Kaelen off of her and rolled over into a sprint.

Her eyes darted from every corner, scoping out her surroundings. *Where is Tate? Where is Mom?* Silently in her mind, she spoke to herself. Then she noticed them. Tate was fighting Seraph in a brutal brawl, blood splattering the ground like droplets of rain as they took massive blows from each other. Evie was being cornered by two hellhounds. Brandon had found a rock and was swinging at a sea of demons that were now snapping their teeth at him. Tess and Kaelen were both now coming for Desti, both looking like they were ravenous animals, and Anthony…

Where was Anthony?

Everything was happening too fast. This was too much. A sob tore from Desti's chest as her world crumbled before her. "Anthony!" she cried. Desti heard a scream come from behind her, but it wasn't Anthony; it was her mother. Evie's shoulder was in the mouth of one of the hellhounds, its massive jaws clamping down with no remorse, and it was dragging her toward the Master.

"Mom!" Desti tried to run to her, but Kaelen and Tess had caught up to her, snatching up her arms in a firm grip. Their snarls echoed around her head, a reminder that her friends were lost to the abyssal blackness of evil. Tears ran a stream down her cheek as she tried to pull herself away from them.

"It's no use, you pathetic little girl. Did you really think you would be able to beat the three kings of Hell? Kill us?" Amaros sneered. His arrogance never stopped slithering from his lips as he spoke. He took a step forward and lifted his hands, and then snapped. It was like the world stopped for a moment. Silence descended over the chaos. In a way, it was a calm that drowned out the terror that had coursed through the air, but that calm didn't last long. He flashed a wicked smirk, never breaking his gaze with Desti, and that was when she knew that something terrible was about to happen.

Anthony appeared from the rubble of the land, being carried by one of Amaros's demons, its elongated claws wrapped around his frail body like twisted tree branches. Desti's heart sank into her gut. "No," she breathed. Desti had stopped trying to break free from her friends' grip because this had now stolen all of her attention.

"Please let him go," she sobbed. If it weren't for Kaelen and Tess holding onto her, Desti would have dropped to the ground.

Amaros only smiled, as if enjoying her delicious suffering from afar. The devil let out a snarl and stepped toward the demons carrying her boy. He slipped a glare of pure evil her way before taking Anthony into his own arms. "You Nephilim are valuable to us. We've been searching your realm for years, hunting them down one by one. You are a threat to our reign, but..." the devil licked his lips, and continued, "that power can be transferred to us for some time. This one has given us quite a delicious power."

The Master, Amaros, and the devil all created a circle and placed Anthony at the center, his limp body barely able to move. Desti's heart ached at the sight of this, her body shaking with terror. She clenched her fists tightly and watched in horror, as she knew what they were about to do. "Please," she begged. Her voice barely came out as a whisper.

They paid no attention to her desperate plea. The Master began muttering a language unknown to Desti under his breath and then carved strange markings on Anthony's arms with his sharp claws—the same runes that were carved on the outside of the cave entrance where Desti had first found Anthony. She then realized that his power could be stolen, using a demonic ritual. Anthony winced the moment the Master sliced through his skin, tiny streams of blood began to trickle down his arm and pooled around him.

Amaros tilted his head back and inhaled, then proceeded to join the Master in his chant. The devil—the most terrifying of them all—began to draw in heavy, ragged breaths before lifting Anthony upwards. Anthony's body started to emit a soft hue of light, but the color of his skin was fading—he was dying. He was too weak for this. Desti tried to yank her arms free but felt Tess and Kaelen dig their nails in deeper at her attempt, growling and hissing in her ears.

In a brief moment, Desti glanced around for the rest of her group, but that only made her sorrows sink deeper into her chest. Her mother was lying lifeless in the jaws of a hellhound, blood coating her body like a second skin, Brandon was on the ground, barely holding off the demons that were attacking him, and Tate was on his knees, taking blow after blow to the head by Seraph's fists. It was her worst nightmare unfolding before her, and it was so horrifying, she almost couldn't believe it to be true.

The chanting stopped, and it was the silence that ripped Desti's gaze back to Anthony. Amaros pulled a silver dagger from his waist belt and hovered its gilded tip just slightly above Anthony's throat. "No!" Desti screamed, but as her scream left her lips, Amaros flashed her a smile, and then sliced Anthony's throat open, forcing her to watch the blood of her sweet boy pour down his body. The sounds of his gurgling and gasping for air sent Desti over the edge. She screamed so loud, so passionately, that it caused everyone to flinch at the sheer terror tearing through the air around them. Desti managed to pull her arms free from Tess and Kaelen for a moment but wasn't quick enough to catch up to the three kings before they began to feast on Anthony's blood. That was what they were after. His Nephilim blood, because it gave them the power of the angels. Desti wasn't sure how long that power would last but right now, she didn't care, the only thing that clouded her mind was the color red. The sweet, tangy smell of blood that coated the air.

Silence overcame Anthony and then his body went limp. Realization struck her like lightning, knowing that he was dead. "No," she whimpered. Sorrow and guilt thrashed around her body like an unrelenting storm of despair. This was her fault. When the three kings had finished licking the blood from Anthony's deceased body, they turned their gazes back to Desti, smiling, and looking…powerful.

"Did you like the show?" the Master called out before Desti felt the grip of his Marked Ones take ahold of her once more.

Chapter Forty One

Death

"You fucking monsters!" Desti screamed with rage, shaking with no amount of fury any person should be feeling, and the more they smiled at her with those wicked grins, the more Desti's anger festered within her.

"Shall we continue, *Escaped One*?" Amaros snapped his fingers, and then the hellhounds growled from her side. Evie was still hanging from the hound's mouth, but a sliver of relief flushed through her when she saw her mother take in a shallow breath.

"Don't get your hopes up just yet. I kept her alive just long enough, so that I may watch your grief drown you as I kill her." A quiet, desperate gasp forced its way down her throat as she had no choice but to watch. The devil strode for her mother and held out his hand. The hellhounds cowered and bowed their heads in the presence of their kings and dropped Evie to the ground. Her body was barely breathing, barely moving, clinging on to the thread of life. "Amaros, please! Stop this! I will surrender to you if you just let them go. Please don't hurt anyone else."

Desti's sobs became unbearably raw, tearing away at her voice as she cried out in desperation, clinging on to hope that he would take her offer, but only the eyes of the evil stared back at her, and those eyes spoke the promise of death. Promise of torture and suffering. There was no use, she knew that now. Desti didn't want to use her powers against her friends, but she had no choice. The devil was going to kill her mother if she didn't do something. Desti glanced over her shoulder for a moment and noticed the same sad expression in Tate's eyes. He looked at her for a moment, and she had never seen him look so sad, so defeated. Tate hung his head as if he knew what was about to happen but couldn't bear to watch because there was nothing he could do. He too was on the verge of collapse from the brutal beatings he endured.

The devil yanked Evie's head up by the roots of her hair, a slight whimper escaped from her, and then he held out his sharpened fingers as if he was going to slash her right open. Desti sucked in her breath in horror, clenching her jaw, and just as the devil's arm came slashing downward, something knocked into him with incredible force, knocking Evie out of his hand. A growl so loud, so full of rage, roared through the air as he rose from the ground.

"Who dares to interrupt me?"

Desti's heart was slamming in her chest as she darted her gaze all around. But then she saw it—the wagging tail, the matted coat of fur. "Jet?" she breathed. Her little furry friend that she had met when first arriving in this city was now here and had just saved her mother's life. But if Jet was here then someone else must be around too.

Desti craned her head back, searching for anyone who didn't look like they crawled from the depths of Hell, but the horde of demons that the devil had surrounding her was overwhelming and made it difficult to see. Then she heard a bark, and then a whistle from afar.

It was like watching everything happen in slow motion as an explosion came out of nowhere and blasted everyone back. The brutal force hit Desti like a punch to the gut, sending her and her captors flying backward. Everything went down and then screaming erupted. Desti stumbled to her feet and found Tate lying on the ground next to Brandon. "Tate, are you okay?" Desti was running for him with her arms out. Brandon looked stunned and was now starting to bring his body back to his feet. "Help me!" she called. Brandon nodded and took one of Tate's arms and Desti took the other until they were able to drag him away from the chaos that was ensuing. Desti managed to drag Tate all the way to the other side of the building and hide him behind a bush.

"Desti, I'm so sorry—"

"Don't. I can't think about that right now. We need to get him out of here, but first, I need to go get my mom."

"Desti, you can't just go back in there. It will be a death sentence." Brandon pleaded, but it was no use. Desti placed her hand on his shoulder and asked, "Will you please stay here with him? Make sure he is safe?"

Brandon didn't respond at first but Desti's pressing stare eventually got him to nod his head. "Don't worry, I will be okay. I am Nephilim, remember?"

Brandon grabbed Desti's wrist before she could stand, staring at her with worry in his eyes. "What about the others?" She knew he meant their marked friends. But truthfully, Desti didn't know what to do about them. If there was a way to reverse their curse, she sure as hell didn't know how to break it. "I'm sorry," was all she said, before darting back into the fiery battle.

There was smoke everywhere, clouding every bit of vision she might have had, so Desti had to rely on her hearing. All around were echoes of snarls and hisses, grunts and yelps. She wasn't sure what was making those noises, but she made sure to stay as far away from them as she could.

I have to find my mom, was the only thought that was filtering through her mind. Desti tried to remember how to get to where she had been standing before the explosion, guessing the number of steps it would take to get to her mother, but then her foot hit a familiar boulder, one that she had tripped on just before being snatched up by Kaelen and Tess. Desti knew her mother had to be about ten steps forward and slightly shifted to her right.

It was only a black plume of smoke mixed with blazing flames licking the sky, but she ran full force into it with no other thought in her mind. A wave of heat blasted through the air, almost burning every time she took a breath, but Desti shoved that pain away and kept searching. It sounded as if everyone was fighting in the roaring flames.

Then it hit her—there were others here now, screaming from the shroud of smoke. "Back up you disgusting motherfuck—"

"Rebecca!" Desti called out. She knew that voice, that sassy and arrogant snarl from anywhere. Desti took a few more steps forward until she came up behind her fiery red-headed friend, and then realized she was fighting off two lesser demons. She had a sword in her hand and was limping on her left leg.

"Oh my God! I thought you were dead!"

Rebecca shot Desti a swift glance and tossed her a dagger from her belt. "Help me kill these things, then we can catch up!" Tendrils of her red hair whipped around like electric bolts of fire, her body twisting and lunging through the air like the fierce warrior that she was. Desti had almost forgotten how intimidating Rebecca was, but seeing her back in full action, fighting these creatures really brought everything back. Desti didn't waste any time and lunged for the demon closest to her. She ran and then slid, ducking away from its viper tongue, and then stabbed the demon in the leg. Black, oozing blood squirted from the demons, but it only seemed to hiss in annoyance at her attempt to injure it.

"You need to go for the throat!"

Desti nodded and tried again. This demon looked like the crossbreed of a snake and a pig, something only you would expect to see in your worst nightmares. Desti cringed as it flashed its razor-sharp canines and jumped back as it took a snap at her. She took her dagger and sliced it down, grazing the side of its face.

This only seemed to piss it off more. Desti hadn't trained as much as Rebecca in battle, but she had a new weapon burning within her. Desti threw the dagger down and drew in a deep breath, focusing on harnessing her energy to the surface. A white light began to start at her fingertips and then eventually surrounded her hands. She could feel it now, the power of the angels flowing so freely within her.

The demon didn't seem fazed as it lunched for her, but Desti was quicker, as she held out her palms and shot a beam of blazing light at the creature. Its body exploded the moment her light touched it, sending its guts and blood flying into the surrounding debris. Rebecca's jaw dropped and she stepped back almost forgetting that she too was fighting a creature of her own, but Desti just said, "Move!" and then blasted that demon with her light too, until they both were left standing there covered in its thick ichor.

"Holy shit Desti."

"Where is my mom? We need to find her." Desti handed Rebecca her dagger back and wiped her hands on her pants. Rebecca's curly hair was now stuck to her face with sweat and God knew what else. She nodded her chin to her right. "I think I saw something over there."

"Come on." Desti pulled Rebecca into a sprint, her chest heaving as her lungs begged for clean air. "Where did you come from?" Desti asked.

"I found this group in the city. I was hurt and alone and they took me in."

Still running through the rubble, Desti called back, "Was his name Peter? Lorie?" Rebecca laughed and said, "Yes. How'd you know?"

The last time she saw Peter, he was lying on the ground, beaten and broken, his skin decorated in lacerations. And the burning hatred within his people's eyes for her never left her mind. It haunted her to this day, knowing that she had betrayed them. Him. Desti thought Peter was dead then. She saw the Master take him after eating Lauren, but then again, Desti had run away before watching the horror unfold. He must have gotten away somehow. She just assumed that Peter had met the same fate as his friend, which made her feel all the more guilty. "I left him…" her voice trailed off. Desti cleared her throat and yelled over the chaos of battle, "He took us in too. We thought he was dead, and then everything went crazy—"

"Desti, I see her!" Rebecca darted forward and kneeled next to Evie who was lying underneath a pile of rubble. The explosion must have sent her through a wall or something. A tiny stream of blood dripped from her mouth, and her eyes barely fluttered open. "Hold on, let me see her." Desti took her mother into her arms and pulled away the remaining rubble before focusing her attention on who was lying in her arms.

"Can you help her?" Rebecca asked. Desti glanced over with tears in her eyes. "I'm going to try." Desti closed her eyes and pulled her mother's head into her chest before she began to pray to Seraphiel to give her strength. Desti pleaded to be able to send healing energy from her and to Evie.

Suddenly a white light began to glow around Desti, starting from her chest. She watched as it traveled its way to her fingers until she felt the energy blend into Evie. Desti could feel Evie's body siphoning the strength from her own, but she ignored the growing ache of weakness and kept feeding that light to her mom.

Evie gasped, her breathing becoming more regular, and even the color of her skin was now less gray, but as Evie seemed to grow stronger, healing from her wounds, Desti's body began to crumble. Rebecca shoved Desti back and took Evie from her grip. "You're giving too much. You will kill yourself."

Desti fell back, dizzy, and disoriented, and as she tried to stand up, she felt the ground shake from behind her. "There you are," the devil growled. His hooved feet were rumbling the ground as he ran full force toward her. "Run!"

Rebecca took Evie into her arms and disappeared into a wall of smoke as Desti stood and turned to meet her fate. This time was coming, she knew eventually this war between good and evil would ensue. Screaming reverberated all around this chaotic storm, and Desti now knew that this was the sound of war. Peter and his people had finally waged their war on the evil of this city, and Desti was now about to meet the same fate.

As the devil came rushing for her; the last thing she saw before being ripped into battle was Tate being dragged by his hair off in the distance.

Chapter Forty Two

Good vs Evil

There was no time to act before his clawed hands surged forward in a striking swipe. Desti ducked and fell backward, just barely missing the hit. "Tate!" she called out. She thought he had been safe where she left him, but maybe something found him. The devil snarled, stealing her attention back to the battle, and took his other clawed hand, swiping at her, aiming for her neck. Desti shoved out her hands and blasted the demon with what little bit of power she had left in her body—which was not much, since she had given most of it to her mother. It would take time to replenish her strength.

The devil hissed but was merely unamused at her attempt to harm him. "You're weak," he sneered. There was no hiding the exhaustion that hovered over Desti like a cloud. Her energy was gone, her light was gone, and now her hope…

"Never underestimate your opponent," she hissed, knowing that the wavering in her voice betrayed her. There was no hiding the exhaustion that now clung to her like a weight.

The devil chuckled, now swaying from side to side as if trying to confuse her. Desti desperately wished she hadn't let go of that dagger now. As the smoke began to clear from the gusts of wind blowing through, the true terror was now unfolding like a scene from a nightmare.

Bodies laden the ground in guts and blood, crimson red seemed to coat every porous surface of the land. Some of the faces she recognized to be Peter's people scattered along the rubble and the deceased. But not only the good lay in their own blood. Demons of all shapes and sizes were among the slaughtered, which made Desti pull in a small breath of relief. "Your people will burn for what they did. Their souls will be *mine* to torment for all eternity once you are dead."

Desti flinched. Was her life really the only thing that stood in the way of the rest of these people suffering? She had no idea how she was going to save the entire world from this hell but killing the devil would be a good start. Desti hardened her stare and flashed the devil a smirk, "I'm not that easy to kill if you haven't noticed." Desti drew in a large breath and thought of her light, her power, and begged for it to come to the surface. Just enough rushed to her fingers and she shot her light right into the devil's eyes.

He screeched in agony and staggered away from her. This was her chance to run. While the devil was temporarily blinded, Desti took the opportunity to hurtle her body as fast as she could manage toward Tate, toward the love of her life. He was her everything, and if he were to die at the hands of these creatures, then she didn't know what she would do.

The city was a disaster—half-blown-up buildings and rubble littered the streets, the ground was split as literal Hell spilled into their world, and bodies—hundreds of them, littered the ground. Tate had to be somewhere.

The longer she searched for him, the quicker her heart sped up, fear now exploding throughout her body with the thought of losing him. "Tate!" she called. Desperation had fully taken hold of Desti, and she didn't care anymore about being quiet.

Desti yelled as loudly as she could, her voice wavering with worry and sorrow. "Tate, where are you! Please!" Just as she thought she was about to scream from the pressure of her worries building, she heard chatter around the bend of a building. Desti quieted herself and followed the noise, but when she peered around the bend, what she saw was like a dagger to the heart.

"Ah, we meet again. I sure do miss having you around, *Pet*." Amaros stood before Tate, seemingly unharmed, striding around in his pressed suit, wearing his arrogance like a cologne. Tate was on his knees, and his arms were being pinned behind his back by the Master. His snake-like tongue whipped out and shot to Tate's face as he tasted his flesh. The Master leaned his head back, inhaling as if really tasting the fear coming from him.

If Tate was scared, he sure didn't show it on his face. Even now, he was a master of facades. Desti knew she had to get close to him, but now with the smoke cleared, visibility was an issue. She would have to take a longer way around, behind the buildings, and snake her way to the other side. Desti ducked off behind the closest building to her down an alleyway and sprinted as fast as her legs would let her.

"Come on. Hurry," she told herself. Silence was like a mist now, seeping its way slowly over the land; the screaming and sound of war fizzled away like a distant nightmare, which was not a good sign. This meant death. Desti knew hundreds had probably died fighting the demons of Hell, and at this point, she wasn't sure which side was winning, because when she glanced around, every street had bodies—human and demon—lying there like an offering to the darkness.

She desperately hoped that Rebecca got her mom out safely, that Brandon—wherever he was—made it out too. And as for her marked friends, that was something she would have to learn to let go of and welcome grief into her heart once she was safe. Maybe they were killed in battle. She wondered if their souls were now damned to Hell forever if they had been, but Desti shook her head and tried to focus on what was imminent—saving Tate.

She was now around the other side of where they stood, and it still seemed Amaros, and the Master were toying with him. Drawing out whatever torment they seemed to be enjoying causing him. It angered Desti to her core to see Tate being held down like this. To see Amaros sneer in his face. Anger was the only thing filling her body and right now; she didn't care about the chaos around her. Her focus was solely on the love of her life.

She listened.

"I already told you. I don't know where she is, and even if I did, I would never tell you." Tate spoke so strongly in the presence of such evil, holding his chin up high as the wind blew his midnight hair around like whips. The Master tightened his grip on Tate, and she noticed a wince from him. Was he in pain? She thought.

Amaros took a step backward for a moment, a sneering smirk plastered on his face and reached for something from behind him. "If you won't tell me where your precious love is, well then you are no good to me anymore. I am growing bored of this war. It's time to end it." Amaros pulled out a long spear, its tip gleaming with fury under the blazing sun rays. Desti immediately sucked in her breath as a rush of adrenaline coursed through her.

He was going to spear Tate. Desti couldn't bear this. She couldn't bear to watch another person she loved being slaughtered by the hands of them. The image of Anthony's blood streaming from his mouth before taking his last breath flashed through her mind. It was a painful memory…so new, so raw. Almost too painful to think about. Desti blinked away her tears and panicked as she was now watching the same horror unfold before her again.

She had to do something, but it was as if her body had already made up its mind, because before she knew it, she was sprinting toward Tate, toward Amaros and the Master, and as Amaros had lifted the spear above his head, bringing the spear down to strike Tate, Desti leaped forward and took the spear into her chest instead.

Pain immediately sent a shock to her system. A sharp ringing blared in her ears and breathing became painful as she gasped for a breath. She felt Tate and the Master stumble back and the last thing she saw before being sucked into death was the look of horror in Amaros's eyes. She had never seen a look like that come from him. This was the look of fear.

Coldness descended upon her, a gradual surrender to stillness as Desti felt her body sway backward. She hit the ground. Her grip on the world was slowly unraveling, blackness now spilling into her vision like spilled ink. And before her body slipped into the void, the sound of Tate's agonizing scream was the last thing she heard before death claimed her.

Chapter Forty Three

No More

The first thing that Desti noticed was a sweet and sultry smell that lingered in the air. She inhaled deeply and cracked open her eyes as she sat up from the ground. Her fingers padded the soft, green bed of grass and then danced their way toward a blooming flower—white petals with a yellow center. A gentle breeze blew through the meadow, twisting her loose strands of hair in a delicate dance around her face.

Where am I? she thought.

Desti's memory was foggy, but slowly, bits and pieces began to trickle their way back into her mind.

The war. Anthony. Me.

"I died…" A realization came crashing into her full force. Despite being in this serene landscape, fear rushed through her body, but just before she felt she was about to go over the edge, a hand rested on her shoulder, bringing her back down.

"Don't worry, child."

Desti knew that voice. The velvety smoothness of his tone. Desti turned around and blew out a sigh. "Seraphiel." A brilliant white light outlined his body as if he were part of the sun. Seraphiel held out his hand and said, "Come. There is much that you should see." Desti nodded, wide-eyed, stunned. She slipped her fingers into his hand and pulled herself from the ground.

"What happened?"

There was silence, but this silence wasn't like an eerie silence that seemed to creep over your nerves like how it did down in Hell. This silence was…calming. Seraphiel led Desti down a path of soft grass and toward a massive structure— marbled pillars soared through the sky that seemed to have no end, its gilded design glistened under sunrays that seemed to have no specific source. Desti peered around her, taking in the peace and the beauty that stretched across the land.

"Come child. You will see."

Desti continued to follow Seraphiel into the massive structure and ended up standing before some kind of translucent orb connected to a marbled stand. A gentle hue of lilac and baby blue seemed to pulse and swirl within the orb, as if it were dancing, and as Desti stepped closer, it became clearer what she was gazing upon.

"Is that the Lux?" Seraphiel smiled and lifted his hand to touch the Lux. "Because of you, our Light has been restored. When Amaros was cast down, he stole our Lux thinking that he would be able to control all the realms, but he didn't consider the curse that tainted his blood then, tainted his power. We have been searching for it for many years. With us unable to enter the demonic realm, our only option was to hope that someone born into your world would help bring it back."

Everything was now clicking, like a puzzle piece sliding into its perfect spot. Desti shifted her gaze up and asked, "So that was why the angels started creating the Nephilim. So that one day, someone would be able to enter both realms and bring this back to you."

Seraphiel offered a gentle expression and nodded "Yes. We took a more human form, and went across the land sprinkling our prophecy around in hopes that it would one day make it to the right person. A true Nephilim. Our angels, in the beginning, were able to create offspring, but the longer our bodies were away from Heaven, the weaker we became. We had no choice but to retreat back to our realm."

"So, how come there were Nephilim in my generation then?" Seraphiel placed his hand on the Lux and sighed. "Some of us waited years for the prophecy to start, but as the years went on, we realized that that person must have not existed yet. I and a few more of my angels set out to your world, one more time, to plant our seeds, so to speak." There was a pause of silence, as if Seraphiel were contemplating his next choice of words wisely. "When I found your mother, I didn't expect to…"

His velvety voice slowly faded, but Desti filled in the missing pieces. "Fall in love?" There was a glimmer in his brilliant eyes. A look that spoke of regret and longing. And then like a rolling storm, it hit her. Desti gasped and staggered back. "Wait. Are you my…?"

He couldn't be. Desti held her necklace between her fingers and drew in a ragged breath. "You're my real father?" A gust of wind seemed to blow through out of nowhere, whipping his magnificent hair around his face. He nodded, a calming expression in his eyes. "Child, please." Seraphiel held out his hand. Desti was reluctant to take it at first as this swarm of information was ravishing her from the inside.

And then a sob ripped from her chest. Desti sprinted forward into Seraphiel's arms. His embrace was warm and powerful, everything that she needed in this moment to comfort her sorrows. Desti wasn't sure why she was crying. Her body had suffered so many years of abuse; so many years of living in a hate-filled world, so to finally feel the embrace of her true father's love, it brought everything to the surface. A salty stream dripped down her face, but she didn't bother to wipe her tears, instead, she buried her face deeper, inhaling the sweet scent of her dad.

Desti pulled away, hardening her face. "Where were you?" Seraphiel's expression dropped. Before he could speak, Desti interrupted. "You let me live my life thinking that *he* was my father. Let me live day by day being beaten and hurt." She stepped back as a new fury began to fester and continued. "You let my mother, the woman that you love, be poisoned by demon's blood, turning her into some kind of mindless slave for him. Why didn't you come for us?"

"Desti, please." He stepped forward. "I had to return to where I belonged. I could not intervene anymore, and with the Lux stolen, I did not have what I needed to see what was happening."

Desti's heart was now slamming in her chest, beating with rage and hurt all at the same time. "What do you mean, *you didn't have what you needed to see*'?" Seraphiel strode over toward the Lux, hovering his hand just slightly above it. "The Lux allows us to see into your world, any time, present or past."

Desti let her arms fall to her side and she closed the space between them until she was gazing upon the glowing orb. "So, you can see my friends? The world?" Speaking of the world felt wrong, causing a bad taste to form in her mouth as her lips slipped the last syllable. She knew the world was destroyed, that she had failed everyone. Amaros had killed her before she had a chance to take out the three kings of Hell.

Desti noticed a smirk tugging at Seraphiel's mouth, and she knew he was about to pull up the image of her world, but Desti shoved out her hand and looked away. "I can't see it. I don't want to see what I have done to them."

Seeing the devastation, the death, the blood, would only cause more heartache, maybe more than what her soul could handle. "Come. It may be different than what you are thinking." Seraphiel held out his hand and motioned for Desti to walk closer. Reluctantly, she stepped closer to the Lux, closer to what she feared the most, but when she gazed into its essence, it was as if she were sucked right back into her world.

An eerie silence instilled upon the land. No more screaming. No more war cries. Just complete silence. It was as if Desti was hovering above the city, seeing the destruction from the cloud's point of view, but something was different. As she shifted her attention to her right, that was when she noticed that the ground had begun to heal, sealing the cracks that allowed Hell to spill on the land. The inferno flames no longer burned throughout the city, and then she realized something.

There were no demons. None. It was as if the carcasses that had laden the roads had just disintegrated into nothing, leaving the streets empty. Even the bodies of Peter's people were gone. Desti's eyes sped up, frantically searching for her friends—her family. And that was when she saw him.

"Tate," she breathed. She went to reach for him but then remembered that her body wasn't physically there. He was kneeling on the ground, holding Desti's body in his arms, crying. Seeing her body like this was a shock to her system, a reminder of what had happened to her. She had jumped in front of a spear, taking the tip into her heart, sparing Tate's in the process.

Desti was suddenly pulled back to the room where she stood. Seraphiel removed his hand from the Lux, and then the image of her world disappeared. "What happened to everyone?" she asked.

Surely the war would have still been going on, so why was there no reminiscence of it now? "The prophecy was fulfilled. The demons can no longer roam your world." Seraphiel's voice was smooth and sultry, but it still struck her like a whip. Desti narrowed her brows.

"Wait. What? The prophecy was fulfilled? But how? I didn't kill any of the kings."

A chuckle escaped from his chest before he answered. "In order to fulfill the prophecy, to win this war against the evil that reigned upon Earth, a true Nephilim must make the ultimate sacrifice in the name of love."

Flashes of the moments just before getting speared rushed to her mind; the sorrow that she felt as she barreled her body to save the love of her life, the way Amaros's smirk promised death and pain, but what really stood out to her was the moment right before the spear hit her. Amaros, for once, looked scared.

And that was when it hit her. Amaros had the look of fear etched into his eyes because *she* had made the ultimate sacrifice for true love. It was the one thing that would fulfill the prophecy. Desti gasped and cupped her mouth. "When I saved Tate…"

"You sacrificed yourself. Selflessly, in the name of true love," Seraphiel finished. "So, what happened to everyone else?" For a moment, Desti had forgotten about Peter's people, and that they too, had immersed themselves within this war. When Desti's eyes reached her father's—her *true* father's—she saw something hopeful in his gaze, staring back at her.

"When the prophecy is fulfilled, a reset will happen. First, the demons will be cast away from your world, forever trapped in their realm. Second, the humans living on this land will be sent back to a time before the world was destroyed. Third," Seraphiel paused and smiled. "Any who have fallen in battle may be brought back, if you wish it."

This was a lot to take in. Everything around her began to go fuzzy, as she felt a wave of dizziness rush through her. She grabbed onto the marble stand to keep herself from falling, realizing what this meant.

"I can bring Anthony back? Peter's people? My friends from Mors?" she asked, her throat constricting as she tried not to cry. Her sweet boy, to be brought back to her, and back to a world with no evil, it felt like the missing piece to her broken heart. Desti tried to keep the images of his blood out of her mind. She had to fight away the memory of his brutal killing as it tried to creep its way to the surface. She shook her head. Seraphiel nodded. "If you wish to bring him back, then so be it."

"What about me? Am I stuck here, or can I go back too?" There was nowhere that Desti would rather be than with Tate and Anthony. Her mother, and friends. She wished to start this new world with all the love and all the hope that she had and put it into building a new life. A new world. With them.

"Only if you wish to. Or you could remain in Heaven with me." Desti had only learned that Seraphiel was her true father. Her entire life, she yearned to experience what love felt like, what a father's true love felt like, but if she chose to go back to her world, that may never happen. A single tear gathered but Seraphiel wiped it away.

"Do not cry. No matter where you are, my love for you will always be there. Whenever you feel as though you need me, pray. You will feel my love reach out and touch you." Then memories of the voices came trickling into her mind, the voices that had helped her in her times of desperation. Desti gasped.

"It was you."

She looked up at Seraphiel, finally realizing that *he* was her guardian angel. "The voices. They were you talking to me." Seraphiel only nodded.

Desti embraced her father into her arms and squeezed him tightly. She knew what she wanted. Her heart needed to be with Tate. With her friends. Her mom. As Desti pulled back slightly, she questioned, "How come Tate is still there, with my body?"

Looking up at someone so holy, so powerful, sent a shiver down her spine. "Your love for each other is like a rope, connecting your souls together. Until you sever that connection, he won't be able to go. But if you go back to your body, you and Tate may be with your people, on your new Earth."

"What about the people from Mors, and all the other cities from my time? Are they stuck there?" This thought was something that was pressing Desti. It would be awful to think that all those people would forever be trapped living in their perpetual hell, but the look on Seraphiel's face gave Desti a sliver of hope.

"Past, present, and future will merge, and only the true timeline shall exist from here on out." Desti clutched her cross necklace and held it, saying a silent prayer under her breath. After an entire life of torment and pain, after all the death and sorrow, Desti had not only saved herself from her insufferable life, but she saved every soul of every human who had suffered along with her.

"Thank you. Thank you. Thank you." Desti pulled him in again, taking in his scent just one more time. She knew this was goodbye, and as she opened her eyes, she wasn't in Heaven anymore hugging her father. Desti was now staring a blue sky, casting delicate shadows from the puffy clouds above.

It was one word that tore her gaze from the beauty above her. One word that made all her fears and pain melt away until she only felt love. It was the voice of her true soul mate.

"Desti!"

Chapter Forty Four

Fulfilled

"Tate?" Desti's voice whimpered. A sob ripped from her chest as she felt Tate pull her into his chest, crying. His arms wrapped around her body as if he were scared she'd float away from not holding on.

Tears splashed along her skin like rain, trailing up her shoulder and onto her cheek. "You were dead. Amaro's…he speared you." Tate pulled back, now analyzing Desti, as if he couldn't believe what he was seeing. "I saw you take your last breath. How are you here?"

Even with all the blood and dirt caked on his face, he was still the most handsome man she had ever seen. Maybe it was the way his black hair hung so freely around his face, or the sharpness to his features. Or it was the way he looked at her, as if she were Heaven itself, truly making Desti feel loved. She reached her hand and placed it gently on his cheek. Tate leaned into her touch and inhaled.

"I'm here. I'm really here. We did it," she softly spoke. When Desti finished, Tate's eyes grew larger. "We, did it? You mean we won the war?" Desti could see the desperation that lingered in his eyes, the twinkle of hope that he clung to, and it was almost as if he didn't want to believe her. How could she blame him for what kind of life he had lived.

"We really won the war. Amaros, the Master, the devil, they are all gone. Trapped in Hell forever." Tate sighed and a smile stretched across his face. "You did it, Desti. You actually save the world. I can't believe that after everything we have been through, we finally won."

The air stilled. Silence swept over like a rolling storm, and Desti was now feeling all her emotions rush to the surface. "I love you. So much. I never want to be without you again," she said. Desti twirled her fingers into Tate's messy hair and pulled him in, their lips crashing together as if it were their last time they would ever touch each other. The world outside faded away into the abyss of desire, and for a brief moment, it was just the two of them. Tate pulled Desti in closer, deepening the kiss, capturing her escaping moans with his mouth. Desti pulled away slightly, placing gentle open-mouth kisses along his jaw. "I missed this."

"I missed this too," he groaned. Tate pulled Desti's face back into his until his mouth claimed hers in an all-consuming kiss, passionately deeper and more fervent than the last. His fingers clasped onto her, holding her tight, as he traced delicate swirls along her back.

When his hand reached the small of her back, he pulled her into his body until she was pressed against him. "You saved me. You risked your life to save me." His words came out as breathless whispers. Desti nodded. "I couldn't let them hurt you. I just reacted."

"Now it's time for me to take care of you." Tate lifted Desti in his arms and surprisingly she felt completely normal, as if her wounds had already been healed. In fact, she felt fantastic. While carrying Desti, he grazed his teeth along her jaw, trailing his teeth down to the hollow of her neck, nipping and nibbling all the right spots. Desti moaned and leaned into his touch. His breath, his body, his scent, everything sent her over the edge of pleasure.

Desti felt herself being gently let down and so, she wrapped her arms around his neck, just gazing into his brilliant green eyes. And he stared right back at her with pure love burning beneath. "I am so proud of you, Desti. For everything you have done. You gave me a world worth living in," Tate played with a strand of her hair, wrapping it around his finger, and continued, "although, I would have settled for just you."

Desti smirked, giggling at the butterflies he gave her. "I came back for you. I would rather live here with you in this world than up there without you by my side." Desti glanced up, gesturing toward the clouds.

"Do you mean Heaven?" Tate tilted his head and pulled his body back slightly. Desti was silent, just nodding her head slowly at his question. "You went to Heaven, and you chose to come back to me?"

"Of course. I couldn't bear to be even one more minute without you."

"Was that how you did it? Win this war, I mean." It was as if Tate was finally connecting the missing pieces. Desti pulled his fingers into hers, interlacing them, holding them firmly. "The prophecy predicated a Nephilim sacrificing themselves for true love. When I jumped in front of the spear…"

"You sacrificed yourself truly out of love for me. And nothing else," he finished. Desti nodded, tears now lining her eyes. She loved this man so much it hurt. "I couldn't let them kill you. It would have killed me, and so I just ran, and that was when I felt the tip pierce my heart."

Tate pressed his open palm against Desti's beating chest, as if feeling for her wound that was no longer there. Even though she had healed, he still was so gentle. "So, the prophecy was real. Our world is now safe?" He said it as if he almost didn't believe it.

"We are safe."

"Then where is everyone?" When Desti dropped her hands and gazed around her, it was like the desolate world—a world of destruction and death, or fire and pain—melted away, the scene before her literally dripping from the sky, revealing a new world in its place.

She stumbled back and gasped. Tate did the same.

There were no more flames. No more demons. No more decayed land. When Desti glanced around she was surrounded by undeniable beauty, and the closer she looked, she realized that she wasn't alone.

"Desti!" she turned her head to see Anthony running full force toward her, arms stretched out and a smile stretched across his face. Anthony collided with Desti as she pulled him into her arms. "Oh my God, Anthony," she cried. Desti wrapped her fingers around his face and stared at him as if he weren't real. " I am so sorry for everything. Are you okay?" Desti's fingers poked and prodded his face as she searched for any marks or wounds, but he looked perfect. When Anthony pulled away, his next hug was Tate. She watched as her two favorite men welcomed each other in the purest embrace.

"Oh, it's so good to see you," Tate said. Anthony pulled away and asked, "Did she, do it? Did she kill the kings of Hell?" When Tate glanced back at Desti, as if waiting for her nod of approval, he smiled and said, "Yes. She did it. She saved everyone."

Anthony opened his mouth as if he were going to speak, but the sound of Evie yelling from the distance interrupted. Desti jolted her attention to her side to see her mother—who looked perfect—running toward her. "Desti!" Evie wailed, a sob escaping her chest. The last time Desti had seen her mother, she was being dragged away by Rebecca, teetering on the verge of death. Evie slammed into Desti almost hard enough to knock her over and squeezed her until she couldn't take a full breath of air in. Splashes of tears trickled down her shoulder as her mother cried in their embrace.

It was like a sea of the purest of emotions, all rushing toward her in intervals. The first wave was shock, but as more and more of her friends and family began to emerge, Desti felt all the sorrow and tension that she held onto, simply fizzle away. One by one, familiar and unfamiliar faces rushed toward Desti and Tate, thanking them for offering the chance at a new life. Rebecca and Brandon came next, not a single scratch along their bodies.

"Thank you, for bringing my mom to safety, Rebecca." Desti placed her hand on Rebecca's shoulder, and smiled, receiving a soft expression of endearment in return. "Desti, I would do anything for you. You got me out of my hell and saved me. It's the least I could have done."

Desti smiled and glanced over her shoulder to see Tate's and Brandon's faces buried in each other's shoulders. "Looks like they missed each other," Desti giggled. Rebecca laughed and pulled away to go see Tate, and then one by one, people greeted and thanked Desti for her bravery. There were hundreds of bodies lined up, waiting to thank the angel-blessed warrior who saved the world, starting with Peter and his people.

"Peter...I—"

He held up his hand. "It's okay. I understand why you left me now. No hard feelings darling." Peter carried along, person after person, pulling Desti into a hug, but when Desti shifted her gaze up, she caught the eye of someone who made her breath hitch in her throat.

"Tess," she breathed. There stood Tess, Kaelen, and Seraph, smiling, clean, and unmarked. No longer were they these creatures of rage controlled by the devil; it seemed as if Desti had broken their curse after all. There was no holding back the emotions now, because when she realized that she had saved everyone—including her Marked friends—it was the last piece of her broken heart that she needed to heal the guilt within her.

Tess offered a gentle smile and wrapped her arms around Desti; Kaelen followed, and then Seraph, until Desti was feeling the full embrace of her friends. "I did it," she cried. "I can't believe I did it. Are you guys, okay?" Desti pulled herself back so that she could meet their gazes. "We are fine. Perfect actually. I have never felt better." Kaelen laughed and nudged Seraph in the shoulder.

"We are grateful for you." Seraph placed his hand on Desti's shoulder before his attention was snatched by Tate calling him over. Desti looked up, embracing the warm, gentle sunrays kissing her skin. A gentle breeze blew through the land, fields of flowers and grass dancing to the rhythm. This would have all been a wild fantasy not too long ago; green grass and birds chirping melodies. They were just a myth in the land of Mors, but looking around, Desti knew that she was no longer standing in that corrupted world, and neither was she in the world in the time before. Seraphiel had said she would be in a new time. In a world unscathed by the evil of Hell. Somewhere pure, untouched. Peaceful. And that was exactly what she felt in her heart now. Complete undeniable bliss.

Surrounded by her friends, her love, and her new companions, there was no more room in her heart for the fear that used to live beneath her skin. No more room for the stress that clouded her mind. This world was a gift from Seraphiel. A gift from herself.

"Desti, you okay?" Tate was walking over to her, his jet-black hair gilded by the beams of sunlight, sparkling like the midnight sky. In his eyes, there was a glimmer of something Desti hadn't seen before. She turned to face him and smiled. "Yeah, I'm okay. I just…it's hard to believe this. To feel…safe."

Tate interlaced his fingers with hers and pulled her into his chest, feeling the rise and fall of his even breathing. "I know what you mean. I still feel as though this is too good to be true, but we can't live like that. We deserve to be happy."

She felt his hands travel up the curve of her silhouette, trailing his fingers along the small of her back until they found their way to her chin. Gently, Tate guided Desti's chin up until she was now staring into his eyes, all-consuming, loving, pleading. She could get lost in the jade hues, the golden specks, forever entrapped in the beauty and fierceness of them, but before she let herself fall too deeply into him, Tate had captured her mouth in the purest of kisses. A kiss that spoke of the promises to come. The warmth of his skin was electric, his soft groans pulling her deeper into the kiss. She twirled her finger in his hair and devoured him. Every inch of him as his lips danced with hers.

Tate pulled away slightly, just for a moment, and asked between breaths, "So, what do we do now, my angel." Desti smiled and replied, "Now, we rebuild."

Epilogue

Five Months Later

"Mom, come on. We are going to be late!"

Desti was waving her hands for her mother to hurry. It was the most beautiful day in the midst of Fall. Desti had never experienced a true season other than the blazing perpetual summer that lingered in Mors, so to be surrounded by shifting colors of auburn, orange, and yellow, was all the more magical. The land, decorated with hues of golden leaves, and amber trees, was now transforming into another type of beauty. The air was crisp, just enough to cause a stream of chills to run up her arms.

Desti wrapped her arms around her chest and shivered. Thank goodness Tess had knitted Desti this cotton dress. It seemed as though Desti, and her people had been placed in a world designed perfectly, just for them. Cotton fields on the outskirts of her land surrounded them, followed by a garden that could feed thousands, with every colored vegetable she could think of and some that she didn't even know existed. These past eight months have been the best in her existence. Memories of her life before now were distant, fading away into the darkness of her mind, and that was where they belonged. Desti didn't dwell on her trauma, she thrived off the strength she gained from fighting all those years and promised herself to truly enjoy her new life.

Evie came rushing forward. "Oh Sweetie, you look beautiful. Tess did an amazing job on your dress." Desti did a little twirl, placing her hands over her belly. Evie smiled as she approached and placed her hand along with Desti's. "She is getting so big. How many months are you now?"

"She? What makes you think it's a girl?" Desti joked. The thought of bringing a baby into this world would have frightened her to her core if she were still living in Mors, but now, knowing that she was carrying a life inside her, she couldn't wait to bring this child into existence. They had created a paradise here, a community where everyone helps and everyone contributes, a life of peace and happiness.

"I can tell by the way you carry her. Now come on, you can't be late for your own wedding. Everyone is waiting." Evie looped her arm through Desti's elbow and guided her down toward the village garden. Rebecca had spent most of her time tending to the garden, with the help of her fellow neighbors, and Desti had to admit that it sure was lovely—the perfect place to hold a wedding.

"I still can't believe that I am getting married."

"I can. That boy loves you with every ounce of his soul." Evie had slowed her pace as she came up to the entrance to the garden. Radiant lilac, white-, and blush-colored roses lined the pathway, Desti taking delicate steps forward, careful not to step on the fallen petals. Desti gasped. "It's beautiful."

"It sure is Sweetie. Rebecca and Kaelen did such an amazing job. I can't wait to see the look on Tate's face when he sees you in your dress."

Since Tate proposed, Evie had taken over planning the wedding, something that she never got to do in her lifetime. This was probably the first wedding to happen since the end of the world, and to be able to spend it with her loved ones was all the more special. "I'm going to take my seat. You look radiant. You've got this."

Evie slid next to a couple who were gazing up at Desti with wide eyes—a look of endearment mixed with their soft expressions—and as Desti drew her gaze along the crowd she inhaled. She had learned about weddings back when she was young. They were forbidden in Mors, in the land of the demons. The thought of attending one, let alone having her own wedding, would have never crossed her mind. But here she was, draped in a white cotton dress, surrounded by family and friends, staring down the aisle as the love of her life waited for her. It was like a dream, and at times Desti had to remind herself that this life was no illusion. She fought for this world. Fought for her people, and she deserved the happiness that came with it.

Everyone stood and turned to look toward her. Like a swan gliding on water, Desti strode down her aisle, guided by the color of flowers that led the way, and when she had made it to the end, there stood the one person who could make her heart melt with just one look.

"Everyone is staring," she whispered. Tate reached for her hands and took them into his, smiling softly from the corner of his mouth. "That is because you look like an angel from heaven." His eyes, jade, and gold glimmered as the sun rays glistened across the garden. Her heart was fluttering, nerves rushing to her core, but it was his eyes that centered her nerves, bringing Desti to a sense of peace.

"You look," Desti traced her eyes up and then down over Tate—dressed in a soft cotton shirt and trousers, stained a dark crimson red from the flowers nearby— "amazing." Her breath caught in her throat at the sight of him. "I can't wait to be your wife."

Tate took his hands and grazed them across Desti's belly. "I can't wait to be your husband, and a father to our baby. You have given me the world Desti Anderson, and you deserve every bit of happiness that comes your way."

It felt as if the minutes stretched to hours as she waited for the ceremony to start. Weddings were a forbidden event in the land of Mors, and the only thing Desti truly remembered about this sacred ceremony was that the unification of husband and wife was sealed with a kiss, so Desti placed her hand on Tate's cheek, feeling him mimic the same gentle touch. She melted into his eyes, getting lost in the dreaminess of his stare. "From the moment that I met you, I knew that you were special. We were only kids, but I could feel something between us that was powerful. All my life you had been there to pick me up when I was down, and put me back together when I was hurt. You are my place of security, my place of happiness. I never thought that living where we did, we would end up finding love, but you made it so easy to fall in love with you. I would do it all over again just so that I could experience that fall for the first time again." Desti wiped away tears that lined her eyes and continued. "Do you, Tate Mitchell, take me as your wife, for you to love and care for, for the rest of our lives?" Tate leaned into her touch, softly speaking, "I do." His tousled midnight hair was magnificently gilded by the sun's light spilling onto the land, and when he leaned in a little closer, Desti could see just how deep the gold in his eyes traveled. He was her savior, her perfect soulmate.

"I know you mentioned that I was the one who had been there for you when growing up, but you too were my rock through our hard times. I had always felt as if a piece of my heart was missing, but when I met you, it felt as though something had filled that void within me. You are strong. You are beautiful and brilliant. You are brave and your heart has enough love to fill this entire world. I fell in love with you way before I wanted to admit it, but you made me feel safe in our world, safe enough that I couldn't walk away from this. No matter what we went through, I would do it all over again, because you are worth it." Desti happy-cried and watched as Tate's eyes glossed over. He drew in a large breath and said, "Desti Anderson, do you take me as your husband, and do you promise to love me and take care of me for the rest of our lives?" Desti sucked in a breath, an explosion of feelings swirling around in her mind, and cried, "I do."

"Just kiss him already!" yelled Tess from the crowd. Desti smiled, seeing all the smiling faces looking back at her—Anthony and Tess, Kaelen and Seraph, Brandon, and all the others. They had become her family these past few months, and to see them here, now, supporting this wonderful event, filled Desti with an unexplainable amount of joy. When she returned her gaze toward Tate, he was staring, right at her. Truly seeing her for who she was. The tension between them was electric and she could barely hold herself back any longer.

She locked her fingers into his hair and whispered, "Just kiss me already." Desti pulled Tate into her, his lips pressing the gentlest of kisses, and as gentle as it was, this kiss lit a fire within her. This man was her soulmate, her true love, and now, her prayers were answered. Her lips didn't want to pull away as Desti melted into his touch, her fingers clinging on to him as if he were going to float away, but suddenly, a brilliant white light seemed to drown out the land, causing Desti and Tate to stagger back.

Audible gasps echoed throughout the garden, and at first, Desti wasn't sure what was going on, but when she heard her mother cry out, everything began to make sense.

Evie stood from her chair, eyes wide and in disbelief, as she cried out, "Jonathan? Is that you?" Evie was now walking toward Desti, but she was focused on something behind her. Desti turned around, and when she did, her heart melted just a little more.

"Dad," she breathed. Desti let go of Tate's hand and ran into Seraphiel's chest, breathing heavily as she held back tears of joy. "I never thought I was going to see you again. How are you here?" She pulled back, tears now streaming down her face. Seraphiel placed a gentle hand on her head and smiled. When he opened his mouth, the rush of Evie's body running for him snatched his focus.

"Jonathan!" Seraphiel stepped back and held open his arms, embracing Evie with the gentlest of hugs. "My Darling," he spoke. His voice was deep and soothing. For the most part, he looked practically human, save for the dim glow that surrounded his body. "I thought you forgot about me," Evie cried. Seraphiel offered her a soft expression and placed a kiss on her forehead. "I'm sorry, my love. There wasn't a day that went by when I didn't think about you."

Then Evie pulled away and glanced over at Desti, realization now coming into effect. "He is your guardian angel?" Desti stepped closer and nodded. "Johnathan, huh? Is that your human name?" Desti smiled. Seraphiel held out his hand and pulled Desti in with her mother and held them both. "I have many names."

Desti tilted up her chin and asked, "How are you here? I thought you couldn't leave anymore."

Evie seemed to have the same question burning within her stare, as she just waited for him to answer. Seraphiel smiled and said, "Let's just say that I made a deal up there. I have been able to check in on you, now that the Lux was returned, and I chose to spend my time on these lands with my family."

Desti placed her hand on his chest and asked, "But won't you grow weak? I thought you can't be away from Heaven…"

Evie pulled his chin toward her, tension electrifying between them. "You are choosing to lose your Light, aren't you?" Seraphiel nodded slowly and smiled. "Being with you, growing old with you, it's what my heart wants." Evie happy cried and leaned forward, pressing a soft kiss on Seraphiel's lips. Desti felt a slight touch on her hand, and when she glanced down, she saw Tate's fingers interlacing with hers. He pulled her away into her own embrace of love, his hands now resting on her hips.

"Looks like we've got it all." Tate smirked and tucked her loose strands of hair behind her ear. "You are so beautiful, Desti." Tate leaned down and kissed her belly, holding his lips there just a little longer than he should have, and returned his stare a moment later. Desti could feel the love in the air, the burning desire festering between them. She ran her fingers through his hair and pulled him to her, whispering, "Just kiss me already."

The world around her narrowed until she felt as if it were just the two of them, their two souls meeting within that spark between them. Each touch from his hands as he explored her body was tender and gentle, and as he stepped closer, the heat of his body continued the caressing. "I love you," he whispered, his lips dancing with hers. Desti pulled away slightly and whispered, "I love you too."

Her heart was full. The world was pure and untouched by the horrors that she had endured, uncorrupted by the evil and hate that seeped its way throughout her previous home. Desti had finally gotten it all: Family, friendship, loving parents, thriving lands, and…Tate. The man who had her heart. It still felt like a dream at times, living in this new world of hers, but Desti had to remind herself that it was real. She had saved the world. Saved herself. And as this realization came rushing in, she realized that the thing her soul desired the most was finally right in front of her.

Through all the heartache, through all the pain, Desti had finally found peace, finally able to spend forever with *him*. And this moment, right now, made all those painful memories all the worthwhile.

Acknowledgments

This series has been an incredible ride of emotions these past few months and I want to thank everyone who has supported me along this journey. I put my heart and soul into this series, and I can't wait to share it with the world. First, I would like to thank my family who have supported me unconditionally throughout my publishing journey. Thank you to my marketing team, you guys are the best! Thank you to my editor for making sure that my manuscript is polished and ready to go and thank you to my readers for diving into this post-apocalyptic world of mine and giving me a shot. I truly hope you love Desti and Tate as much as I do.

About the Author

Kay Marrie is a dark fantasy author who pulls her ideas for her books from her wild dreams and nightmares. Her vivid imagination always creates these complex stories in her mind, and when she is not juggling playtime with her three children, you can find her turning these dreams into stories. She is fascinated with the dark and twisted and when you delve into her books, that is what you will end up reading. But don't let her dark mind fool you. She is a loving and kind person who enjoys reading, painting, and anything to do with the beach.

Connect With Kay

https://kaymarrie.com/

https://www.instagram.com/kaymarrie_?igsh=MWJmajRweX
cycml6&utm_source=qr

https://www.facebook.com/profile.php?id=61562340535207

https://www.tiktok.com/@kaymarrie_author?_t=8rTOTzVbuK
E&_r=1

https://www.amazon.com/stores/Kay-
Marrie/author/B0D94SHVRW?ref=ap_rdr&isDramIntegrated=t
rue&shoppingPortalEnabled=true

Loved Era of the Damned? Share your thoughts on Goodreads
here   —→
https://www.goodreads.com/author/show/48734002.Kay_Marr
ie